THE COINCIDENCE

DAVID B. LYONS

Print ISBN: 978-1-9160518-6-7

PRAISE FOR DAVID B. LYONS

"An outstanding novel"
– The Book Magnet

"Keeps you guessing right until the end"
– Irish Daily Mail

"Incredibly clever"
– The Writing Garnet

"Impossible to put down"
– The Book Literati

"Book of the year so far"
– BooksFromDuskTilDawn

For Lin

The coincidence that occurs in *The Coincidence*

was inspired by a true story.

'We all here cos o' coincidence.'

Those were the first words Christy ever spoke to Joy. Up until that point in their brief journey together, Joy had been content to just stare down at the filthy shoelaces of her Converse trainers rather than at the intimidating, lanky woman sat across from her.

'Life for everyone is a gift from God, alright… the God o' coincidence,' she continued.

Christy's accent was a marriage of her natural Nigerian husk to a southern Texan drawl. She had learned to speak English by listening to the sermons of Terence Huntcastle; a famed Christian pastor who hailed from Dallas and who ran one of the biggest superchurches in the whole of America. She played his tapes non-stop on a smashed Sony Walkman during her seeking of refuge from Nigeria over twenty-five years ago, and can still rattle off each of those sermons word for word today.

'A one in five hundred million miracle we all are. You're a one in five hundred million miracle, curly-haired girl, you know that?'

Joy slowly lifted her gaze from her shoelaces and met Christy's bloodshot eyes for the first time.

'S'true. When yo dadda made sweet, sweet love to yo momma and orgasmed his ball sack inside her, five hundred million of his little swimmers began a mega race to yo momma's golden egg.' Christy leaned as forward as she could. 'And you know which little swimmer won that one in five hundred million race, curly-haired girl? You. You, Joy Stapleton! You literally are a coincidence. We all are.'

Joy's heart sank. Not because Christy was preaching, but because she had mentioned her name. Though she knew she shouldn't be surprised by that. Her tiny frame, covered by her oversized curly mane would be, by now, unmistakable to anyone in the country. And likely would be for the rest of her life.

That short one-way conversation was pretty much all Christy and Joy shared while the van chicaned its way around the mazed inner city streets of Dublin, until its engine finally died. Then the two front doors of the van opened and slapped shut in unison, before footsteps clacked against concrete. Christy leaned as forward as she could again.

'Yo gon' be fine, Joy. Just keep yo pretty head down.'

'Welcome home, ladies,' the big fat ginger one said, pulling the back doors open, blinding his passengers with the low sun. When he stepped into the van, it sunk under his weight and Joy had to hold her breath to stave off the heavy stench of B.O. as he bent over to free her wrists. Then he exposed the top of his ass crack just inches from her face when he turned to free Christy.

'Step down,' he said, motioning to the bright outside world. It was freezing cold that afternoon, but the sun was still shining low in the sky, highlighting the cloud of Joy's exhalations as she stepped onto the concrete yard.

The tall cranky looking one was waiting for them, standing with her hands on her hips by the back wheel of the van. She and Fatso then led the women towards a grey stone wall that seemed to stretch as wide as the eye could see. There was a small blue wooden door in the middle of the wall that they made their way towards, then Fatso stared up into the CCTV camera hanging above it and, without much pause, the blue door buzzed open. The four of them entered a much smaller concrete yard, though this time the door on the wall opposite wasn't wooden, nor was it small. It was wide. *Very* wide. And made of steel.

Fatso stared again into a camera that hung over it until another buzz sounded. And when the steel door was pushed open, a chorus of screeches immediately echoed from the distance and within that split moment Joy's whole body paused; her feet, her thoughts, her breathing. The screeches were quite literally her worst nightmare coming true.

'Don't mind the noise,' Christy whispered over Joy's shoulder. 'S'not as bad as it sounds.'

'You first,' a voice from the shadows shouted. Joy blinked her eyes, ridding them of the glare of the outside world, before she could make out the figure of a woman standing behind an arched-wooden desk. She trundled over with Fatso still flanked by her side. 'Well, I guess I don't need to ask your name, now do I?' the woman behind the desk said. 'So, let's start with question number two, huh? Date of birth?'

Joy swallowed, tasting the last of her pride as it slid down her throat.

'First of January. 1986.'

'Well, congratulations, Joy. I can confirm you've definitely come to the right place.'

Fatso sniggered, then covered his mouth with his fingers when the woman behind the desk glared at him.

'Empty your pockets. I need all belongings in here,' the woman ordered as she slid a blue tray across the desk.

'I, eh... I don't have anything on me,' Joy replied, stiffening her nose in an attempt to stall the tears.

'Except for this,' Fatso said. He stuffed his chubby fingers into Joy's jeans pocket, fumbling for longer than was necessary before pulling out a photograph. He carelessly skim-threw it into the tray, and the woman behind the desk took a long stare at it before glancing back up at Joy.

'That it?'

'S'all's she's got,' Fatso replied.

'I, eh... I was told I could take that with me,' Joy said, her voice quivering.

The woman clicked her tongue against the roof of her mouth, then picked the photo up and stared longingly at it before handing it back to Joy.

'Okay, but I'm gonna have to take the laces out of those trainers.'

Joy looked down at the filthy laces she had spent the majority of the van ride staring at, then dipped to her hunkers to yank them from her Converse. She had barely dropped them into the tray by the time Fatso was grabbing at her elbow again, guiding her past the wooden desk with a firmer grip than she felt was necessary and leading her towards another steel door. He didn't have to nod at a hanging CCTV camera to open this one. Instead, he pressed one of his chunky fingers to a keypad until the door clicked open. Then he pushed Joy inside with more force than, again, she felt was necessary, before slamming the door shut.

'Ah, well, if it isn't Joy Stapleton,' a sweet voice inside the hollow room said.

Joy spun around to see another one of them standing in front of her, clad – same as 'em all – head to toe in navy. Only this one looked different. She wasn't menacingly grinning, nor furrowing her brow. She actually had kind eyes; eyes not too dissimilar to Joy's best friend Lavinia – or former best friend as she surely was by now.

'Strip!'

'Huh?'

'Strip. It means take off all your clothes.'

'I know what it means.... It's just... what, here? Now? In front of you?'

The woman smiled her kind eyes. And then a long silence settled between them before that kind smile abruptly dropped from her face.

Joy huffed out a sigh, before pulling her arms from the sleeves of her jumper and lifting it over her head, taking her T-shirt with it.

'Everything else,' the woman said, the glint in her eye threatening to return.

Joy reached around and undid the clasp of her bra, revealing her goose-pimple covered breasts before dropping it to the concrete. Then she kicked off her laceless Converse trainers and shimmied her way out of her jeans.

'Lemme see that bush,' the woman said.

After a pause of silence, Joy plucked up enough courage to hook a thumb either side of her knickers before yanking them down.

'Now turn around.'

'Huh?'

'Turn around. And interlink your fingers on top of those lovely curls for me.'

A chill ran down Joy's spine; partly because of the intimidation, but mostly because of the cold. Though as the goosepimples raced their way around her tiny frame, she relented and finally spun to face the back wall, noticing the yellow paint was stained a vomit-inducing shade of brown in each of the corners.

'Now squat.'

'Sorry?'

'Squat. Bend your knees and lower your ass.'

Joy held her eyes closed and then, widening her stance, began to bend her knees – until the steel door clicked open once again and Christy skidded into the room, pushed in with much the same force as Joy had been.

Joy stood back upright immediately, holding one arm across her breasts; her other hand covering her bush.

'Looks like you gettin' all comfortable up in here already, Joy,' Christy said, grinning her stained teeth.

'You start stripping,' the woman in navy ordered her before turning back to Joy. 'And you start squatting.'

So, Joy refaced the wall, placed her hands back on top of her hair and bent her knees, lowering and pushing her ass out as quickly as she could before standing back upright.

'No, no, no,' the woman called out. 'Slower!'

'Hey, you don't think she got somethin' up there, right?' Christy said, cackling. 'She got such a tight lil ass you couldn't fit a tic-tac in that thing. Ma right, sista?'

Joy stiffened her nostrils with irritation, then bent her knees even further before ever-so-slowly lowering her ass as if she was sitting on an imaginary loo.

'See, not even one of those curly pubes fell out,' Christy said as Joy stood back upright.

The woman, ignoring Christy, paced over to Joy, placed a hand to her shoulder and guided her with a forced shove against the stained yellow wall behind her. Then she reached above Joy's head and pulled a gauge down to the top of her curls.

'Five foot, two inches,' she said before biting off the lid of her pen to scribble on her notes. 'Stand up here,' she said, pointing the pen at the weighing scales in the corner.

Joy stepped onto the board while staring over her shoulder at Christy undressing. She took in the back of Christy's long, brown legs and slowly lifted her gaze up the length of her spine till she was staring at her bowed elongated neck. Christy had the physique and posture of a super model. And probably could have been one too had she trod a path in life that hadn't turned her teeth yellow and her eyes red.

'Seven stone, ten,' the woman said. 'I think you'll need to eat a few McDonald's while you're here.'

'Huh?' Joy said, stepping down from the scales. 'We get McDonald's here?'

Both the woman and Christy laughed so loudly that it echoed around the concrete room. And when the woman had decided the joke was no longer funny, she spun around to pull open a steel cabinet door, from which she removed a neatly rolled up grey jumpsuit.

'Here, wear this,' she said, tossing it at Joy. 'It's the smallest one we have.'

'Oh, yo really gonna look like Krusty the Clown now,' Christy said, cackling from the back of her throat again.

When Joy finally smothered herself in the jumpsuit – the sleeves so long it looked as if she had two baby elephant trunks for arms – the woman turned and snatched at a door on the opposite side of the room.

'Way to break your duck, Aidan,' she called out. 'I've got a VIP for you. None other than Joy Stapleton.' Joy peered around the door frame to see who the hell this Aidan was. He looked young. And fresh; his face still producing acne, his forehead void of wrinkles. He was nice looking in the way Dublin men can be nice looking; black hair, pale skin and piercing blue eyes. Eyes that reminded her of Shay's.

'She's Elm House, E-114.'

'E-114, got it,' Aidan said, nodding. He swallowed and then awkwardly stepped aside, welcoming Joy to join him on the steel-grated landing. As soon as she took one step on to the grate, the screeching that had earlier sounded distant raised intimidatingly in volume.

'Oh wait,' Joy said, gasping and spinning back. 'I forgot my photo. I need my photo. It's in my pocket.'

The woman knelt down and felt around Joy's jeans before retrieving the polaroid. She stared at it and paused, before eyeballing Joy.

'Whatever makes you sleep at night,' she said, handing the photo back.

Joy crossed her brow as she snatched at it, then whispered: 'It was a coincidence.'

Then the woman shrugged one shoulder before slamming the door shut just inches from Joy's nose.

Aidan was looking sheepish when Joy turned back around to face him, then he motioned towards a large steel staircase at the far end of the landing.

'Don't worry,' he said, as they took the first step. 'They say the noise isn't as bad as it sounds.'

'Jaysis, it's yer one, innit?' a voice called out when Joy and Aidan had reached the top of the stairs. And then, without pause, a cacophony of wolf whistles echoed, bouncing around the landings both above and below them.

'Ignore them,' Aidan said out of the side of his mouth. Then he stopped in his tracks suddenly, causing Joy to crash into the back of him.

'Sorry,' he said, 'it came on me all of a sudden. E-114. This is you.'

He pushed at the door and stepped aside, inviting Joy to enter first. It wasn't as grim as she had feared it would be; brighter and actually roomier than she had imagined. But she mostly felt relief when she first stepped inside; relief because there was only one bed in there.

'You'll, eh... you'll get three rounds of clothes brought in... so you won't have to wear the jumpsuit all the time,' Aidan informed her as Joy stared into the lidless steel toilet bowl in the back corner of the room. When she turned back around, she met Aidan's blue eyes and he nodded kindly before taking two steps backwards.

'This has to be locked,' he said gripping the door. 'It's just precautionary for the first twenty-four hours. It's what happens when you're high-profile. We'll, eh... we'll bring you some food in the next couple of hours.'

'Can you, eh... get me some sellotape or Blu-Tac or something? I just wanna hang this on the wall beside my bed ... please?'

She held the photograph up and Aidan blinked at it, before slowly nodding.

'Lemme see what I can do,' he said.

Then he took one more step backwards, dragging the door with him and slamming it closed with an echoed clank.

And that was it. She was alone. Finally. Her freedom well and truly taken.

She attempted to look about herself, only there wasn't much to look at. So, she ran her fingers over the thin blue mattress laying on top of her steel-block bed, before opting to perch her ass on to the edge of it.

'Hey,' a voice yelled before loud banging slapped against Joy's steel door. 'I think I know your face from somewhere... or is that just a *coincidence*?'

The cacophony of laughter that followed shook Joy more so than the banging against her door had.

'Yeah, I know who she is,' another voice shouted when the laughter had died to near silence. 'Wasn't she in all the papers for winning Mother of the Year or somethin'?'

The cackles grew in volume, as if all the women outside were competing for the loudest laugh.

To drown the noise out, Joy dropped the photograph on to her thin pillow, then lay her face beside it, wrapping her elbows around her head to smother her ears. Sometimes, when she stares at the photo long enough, she can hear Reese's laugh. And Oscar's giggle.

'Hey, child killer,' a voice roared, before the door received another bout of slapping. 'Don't you dare think you're gonna have an easy time of it in here, ya hear me?'

❖

'Your Honour, my client,' Gerd Bracken says, while remaining seated, 'has spent the last eight years and two months incarcerated in Mountjoy Prison because of nothing more than mere coincidence. A coincidence, I should add, that in the grand scheme of coincidences is not even that coincidental.'

He scoots back his chair, gets to his feet and strolls, slowly, to the middle of the courtroom floor. Judge Delia McCormick peers over the rim of her retro 1950s-style glasses to squint at him, already intrigued. She'd been working up to this trial for months, was staggered it fell into her lap. A retrial – *the* retrial – of the biggest mystery that has plagued the entire nation for well over a decade. She was initially hesitant to take on the role, especially as it was all on her; no fellow judges to debate legal arguments with; no jury to rely on for a verdict. But after careful consideration and painstaking research – not to mention discussion after discussion with both her annoying son, Callum, and her persuasive boss, Eddie – Delia finally accepted the pressure of presiding over the Joy Stapleton retrial. She knew the weight of the world would push hard onto her shoulders, knew the media would sensationalize every word she'd speak, and that the judicial system would scrutinize every move she'd make. But as both Callum and Eddie repeated to her regularly during her dilemma: why become a trial judge if you don't want to preside over the biggest case there's ever been?

So here she finally was; sat in the overly large velvet-cushioned judge's highchair at the back wall of the largest trial room in Dublin's Central Criminal Courts, squinting at Gerd Bracken – a defence lawyer she knew all too well – as he began his opening argument.

'Imagine, if you will for one moment, Your Honour...' Bracken forms a steeple with his fingers and frames them around his navel, 'you call out for your two beautiful young sons, and they never answer back. Two years go by and you are still calling out for them... and they still don't answer. Then a detective knocks on your door one morning, informs you your sons' bodies have been found in wasteland high up in the Dublin mountains.' Bracken shakes his head. 'Sounds like Hell on earth, doesn't it, Your Honour? But imagine that was only half of the story? Imagine six weeks after hearing such devastating news, the same detective knocks to your house again, this time to arrest *you* for the double homicide of your sons. And imagine, eighteen months later, despite the fact that there was *zero* forensic evidence and *zero* eye-witnesses, a jury of twelve find you guilty. And then you are sentenced to two life sentences in prison – unlikely to ever get out. That's a lot for me to ask you to imagine... but I would ask you, Your Honour, to imagine one more thing if you will... imagine this... imagine you were innocent all along?' He allows a silence to wash over the court room as he subtly shakes his head again. 'Your Honour, my client has so far spent over eight years in prison for the most heinous of crimes that she simply did *not* commit. And the only reason she has spent over eight years in prison comes down to mere coincidence. *Coincidence!*'

Bracken kisses his own lips before shaking his head again. Judge Delia doesn't react at all; not to even blink her eyes, which are still peering over the rim of her glasses at the lawyer in the pin-striped suit.

'Your Honour, Joy Stapleton – who may I add is still in the process, many, many years later, of grieving the loss of her sons –

has only been convicted of this crime for the simple reason that somebody else out there was wearing the exact same hooded sweat-top to one she happened to own at the time. That's it. That is the *only* reason she was arrested. It is the *only* reason she was convicted. There wasn't one jot of forensic evidence that links Joy to this crime. Not one eye-witness who can link Joy to this crime.' He lowers his voice, and his tone, 'not one credible motive that links Joy to this crime...'

He pauses, then fills his cheeks with air before slowly exhaling; displaying a show of anguish. But this sort of act won't do him any favours. Bracken's melodramatics might work on jurors; in fact, his melodramatics almost *always* work on jurors – he's only lost one trial out of thirty-three over the past ten years. But his melodramatics won't work on Judge Delia. She knows him well; has presided over two major trials he had been the leading defence lawyer on. Still, she has always been professional enough to not allow her own personal feelings on individuals to cloud her judgements. Bracken may well be a sleazeball, he may well love the sound of his own voice and the attention he gets from the media as much as he loves a sunbed, but Delia has evolved an envious ability to shove all of her peripheral thoughts to one side so she can focus solely on the facts of any matter, let alone the matter of a major murder trial.

'Your Honour,' Bracken says, 'I and many, many other people, in and out of the judicial system, have felt, for years, that Joy Stapleton is innocent of this crime. We can't quite understand how or why our judicial system could put a young grieving mother behind bars based on evidence so minimal and so trivial. But I am now glad we have won the opportunity to be here today in front of you at this retrial, so that we can bring, to you, undoubted evidence of this mother's innocence. A cadaver dog, Judge Delia. *The* cadaver dog – a dog named Bunny who helped detectives push their narrative that Joy Stapleton was guilty all those years ago – has since been exposed as not having the adequate training required to determine anything about this case. Bunny, y'see, Your Honour, was said to have found evidence of decomposing bodies in the Stapleton family home back in January of 2009 – mere months after poor Reese Stapleton and Oscar Stapleton were first reported missing. Bunny's findings played a major role in the original trial. But we will bring to you evidence that Bunny didn't know what he was doing all those years back. Because another trial, in London, Your Honour, collapsed four years ago when Bunny's findings in that case were found to be useless... pointless... meaningless... redundant. We will prove to you that Bunny's findings in the original trial concerning Joy Stapleton were just as useless, pointless, meaningless, and redundant. I will also bring forward, Your Honour, a former member of An Garda Siochana who assisted in the original missing persons case of Reese and Oscar Stapleton who will detail to this court that the original investigation got this wrong from the very outset. That's right! A former detective will sit in that seat there,' Bracken points his whole hand to the witness box to the judge's right, 'and tell you that she and everyone else she worked with got this case wrong from the very beginning. I will also bring evidence that the coincidence upon which Joy Stapleton was arrested certainly *was* a coincidence. The girl seen in the CCTV footage wearing a pink hoodie was not Joy Stapleton at all. It couldn't have been. Over the course of this retrial, Your Honour, it will be proven to you that my client did not kill her only two children in November of 2008. Thank you.'

Bracken almost bows – as if he's just nailed one of Shakespeare's most renowned monologues on the stage of The Globe Theatre, before spinning on his heels and walking back to his desk, where he plonks himself next to a sombre-looking Joy.

Judge Delia deflects her gaze and purses her lips at the desk adjacent to theirs.

'Mr Ryan. Your opening statement, please,' she says, before scribbling some notes onto the top sheet of the mountainous paperwork in front of her.

Ryan rises from his chair and clips open the two buttons of his suit jacket before he strolls his way to the centre of the courtroom floor. The courtroom is deathly quiet, despite the fact that not only is it packed inside, but the doors outside of the courts are almost bursting with reporters who couldn't quite get a seat in the arena today.

'Your Honour,' Ryan says, 'Joy Stapleton has spent the last eight years in a cell in Mountjoy Prison for one simple reason. In November 2008, she killed both of her sons – Reese, aged four and Oscar who was eighteen months old – in cold blood. We believe she rendered them unconscious using chloroform, then likely suffocated them to death. She brought them to the Dublin mountains and disposed of their bodies. On the day we believed this happened, we know that Joy Stapleton was wearing a unique pink hooded top. Very unique. So unique in fact, we know Joy to be the only person in Ireland who owns one. Let me say that again. Joy Stapleton is the *only* person in Ireland to own the top that was caught on CCTV footage close to where the bodies were found, on the night we are certain the bodies were buried there. Your Honour... for years, the defendant's argument has always been that this is mere coincidence. But that's hogwash. And we will be able to prove it. The probability of her defence of coincidence is so low, Your Honour, that it simply can*not* be considered coincidence. And I will be able to prove that once and for all in this retrial. I do not wish at any stage to insult the intelligence of this court. But this must be said... In mathematics, two angles that are said to coincide – and note the word *coincide* – fit together perfectly. The word coincidence does not describe luck, or misfortune, Your Honour. The word coincidence describes that which fits together perfectly. We,' he says, looking back to his desk where his assistant Brigit is sitting staring at him, 'will be able to prove to you that Joy Stapleton not only deserves to have spent the last eight years in a prison cell for killing her two young sons, but that she deserves to spend the rest of her life in that prison cell, to see out the double-life sentence that was handed down to her in her original trial.' Ryan takes two steps nearer the judge. 'The detectives during their investigation got this case right. The judge sitting on the original trial called this case right. And the jurors sitting on the original trial called this case right. Your Honour, we're not going to bring witnesses second-guessing the sense of smell of a dog to this court, like the defence team will. We are not going to bring bitter ex-employees of the police force to this court, like the defence team will. We will be putting professionals in that stand; professionals who know this case better than anybody else. And those *professionals* all agree on one thing, Your Honour. And that is, that on the second of November in 2008, Joy Stapleton murdered and then disposed of the bodies of her two baby boys, Oscar and Reese Stapleton.'

It was the door clicking open that woke Joy inside her prison cell for the very first time. She lazily stirred on her plastic blue mattress, then – in stark realisation of where she was – jolted her back against the wall and brought her knees up to her chest. Though much to her relief, somebody outside pulled at her cell door, slapping it back shut.

She panted for breath as she listened to the melee of shuffling feet in the landing outside, and before long that distant screeching that she heard as soon as she had set foot inside the prison the previous evening struck up. She had no idea what time it was, but it sure did seem as if everybody got up and about at the exact same time. Perhaps a prison officer, stationed outside her cell, slammed her door shut. She had been told she wouldn't be mixing with the other prisoners – not for at least twenty-four more hours anyway. And even following that she would be accompanied by an officer everywhere she went.

She spent the majority of her first full day in the exact same spot she had spent her first night – in a foetal position atop that blue plastic mattress. Though there were two breaks – both for half an hour; once in the morning and then again in the afternoon – in the small yard. It allowed her to stretch her legs and breathe in fresher air.

Aidan had joined her for her first half-hour out there, looking as nervous and uncertain of procedure as she was. Yet, somehow, she felt a sense of comfort around him. He had a warmth and was certainly open for conversation. He confided in Joy that the previous day was his first day working as a screw in Mountjoy Prison.

'Your first day as well? And your first job was to take me to my cell... wow, that's a coincidence,' Joy said.

Then she immediately looked down to her feet, as she realised she would for the rest of her life every time she muttered that word.

There were meals each side of the two breaks, too, brought to her cell and left on a flimsy plastic tray atop her flimsy plastic mattress: a breakfast that consisted of toast so dry it may as well have been cardboard, and a reheated microwavable lasagne for lunch that was so congealed it may well have been a stew. The dinner wasn't too bad, though; Indian samosas with fragrant yellow rice. And there were afters too; a large scoop of vanilla ice cream, stabbed with a diamond-shaped wafer.

She had been offered the chance of a shower on three separate occasions, but refused each time. That had always been her biggest fear as she lived through her ordeal. It wasn't the monotony of being holed in a prison cell that frightened Joy. It was the showers.

'There'll be no other prisoners in there,' Mathilda, the female officer who had signed her in at the front desk the previous day, said to her. 'You are being kept from them for the first twenty-four hours.'

'No. I'm okay,' Joy said, sucking up her tears. 'I think I can do without showering for the rest of my life.'

'They all say that... till they start smelling themselves,' Mathilda said. Then she walked out of the cell, slapping the door shut behind her.

Joy lifted her arm above her head and sniffed.

'Okay, okay,' she said, leaping down from her bed and knocking repeatedly at the cell door. 'I'll take one. I'll take my shower now.'

Mathilda chuckled.

'Too late, Stapleton. You had your chance. You'll have to take one with the rest of the girls in the morning. Now why don't you get some sleep. I've a feeling you're gonna need your energy – and your wits about you – tomorrow.'

2,998 days ago...

Her hands were visibly shaking as she reached to take the towel from Mathilda. The prison officer had visited her cell first thing the next morning, as she promised she would, to ensure Joy joined the queue for the showers.

Joy expected 'child killer' shouts as soon as she stepped onto the landing, but the other prisoners were oddly subdued as they brushed past her, probably because it was too early for them to be bothered.

She didn't stand under the water. She just let it fall to her chest, all the while shifting her eyes from side to side, darting glances at the prisoners showering next to her. One of the prisoners met her eye and turned out her bottom lip, accompanying it with a nod. It came across as a sympathetic gesture, but Joy couldn't be sure. It was only when she was dabbing her chest dry with her towel that she was first spoken to.

'I told you we all a coincidence.' Joy looked up to meet the bloodshot eyes of Christy. 'Me 'n' you on the same wing, sista. I think God sent me to protect yo lil ass, huh?'

Joy stood there, naked. And vulnerable. And damp. And cold. Damn cold. The water in the prison's showers never raised to a level beyond lukewarm.

'Hi, Christy,' she said.

And then those drying around her mimicked her.

'Hi, Christy,' they said, their voices mocking and high-pitched.

And almost immediately that horrible cacophony of immature laughter cackled again, sounding even more echoey bouncing off the shower tiles than it did bouncing around the landings.

'Alright, bitches, cut it out,' a middle-aged, flaming red-haired woman, with one foot up against the tiled wall, flossing the towel between the pits of her groins, said. 'If it makes ya feel any better, love, I'm not entirely sure whether you did or whether you did not kill those little kiddies of yours. But I am pretty sure you shouldn't be here. I read all about your trial. I don't think the prosecution offered up enough evidence to send you down. Those jurors, whoever they are, they screwed you, honey.'

'Eh... thanks,' Joy whispered back, before Christy tugged on her shoulder.

'C'mon, get yourself dressed, Joy. We gonna eat some breakfast together.'

They sat on the end of a long bench in the canteen; Christy scoffing her porridge within a matter of seconds, Joy still tonguing spoonfuls of it from side to side in her mouth, her lips turned down in disgust.

'Doesn't all seem so bad in here, now does it?' Christy said, swiping the sleeve of her jump suit across her mouth. 'I know some of 'em been calling you a child killer but I also hear some of 'em say you didn't do it; that you didn't kill yo boys.'

'Seems as if I've split the prisoners...' Joy said before swallowing a mouthful of porridge.

'Split the prisoners, sista? You split the whole darn country. Half the people on the streets saying such a young pretty little thing like you could never do such a thing. Other half think you a stone-cold killer, girl.'

Joy fed herself another spoonful of porridge and allowed it to swirl from cheek to cheek again before swallowing.

'I didn't do it, ye know? That's not me in that CCTV footage. I swear. I've sworn to everybody. I swear to you.'

Christy raised one eyebrow at Joy, then looked around at Mathilda who was standing against the wall next to them – Joy still under guarded supervision when outside of her cell.

'You know you the only person with one of them hooded tops in all of Ireland,' Christy said.

Joy looked down. As she always did when she was lost for a word other than 'coincidence'. Then she changed the subject, by asking Christy about visitation rights. Though she wasn't quite sure if anyone was ever going to visit her. Shay had pretty much refused to believe his wife had murdered their two sons, and even after her arrest had stayed somewhat loyal. But it was noted by everyone in attendance – and certainly by those from the media – that he wasn't present for any of the trial. He had been asked to testify in favour of Joy – to say on the stand that he didn't believe his wife was capable of murdering anyone, let alone their two precious sons. But he stayed away from the court entirely, and indeed cut off any line of communications with his wife. His silence was eating at Joy, even though she knew that there was no chance of them ever getting back together. Not even if she could prove her innocence. Their lives together ended the day Reese and Oscar were first reported missing. There was no chance of them ever going back to where they once were. Despite that, she was hopeful that one day she'd get a tap on the shoulder from one of the prison officers before being told Shay was in the visiting room, waiting for her. Her best friend – or former best friend as she was by now – certainly wasn't coming to visit. Lavinia did appear on the stand, to testify that Joy's personality had changed before her boys were reported missing.

'You think you know who the closest people are in life,' Joy whispered to Christy while pushing her plastic bowl away from under her nose. 'But...' Then she shrugged. Christy nodded, before picking up Joy's bowl and literally digging into her porridge. 'How dare Lavinia testify that I was suffering with depression. I've never suffered with depression. They tested me. I didn't have no postnatal depression.'

'But they tested you two years later, right? After yo boys' bodies were found, not at the time they went missing?'

'You don't believe me?' Joy said.

'E'ryone round here says they innocent, Joy.'

'I *am* innocent!' Joy snapped.

'Calm down, girl. You at risk of losing the only friend you got in the whole world right now.'

Joy unclenched her fists and tilted her head backwards, a groan growling at the back of her throat.

'I'm sorry, Christy. Thanks for... I don't know... thanks for talking to me.'

'Thank *you*, girl,' Christy replied. 'When I do time in here, I normally keep maself to maself. People up in here think I'm all kinds o' crazy. Just me and ma bible when I'm in here normally. S'nice to talk to someone... even if they are a chi—'

Christy stopped herself.

'A child killer... is that what you were gonna say?'

'I didn't say that.'

'You were about to.'

'Well, ya know what, girl?' Christy said, leaning forward and resting her fingertips onto Joy's forearm. 'I actually haven't worked you out yet. Ma visions will tell me in time if you guilty or not. They always do.'

'Visions?'

'God talks to me. Lets me know what's what. I pretty much know all the girls in here. See Linda o'er there, the brunette with the short bob? That bitch says she didn't slit her boyfriend's throat. She be lying. I know she did it. I saw visions o' her doin' it.' Joy squinted at the middle-aged woman sat eating a slice of cardboard toast on the far end of their bench, noting she didn't look too dissimilar to Joy's own mother, whom she had sorely missed every day of the past sixteen years. Breast cancer had taken her. Breast cancer that was caught too late. Joy's father was still alive, but he was in a nursing home, aged only fifty-five years, unable to cope with the continued drama that kept unfolding before him. He lost his wife to cancer, his two grandsons to murder and then his daughter to the judicial system in the space of four years. 'And Stella, this one over here, she's down fo' attempted murder. Put a young girl in a coma in a bar one night. Glassed her, then jumped on top o' her and kept punching at her face until all her lights went out. I saw that in a vision too.'

'And what about you? What are you in for?' Joy asked, turning back to face Christy.

'Me?' Christy said. Then she glanced upwards, to eyeball Mathilda over Joy's shoulder. 'They say I held up the petrol station in Glasnevin. My third one they caught me for, they say. I had a sawn-off shotgun, they say. Didn't fire it though. Still got sent down for seven years. Highest sentence I cudda bin given.'

'Seven years?'

'Uh-huh. It's cos I'm black. But I don't like to moan 'bout it. God will see me right in ma next life. Right now, me 'n' Him tryna get me through this one. Seven years for armed robbery... it's a long stretch. Though I bet you with yo double life sentence you prolly think seven years is nuttin, right? But I'm gonna be sixty years of age in seven years. Ma life's clock is tick-tocking away.'

'What about her, the red-headed one?' Joy asked, nodding towards the woman who offered an ounce of sympathy her way whilst floss-drying her under regions in the shower room that morning.

'Oh... That's Nancy Trott. You don't wanna be dealin' with Nancy Trott. You stay well the hell away from that crazy red-headed bitch, ya here me?'

Joy turned back in her seat.

'Why?'

'She nasty. Bitch prolly be raping yo pretty ass right about now if I wasn't here beside ya. With you all tiny and pretty, I bet yo just her type.'

'You serious?' Joy asked, raising an eyebrow. Though just as she did, she noticed Aidan nod his head at her as he stood against the back wall, relieving Mathilda of her duty.

Christy noticed them glancing at each other and did a double-take.

'You fancy that white boy?' she said, a little too loudly.

'Shhh,' Joy hissed, stifling a smile. 'Course not, don't be silly. I'm married.'

Christy tucked her chin into her neck and gurned a face at Joy.

'You are? I don't think the newspapers know whether you married or not. They say yo husband didn't show up to any o' yo trial.'

Joy puffed a small laugh out of her nostrils, then a long silence settled between them before Christy broke it, using the thickest of her Texan drawl.

'Don't know what all y'all see in those skinny ass white boys anyway,' she whispered. 'They so ugly all bright pink 'n' naked. Can you believe I actually escaped a country of big black hunky men to come live here, in sunny Dublin, where all the boys' skin so white sometimes I think I can see right through 'em. But a woman gets horny, don't we? So, fuck skinny ass white boys I do. Though I have to say,' Christy leaned even closer. 'I don't even feel some o' they white dicks when they all up in there, sometimes.'

Joy held her stomach while laughing and reeled back on her bench. But just as she did, somebody grabbed a fistful of her frizzy hair from behind and slammed her nose to the corner of the table.

Delia exhales loudly as she pushes through the door to her office.

She leaves her briefcase, as she always does, resting against the balled leg of her oak desk, removes her robe, which she drops to the floor, and then sits into her padded leather chair; her elbows on her desk, her hands slapped against her cheeks.

It's been a long day, even for her.

Her overall feeling isn't exhaustion though. It's frustration; frustration because the trial hadn't covered as much ground during its opening day as she had hoped it would.

After opening arguments, both sides of the court detoured into an array of legal spats that seemed determined to test the judge's patience. Although the retrial had been granted two full years before it made it to court, the prosecution and defence teams were still, today, discussing minute details from the original trial, arguing whether or not they should be considered by the judge during her retrial deliberations. The paperwork Judge Delia had to contend with for any major trial was often labour-intensive. But for this retrial it had trebled in size; only because parts of the original trial had to be considered, too.

The opening arguments Delia had heard earlier failed to unearth any surprises. Not that opening arguments usually do. Lawyers just like to draw a rough outline of the arguments they will be bringing up in the trial, and very rarely hit a judge or jury with a key twist so early on.

After removing her hands from her cheeks, Delia wiggles her mouse to blink her computer screen to life. And in the time it takes for her old Apple Mac to refresh, she gazes around her desk – a ritual she isn't even aware she goes through every time she reawakens her computer.

It's a grand old oak desk she gets to look around, worth thousands of euros. Not that she paid for it. It became hers when she inherited this grand office at the back of Dublin's Criminal Courts from her predecessor – Judge Albert Riordan. The office was always densely lit, because the bulb hanging above the desk when Delia first entered was too weak to light the room adequately. But she liked the dimness and the warm ambience it brought to her work environment and so has, for the past nine years, purposely reordered the wrong bulb every time one blows. The dim orange light casts sharp shadows across the old desk; a shadow of the giant computer monitor; shadows from the two cupfuls of pens and pencils that sit beside her computer monitor. And the shadow from the photo frame that stands on the opposite side of her keyboard – framing an image of her and her now deceased husband Ben with their arms wrapped tightly around their only child Callum as they celebrated his graduation from Trinity College back in November, 2008. Although she doesn't like how she, personally, looks in that picture – not with her standing outside the Windmill Pub freezing cold and all hunched up in her winter hat and scarf – the image is as special to her as anything in this life. The flash of a camera. A moment in time captured forever. It's not a special moment to her because the two men in it happen to mean more to her than anything or anybody else; it's special because it's the last image that was ever captured of the McCormicks together. Ben passed away three weeks later, collapsing to a stuttering heart while sat at a conference table in his firm's head office, surrounded by twelve of his colleagues. One tried to revive him after his forehead had slapped to the table, but it was too late. Ben was gone. And has been gone for the past twelve years.

Friends have tried to fix Delia up on dates since she became a widow, but she genuinely isn't interested. She claims she's married to her profession. Besides, she has a man in her life. Callum. He hasn't quite moved out of the family home yet, even though he earns almost a quarter of a million a year and has just turned thirty-five. Despite numerous liaisons with the same sex, Callum is yet to find Mr Right and is way too needy to live alone. Besides, he knows all too well that his mother enjoys having him with her in their family home.

When her ritual of gazing at the items casting shadows on her desk is distracted by her monitor blinking to life, Delia exhales a sigh to reset herself, then begins to tap away at her keyboard. But footsteps cause her to pause pretty much before she has even begun. Then there's a beat of silence before knuckles rattle against the door. She doesn't need to call her visitor in to know who it is. She can always tell by the knock.

'In you come, Eddie,' she shouts.

Her boss grins at her after he's pushed his way through. He's a heavy-set man, is Eddie – over six-foot tall and at least twenty stone in weight. He's just one of those guys who's always been big all over; big shoulders, big hips, big ass. He has worn his greying hair neatly parted to one side in all the time Delia has known him and has immensely bushy eyebrows – shaped like an inverted hairy V.

'Why don't you get a proper light in here, Delia,' he says, staring up at the dim glow above her desk.

'Change the tune, Eddie.'

Eddie closes the office door gingerly, then grips the back of the chair opposite the judge.

'Didn't quite get to open the floor today, huh?'

Delia thins her lips.

'Paperwork and more paperwork. Seemed to me Bracken was trying to delay the day. He kept arguing over the order of the witness list – obsessing about it, truth be told. It was all a nonsense. I think he was trying to delay the beginning of the trial until tomorrow... probably needs more time vetting his witnesses.'

'Wouldn't put it past him. He eh... kept his opening argument pretty close to his chest though, huh? Do ya think he has something up his sleeve? Can't imagine Bunny is his only ace card. A dodgy dog might have been enough to win his client a retrial, but it won't be enough to acquit her.' Delia rubs her fingers across the deep wrinkles of her forehead, then raises an eyebrow across the desk. 'Sorry,' Eddie says. 'It's not my place to say what will or what won't be enough to acquit Joy Stapleton. That power is all in your hands.'

Eddie holds his palms outwards, then scoots himself around and sits into the chair he'd been gripping the back of.

'Defence team didn't say much in opening either, did they?' Delia offers up as she begins clicking at her mouse.

'They don't have much to do, though. As long as they stay firm on why Joy was convicted in the first place, they'll be fine. Onus is all on Bracken to prove Joy shouldn't be behind bars. But he's not gonna be able to do that. I know this is a massive case and the – excuse me for cursing – but the fuckin' media vans outside – did you see 'em?' he asks. 'Never seen so many vans in my life. But truth be known, you don't need to feel a huge amount of pressure on this, Delia. As big a story as it is. This is an open and shut case for you. Take all arguments into consideration and then do what you gotta do...'

'Yes, thanks, Eddie. I do know how to do my job.'

'Course ya do,' he says, chuckling from the back of his throat. 'It's just...'

Delia's breathing pauses, and her fingers hover over her mouse.

'It's just what?' she says, peering over her glasses at him, as if he's one of those chancer lawyers she likes to stare down to exert her dominance. Except she doesn't have dominance in this room. Eddie Taunton does. He's the Chief Justice – is literally responsible for keeping the cogs of the whole judicial arm of the nation turning, and has been doing so for the past twenty years. He has a jovial manner most of the time, but even the most high-profile of figures know he's no pushover. No matter who's in the room, from Supreme Court judges to the President or even the Taoiseach, Eddie Taunton always assumes the role of authority.

'You remember all those years back, I interviewed you for a Supreme Courts Judges Panel chair?' he says.

Delia's hand remains hovering over her mouse, her breath still held.

'Yes,' she says.

'Remember I asked you about this trial in particular... the original Joy Stapleton trial? I knew you'd studied it.'

'Yes.'

'You told me you were sure she did it – that Joy Stapleton was guilty. That the jurors got it right.'

'Yes.' Eddie shrugs. And then Delia finally exhales a long, silent breath through her nostrils before her hand finally rests on to her mouse. 'What are you trying to say, Eddie?'

'I'm not trying to say anything. Just that you believed her to be guilty—'

'This is an entirely different trial, Eddie. What are you trying to suggest?' Judge Delia gasps, then whips off her glasses and leans forward – her eyes wide. 'Eddie, did I get awarded this trial because of an answer I gave to you in an interview seven years ago? Oh my word... that's it, isn't it?' She sits back in her chair and stares up at the dim bulb above her. 'Wow. You decided there'd be no jury on this retrial. You decided on one judge. You decided on me. Eddie... did you set this up because you assumed I'd deliver a guilty verdict?'

'That's not what I've said at all,' Eddie says, holding his hands up. He raises one of his V-shaped bushy eyebrows into a more prominent arch, then creases his chubby cheeks into a grin.

'Eddie... you did, didn't you? You want a guilty verdict. You've played for it?'

'Don't be paranoid, Delia,' he says.

'Why no jury?'

'You know the answer to that quest—'

'Why no jury?'

'Because the whole bloody nation knows about this case. We couldn't get twelve unbiased views. There was never going to be a retrial if a jury couldn't be found.'

'Why me?'

'Delia, forgive me for cursing again, but for fuck sake, we've had these conversations. You were chosen because you're the best bloody judge in the country. Probably one of the best there's ever been. You got chosen on merit.'

Delia squints at her boss, her forehead dipping.

'Eddie, I will be judging this new trial with the freshest of eyes.'

'Course you will. Course you will.'

It comes as no surprise to Delia that Eddie would have preference for a guilty verdict. It'd be less mess for him to clean up as Chief Justice. Delia has been aware for years that Eddie doesn't play every game inside the lines, but surely he wouldn't be so brazen as to ask her out straight to deliver a specific verdict on any trial? Let alone the biggest retrial the country's ever witnessed...

'Well... if... there's nothing of urgency, Eddie, I must get back to...' she points at her computer screen which has by now blinked back off again.

'Sure, sure.' Eddie heaves his large frame out of the chair and rises to his feet. 'Eh...' he scratches at the stubble of his chin. 'You know she did this right? There's no doubt about it all—'

'Eddie—'

'Regardless of what doggy tales or new technology Gerd Bracken brings to this retrial, that's her in that CCTV footage.'

'Eddie!'

Eddie shows her his palms again.

'Alright, alright,' he says. 'I get it. You're the judge.'

Delia grins her teeth and offers him a friendly blinking of the eyes. But Eddie just shakes his head back at her, then he grunts as he pulls open the office door and strolls out.

Delia leans her head back to the top of her chair and puffs out a snort of laughter. Then she wiggles at her mouse again, for her screen to blink back to life, and in the time it does, she stares around her desk again, following her usual routine.

'That was odd,' she whispers to herself.

2,860 days ago...

Joy had been slowly and carefully reintroduced into Elm House; starting with her rejoining the prisoners for lunch in the canteen, flanked by two officers, then being allowed an hour in the games room with the other prisoners, flanked by two officers. And last week she was allowed to take breaks with other prisoners in the yard for the first time – again, flanked by two officers. Each transition passed seemlessly, even if she was shitting herself throughout.

Incredibly, given the force of the smash, her nose hadn't broken. Though it did suffer a severe cut right across the bridge that was only fully healing over now – four months after the attack. The purple and yellow bruising under both of her eyes hadn't relented for well over a month. It was odd that she had been placed in isolation, given that that was the exact same punishment her attacker had received. Stella, her name was – a close associate of Nancy Trott. She was so enraged that Joy had killed her two boys and yet had the audacity to sit in the canteen brazenly laughing with Christy Jabefemi that she waited until the new prison officer relieved Mathilda from her shift of protecting Joy before running over and grabbing Joy by the hair and slamming her face to the corner of the bench.

While Stella's isolation was deemed punishment, Joy's was for her own safety. She resided in a cell that sits between a janitor's storage unit and a prison officer's station on the other end of the gate that leads into Elm House. She spent most of her days in that cell; though she did have the luxury of a TV screen for company with six channels, as well as her own shower. She also had the freedom to go to and from a small yard at certain times of the day that was just on the other side of the janitor's storage unit. After a couple of weeks in, her three rounds of civilian clothes arrived. Three sweatjumpers, three T-Shirts and three comfy pairs of tracksuit bottoms – along with a dozen pairs of underwear and two pairs of trainers. All comfy clothes. And all comfy clothes that finally fit her.

The only people she ever really got to see while she was in isolation were the same two officers she had seen on her first two days on the regular wing of the prison: Mathilda and Aidan. They were both given the boring task of seeing to the lone prisoner as punishment because her attack was deemed their fault. The Governor blamed new recruit Aidan for the attack happening on his watch. But he mostly blamed Mathilda, because she was Aidan's line manager and was supposed to be still training him in. The whole incident was embarrassing for Aidan, though he got over it as time passed. He liked the job of looking after Joy in isolation because it left him with no real mistakes to make. He'd escort her to the yard a few times a day and they'd often sit and talk. He and Mathilda shared eight-hour shifts looking after Joy. Though Mathilda didn't speak much during her shifts, well, certainly not on any personal level. She upgraded her usual stern muteness to a 'Good morning' or an odd 'How are you?' over the months, but the smallest of small talk was about as big as it ever got between the pair of them. Whereas by now Joy had known that Aidan had become a prisoner officer even though his real passion lay in catering and cooking. And he knew that she cheated during her Leaving Cert exams by sneaking notes into the classroom. That was the depth of discussion they had bonded over during those months. She would plead with him to believe her innocence whenever the topic of her sentence arose. But it rarely did, in truth.

It was starting to infuriate Joy that Shay had yet to visit her. Though she could somewhat understand his hesitations. She had spoken to him on the phone, on her first day in isolation after she had been attacked, but she knew by his tone that, although sympathetic and sincere, he was still uncertain and unwilling to commit to her claims of innocence.

The other phone calls she made were reserved for her father. He was a full-time resident in Muckross – a care home for the vulnerable that was situated on the Dublin border. Noel Lansbury was the youngest full-time resident in that home by far, but he took his wife's painfully slow death in the middle of her life so bad that he lost all sense of belonging and began seeking semblances of solace in alcohol. Bottles of it. And then, in the midst of his own depression while slipping into alcoholism, his grandsons went missing two years before his daughter was arrested for their murder. He sunk so low that he was offered a room at Muckross, even though it is essentially a home for elderly folk. The move has worked for him in some respects, though – he has been sober for the past eighteen months anyway. But his life as he had known it has well and truly ended. He didn't make it to Joy's trial, couldn't bring himself to. And despite pleading with his daughter over the phone that he genuinely believed her version of events, Joy has never been quite sure what his true thoughts are.

'Well, if it isn't Annie... "It's a hard knock life, fo' us",' a Texan-Nigerian accent attempted to sing. Joy looked up through her curls to see Christy smiling her yellow teeth at her. 'Welcome back, sista.'

'I'm so scared, Christy,' Joy sobbed immediately. And then Christy grabbed her into a tight embrace, resting her chin atop Joy's curls.

'No need to be scared, come here... sit down, girl.' They entered Joy's cell and both perched on the side of her thin mattress. 'I told ya. That chick – Stella – who attacked you, she gone, girl. After her isolation, they packed her off to a'other wing. They was thinkin' bout sendin' you to a'other wing, too. But I pleaded with them that I'd look after ya. 'Sides, Nancy Trott put in a good word, too. Said she'll see to it that her girls don't go near you again. She says she didn't put Stella up to attackin' you, but I don't know whether to believe a word that bitch says.'

'But if you don't believe what she says, amn't I still a target?'

'Relax,' a strange prison officer said, poking her face around Joy's cell door. 'The whole wing has been swept clean. You have nothing to worry about. Nobody's out to hurt you.'

Joy contorted her face at Christy, then whispered, 'Who's that?'

'Oh, she the new screw lookin' after you. They took that new guy what's-his-name, off your watch...'

'Aidan!?' Joy shouted. And then she flew out of her cell all up in a rage; marching down the steel staircases of Elm House until she reached the officers' station close to where she had spent the previous four months in isolation. The only person she had struck up any bond with, any relationship with, since she'd been inside was gone. She dropped to her knees outside the officers' station – her heart genuinely pained. But her cries fell on deaf ears.

'Don't worry, sista,' Christy said, gripping Joy in a tight embrace as a crowd of both prisoners and prison officers gathered around them. 'I'm yo best friend. Anything you need. Anything you want, Christy's here... ya hear me?'

Joy sniffled and snotted and coughed and cried... then she looked Christy in the eyes and offered a smile through the stray strands of her frizzy hair.

'Why are you being nice to me? You don't even think I'm innocent, do you, Christy? You said you hadn't worked me out.'

'Christy works everybody out,' one of the prisoners shouted. 'If Christy says you're guilty, you're guilty. If she says you're innocent, you're innocent.'

Some prisoners scoffed and jeered.

'It's true. God speaks to her,' another prisoner shouted. 'You want the truth, Christy Jabefemi will give you the truth.'

For most of the crowd, the drama was over, and they dispersed, content to allow Joy to be sucked into the delusional bible-bashing clique if she so wished.

'Well,' Joy said, wiping at her face. 'Have you worked me out yet... do you believe I'm innocent?'

Christy laughed, then took Joy in for another hug, kissing her on top of her curls.

'I haven't seen a vision for you yet, girl... but if you want, and when you want, I'm happy to give it a try. Just lemme know when yo ready.'

It didn't take Joy long to let Christy know she was ready.

'I want you to believe me… to believe I'm innocent. I need somebody to,' she pleaded.

Since Joy had been in isolation, Christy had won over a small number of prisoners by conducting mind readings and telling fortunes. She had surprised even the most sceptical in the prison with a number of nailed-on predictions. She had even predicted that Joy would be attacked the day before she was actually attacked. She said that's why she was befriending her, because she got a sign from God that Joy needed protecting. Then Christy predicted that some famous public figure would die soon which just so happened to be the night before Whitney Houston took her own life. There was also the time she predicted that Michelle Doherty – a heavily tattooed prisoner in Elm House – would get her love life back on track soon. And lo and behold, two weeks later Michelle's ex-boyfriend Darren visited the prison for the first time in over a year to declare his undying love for her – telling her he wanted them to move in together as soon as she got out.

The cult of Christy was small, but it was growing pretty much week on week, though only because it was a case of either teaming up with the deluded following of insane-but-placid Christy Jabefemi, or teaming up with Nancy Trott and her cohorts of untrustworthy scumbag criminals.

It was no surprise that all of Christy's recently-recruited associates were in attendance to watch her grip both of Joy's wrists across one of the dining room benches, but it was a surprise that Nancy and her gang of cohorts had also joined in. Although Christy's gifts had been put to the test plenty of times before – to some shocking successes and some embarrassing misses – trying to get a read on the most notorious prisoner in the country was being deemed as the ultimate test of sorts. Even prison officers who had, in the secure confines of the prison officers' headquarters, snorted at Christy's claims of being able to see visions, joined the growing crowd in the dining room.

'You are really, deeply, sad.' Christy said.

Then she let go of one of Joy's wrists to hold a hand towards the crowd in an attempt to stifle the sniggers that had already ignited.

'No shit,' one prisoner shouted, and the laughter grew in volume.

'I mean, deeply sad. I can tell you certainly believe you are innocent.'

Another jeer went up, but it was silenced by the shushing that hissed through pockets of the crowd.

'You lived a happy life. In Rathfarnham. You married well. You had two boys. You were really happy. Actually... hold on... your husband was a real success story, wasn't he?'

'Ah here, for fuck sake, can you tell us something my nanny Margaret couldn't fuckin' tell us?' one prisoner snidely snapped. And then an eruption of laughter suffocated the eerie tension that had struck up as soon as Christy had sat down to grab at Joy's wrists.

Eventually, those who were desperate to listen, shushed down the jeers, to the point where only the crashing and clanking of the pots and pans in the kitchen could be heard in the distance.

'You are a Capricorn, my visions are telling me, that right?'

Joy nodded once, her eyes widening.

'Cudda read Joy's date of birth in the papers,' one prisoner whispered to another.

'Well, do you know Joy's date of birth?' the other prisoner responded. Then they both just shrugged their shoulders at each other, and zoned back in.

'And you are an only child, that right, Joy?'

'Uh-huh?' Joy said, the frown on her forehead creasing further.

'And I can tell that you always wanted a career... you were ambitious, right? Until you got married and then you became a housewife... a mother?'

Joy nodded again, and as she did she noticed eyes shifting from side-to-side in the crowd behind Christy.

'Oh... I've got it. I've got it!' Christy said, her Nigerian accent taking over, her volume rising. 'The woman in the pink hooded top... I can see her... I see her.'

There were puffs of laughter produced from pockets of the crowd, but nobody was walking away, not yet anyway. 'And the figure is walking. Walking down the mountains. Her hands are dirty... her fingernails are dirty. I can't see her face. Just the hood. But I am running towards her.'

More jeering fired up. More shushing stemmed it.

'Wait... wait... I'm catching up with her,' Christy said, her breaths growing in sharpness as she gripped Joy's wrists tighter. 'Come here you. Come here you.' She released her grip from Joy, stretched her hand out to grab at nothing and then yanked herself backwards.

'Turn around bitch. Turn around!'

Slam!

Christy slapped her hand on to the bench. And the whole dining room fell silent. Then she opened her eyes. Wide; so wide, Joy could see the blood rings around both the top and bottom of her eyeballs.

'Was it her? Was it Joy?' a voice from the crowd asked.

'Did she do it? Did she murder her boys?'

Christy slapped her hand to the bench once more.

'You didn't do it. It wasn't you under that pink hood.'

A yell of hurrays went up – a few in support of Christy's gift, most mocking – before the crowd disbursed, shaking their heads either in astonishment or in laughter. But some stayed, either to touch Christy in her moment of enlightenment, or to embrace Joy in solidarity.

'Must be awful what you've been through,' one prisoner, whose face Joy hadn't seen before, whispered into her ear.

2,858 days ago...

Joy had been tossing and turning on her bed during the two nights she had been back at Elm House. The mattress she had slept on for the four months she was in isolation had been at least two times thicker than the one in her regular cell.

She was still yawning from a lack of sleep, but leapt out of bed as soon as her cell door clicked open. And, with the two officers assigned to her flanked by her sides, she stormed her way across the landing to push open the door of Christy's cell.

'Mornin, sista,' Christy said, looking up from her bible. 'What can I do ya for?'

Joy stepped inside, leaving the two officers standing by the door.

'I've been tossing and turning all night, Christy... I never asked you yesterday, not with all the excitement that was going on afterwards, but... you say in your vision that you took down the woman's hood so you could make out her face... to see if it was me or not.'

'Uh-huh,' Christy said, placing her bible on her pillow and standing up.

'Well... you were able to tell everyone it wasn't me.'

'Yep. It wasn't you, Joy. You innocent. You didn't kill those boys.'

'Then who did?' Joy asks, fidgeting with her fingers.

'Huh?'

'What did her face look like?'

Christy picked up her plastic bottle and took a large swig from it, swirling the warm water from cheek to cheek. When she finally swallowed, she patted Joy on the shoulder.

'Let's go eat some breakfast, huh?'

They sat on the same bench Joy had been attacked on four months prior, but being attacked wasn't on her mind right now, nor were the two slices of cardboard toast that lay on a plastic plate in front of her.

'C'mon, Christy. Please. Tell me. What did the face look like?'

'I told ya, sister... I don't know the face. I don't know her. I just know she ain't you.'

'Please.' Joy pressed her two palms together. 'Just tell me what she looked like.'

'Listen, I don't see a full face. Just some features. I just saw enough to know she wasn't you. She didn't have big curly hair like you under that pink hood. She had straight hair.'

'What colour?' Joy said, her eyes squinting.

'Brown.'

'And you say you see features, what kind of features?'

Christy tore a slice of Joy's toast in two, then curled one-half of it into her mouth and chewed.

'She had kinda like an oval face. Pale. White. Definitely white. Red lips. Maybe lipstick.'

'She was wearing lipstick?'

'Yeah. Think so,' Christy said. 'Her lips were all bright red.'

'Did you see her eye colour?'

'Brown. I'm sure they were brown.'

Joy gasped, then held a hand to her mouth.

'What is it, sista,' Christy said, stopping chewing, 'you think you know this bitch? You think you know who killed yo boys?'

❖

Delia licks the tip of her thumb, then flicks through the papers whilst the gallery wait in silence. They'd spent over three hours in this courtroom the previous afternoon following the trial's opening arguments, watching her doing exactly as she is doing now – rifling through paperwork.

'Now then,' she finally says, her voice booming through the microphone. And as it does, everybody in the gallery sits a little more upright in their benches.

The new courtrooms inside Dublin's Criminal Courts contains rows of pews – not unlike a church – in front of which are two benches where the trial lawyers and the defendants sit. Further in front of those two desks, raised higher than any other chair, is where the judge resides, looking down on everybody.

'Mr Gerd Bracken, can the defence please call their first witness?'

'We can indeed, Your Honour,' Bracken says as he stands. 'The defence calls Mr Philip Grimshaw to the stand.'

A shaven-haired man rises from the gallery and strolls solemnly up the thin aisle of scarlet-red carpet before sitting himself into the witness box adjacent to the judge. After his affirmation is completed, Bracken walks his way to the centre of the courtroom floor and clasps his hands.

'Thank you for being here today, Mr Grimshaw,' he says. 'Can you please state your profession for the court?'

'Of course,' Grimshaw says in a thick northern-English accent. 'I am a dog handler. But a specialist dog handler.'

'Okay, but it is fair to say, Mr Grimshaw, that you don't work for the police in your native country, right? You are a freelance dog handler who has, on occasion, been hired by the police force in the UK, is that correct?'

'That is correct, yes.'

'And it is true to say that in early January of 2009, you received a phone call from a detective of An Garda Siochana here in Ireland, requesting your assistance in what was then a missing persons' case? Two boys, Oscar and Reese Stapleton had gone missing and it was suggested you travel to Dublin to help with the investigation.'

'It is true to say that, yes.'

'Now, you testified at Joy Stapleton's original trial that after spending twenty minutes inside the Stapleton family home, your dog Bunny barked which indicated to you that there was a presence of scents associated with decomposing bodies, correct?'

'Eh, well, I can't be certain of the exact words I used. But it should be stated for the record that Bunny made indications, it doesn't have to be a bark. It may have been a sniff and a long pause. But yeah, Bunny gave me an indication that a decomposing body or bodies had been present in an upstairs bedroom of the Stapleton home.'

'So, Bunny doesn't bark... what does he do exactly when he comes across what he thinks are indications to the presence of decomposing bodies?'

'He stays in or around the area. Then sniffs his nose more forcefully... he might bark. Sometimes he barks.'

'So, his reactions are inconsistent – sometimes he barks, sometimes he doesn't?'

'Yeah, that's right.'

'Well then, how do you personally know the difference with

any degree of certainty? Does a bark not indicate something different to a non-bark?'

'Well... Bunny is a unique dog, he's retired now actually.'

'Oh, I'm well aware of his retirement, Mr Grimshaw, and we'll get to that in just a second. But let me ask you this question first... Who trained Bunny to become a dog who could sense the presence of decomposing bodies?'

Grimshaw's fair eyebrows drop.

'Well... I did. I train all my dogs.'

'And who trained you, Sir?'

'Who trained me?'

'Yes. Who trained you to train dogs?'

'I, eh... well, I did a course back in Leeds where I'm from in the late-eighties and eh...'

'Yes, Sir. I am aware of the course you took. A dog handling course. From all accounts, the training you completed didn't exactly teach you how to train dogs to sniff out decomposing bodies, now did it?'

'No.'

'In fact, it taught you how to train your dog to sit, and roll over, and fetch a stick, isn't that correct?'

'Objection, Your Honour, leading the witness,' Jonathan Ryan calls out.

'You may answer the question,' Judge Delia says, nodding her head at Grimshaw.

'It was a lot more than just asking a dog to roll over and sit,' he says.

'But for the record, you never learned or received any qualification in training dogs how to sniff out decomposing bodies, right?'

'I taught myself all of that. I started to help police with some enquiries back in the early nineties and I liked doing that work... so I branched out, started to teach my dogs new tricks.'

Bracken takes two steps backwards, shuffles some paperwork at his desk, then interlinks his fingers around his navel before taking two steps forward again, leading him back to where he began.

'Right, so what we've established is, not only does the dog,

Bunny in this case, not have official training in the sensing of decomposing bodies, but his trainer or handler doesn't either, would that be fair to say, Mr Grimshaw?'

'I know for a fact that Bunny can sense decomposing bodies. Bunny has helped out with major investigations over the years—'

'He has, yes. Nine murder investigations; seven in England, one in Scotland and one here in Ireland. It's just that four years ago Bunny's evidence in one trial was questioned, as were your credentials on dog training, and the evidence you brought to that trial was thrown out, wasn't it? And that is the reason we are here at this retrial today, isn't it? Because that evidence was thrown out and it now calls into question all of the trials Bunny has provided evidence for, including the trial of Joy Stapleton. Bunny has been retired since he was dismissed from that trial in London four years ago, hasn't he, Mr Grimshaw?'

'Yes. I have said that already. He's retired.'

'Because his apparent skills have been called into question.'

'I know he is a dog who can—'

'Sir, I am not interested in your opinion. I am interested in the facts. Bunny was dismissed from a high-profile case in London because his skillsets cannot be determined... correct?'

Grimshaw sighs, then sheepishly glances up to Judge Delia before turning back to Bracken.

'Yes, I guess that's what the court said.'

'Okay, well, let me repeat that for the ears of our court again, shall I? Bunny the dog's particular skillsets *cannot* be determined. We have no way of knowing for certain if Bunny can or cannot sense the presence of decomposing bodies.'

'Nobody knows Bunny better than I—'

'Ah-ah,' Bracken says holding a finger up. 'I didn't ask you a question that time, Mr Grimshaw.' Bracken takes a step towards the witness box and eyeballs the witness. 'Bunny felt he had sensed a decomposing body in a forest near Kent in England in 2016 and you testified on the stand that Bunny had done so. It was, in that same trial, confirmed two weeks later, that Bunny couldn't have sensed these bodies, because these bodies were never in that forest in the first place.'

'Yes but—'

'Ah-ah, still didn't ask a question.'

'Well you better soon get to asking one, Mr Bracken,' Judge Delia says.

Bracken stares at her momentarily, then pivots his face back to Grimshaw.

'Yes or no, Mr Grimshaw – has Bunny been forcibly retired from this line of work because his findings are not scientifically conclusive?'

Grimshaw stares around himself, then relents.

'Officially, yes.'

'And is it true that Bunny provided evidence in the missing persons case of Reese and Oscar Stapleton?'

'Yes.'

'That is all, Your Honour,' Bracken says before he spins on his heels and walks back to his desk.

'Mr Ryan,' Judge Delia calls out as she scribbles some notes onto her paperwork. 'Have you questions for this witness?'

Ryan rises from his chair.

'You are an upstanding member of society, Mr Grimshaw, correct? You've never been in trouble with police? Never even had a misdemeanour? Never been accused of being anything other than just a bit of a loner because you prefer to spend time with dogs rather than humans, right?'

Grimshaw chuckles.

'I guess you could say that, yes.'

'You've never married so therefore have never been unfaithful. But it is true you have the same two best friends that you've had your whole life?'

'Yeah, we met at primary school and have been buddies ever since.'

'So, you are an upstanding member of society who has been faithful and who has never been in trouble for breaking the law. All accurate statements, right?'

Grimshaw nods.

'Yes.'

'You have never, nor never will intend to deceive anybody. All of the work you have done for the police force in the UK and once here in Ireland, it was all done in good faith, yes?'

'Absolutely. I've never tried to deceive anybody in my life.'

'That's all, Your Honour.'

Judge Delia looks over her glasses at Bracken who stands without hesitation.

'Mr Grimshaw. Deception does not always have to be conscious, would you agree with me?'

Grimshaw's eyebrows dip again.

'Sorry… I…'

'It doesn't matter, Mr Grimshaw. You don't need to answer that question. Thank you.'

Bracken sits again and as he does Judge Delia dismisses Grimshaw from the stand with a nod of her head followed by a subtle waving of her hand. Then she rifles through her paperwork in the resulting silence, taking note of Bracken's tactic of disguising a statement wrapped up in a question. She knew he didn't want to ask Grimshaw if he did or didn't think deception was always a conscious act, he just wanted to make a statement to the court that deception doesn't always have to be conscious. She doesn't want to let Bracken get away with snidey mis-steps, but he covers them so well that she really can't condone him for asking an actual question… even if he didn't bother to get an answer for it. There isn't a more experienced defence lawyer in the country than Gerd Bracken. Although Delia knows she would detest the man if she ever had to spend any time with him outside of a courtroom, she has had to admit in the past that she sure is impressed by his skills when inside that courtroom.

'Recess until after lunch-time, perhaps, Your Honour?' Bracken calls out. Delia squints at him. 'Sorry. Our next witness has had trouble with transportation this morning.'

Delia rolls back the sleeve of her robe and takes note of the time on her wrist.

'It's not even midday yet. Seems awfully early for lunch but ehm... yes, court dismissed for two hours. We will all return at one forty-five p.m. sharp.'

Delia wiggles her mouse as soon as she's back at her office desk, and in the time the screen blinks back to life, she has completed her routine of staring at things she is barely noticing; taking in her cupfuls of pens and the framed photograph of her family – smiling at her husband as he smiles back at her. One of the last smiles he ever smiled. Then, as soon as her hands hover over her keyboard, she hears footsteps outside, followed, annoyingly, by the rap of one knuckle against her door two times.

'Come in, Callum,' she says.

He grins the same grin his father would grin at her when he used to poke his head around her office door.

'So, the dog was dodgy all along?' Callum says. They both offer the same puffed-through-the-nostrils laugh in sync – a habit they have picked up from way too many years of living with each other. 'Doesn't mean anything though does it?'

Delia shakes her head.

'Don't mind that... how was your date last night?'

'Good, actually. He was... what would I say? Genuine. Honest. Didn't seem as if he was full of shit or anything, you know... Nice looking. Nice eyes. Though he needs a beard. His face is a little pasty.' Delia laughs. 'We swapped numbers.'

'What does he do for a living?'

'Listen,' Callum says, smirking. 'You're at the start of the biggest retrial in the history of this country and you wanna talk to me about a guy whose second name I can't even remember.' He cocks his head. 'Go on... tell me. Did the dog testimony have any impact on you?'

Delia removes her glasses, then unclips her pearl earrings and places them carefully to the side of her photo frame.

'It's made an impact. But not a huge one,' she says. 'There were no revelations, were there? Not much we didn't know before today. The dog that sniffed a decomposed body in the Stapleton bedroom all those years ago turns out to be a bit of a fraud. That was pretty apparent in the original trial... to me anyway.'

'Grimshaw was always just a forensic witness fitting the needs of the officers, right?'

'Exactly.'

'But you still think she did it, right?'

'Callum!' Delia barks. 'I am looking at this trial with totally fresh eyes.'

'Course you are, Mum,' he says.

'Y'know, you're not the first one who's dropped by to ask what I'm thinking.'

'Huh?'

'Eddie Taunton... he popped by yesterday. Sounded most suspicious. As if he was leading me towards a guilty verdict.'

'Well, he would want a guilty verdict, wouldn't he? He can't have his whole system come crashing down by admitting we got the Joy Stapleton trial all wrong in the first place. Heads would roll... Lots of them. His would probably be the first to go.'

'Can you imagine the pay-out Joy would get if she was found not guilty after all these years?'

'Tens of millions, right?' Delia turns out her bottom lip and slowly nods her head. 'Taunton couldn't have been leaning on you though, right, Mum? I mean I wouldn't trust him as far as I could throw him, but he's not that dodgy, is he? He wouldn't put pressure on you to deliver a specific verdict, right?'

Delia creases up her nose.

'It was just kind of odd how he spoke to me. He brought up the fact that he asked me about the Stapleton case in an interview years ago. He remembered I was insistent the judge and jury got it right in the original trial; that Joy is guilty of killing her sons. I think that's why I landed this case. He fought for no jury, and one judge. Then he picked me as that one judge, knowing I had once given him a detailed analysis of why the first trial got it right.'

'Jesus. You seriously think he picked you to ensure a guilty verdict?' Callum's eyes narrow, and he sits back in his chair, blowing through his lips. 'He's right in one way though, is Eddie. You're certain she's guilty, aren't you?'

'Callum...'

'Yes! I know... You're looking at this case from fresh eyes. I get it. Of course.' Callum grins. 'So, who's up next after the dog handler?'

'Ehm...' Delia picks up her paperwork and begins to file through it.

'Geez, Mom. How can you be somebody with brains to burn, but no idea how to ever get your paperwork in order?'

'Ah, here, I got it,' she says, removing a sheet from the pile and bringing it to the top. 'Bracken is going to call an ex-detective who was involved in the original case. A Mrs Sandra Gleeson.'

SANDRA GLEESON

I'm not nervous. The opposite in fact. I'm bullish. Determined.

I actually wasn't invited to give evidence at this trial, I offered to do so. As soon as I heard there was going to be a retrial – and that Gerd Bracken would be defending Joy Stapleton – I immediately picked up the phone.

I sheepishly take a peek at Joy as I sit. She hasn't changed. Well, not really. You'd still know it was her. Big bushy curls smothering her tiny features. Though I can tell from here that her skin looks drier, as if she's been parched of fluids for the entire eight years she's been inside. She has one deep lined wrinkle that runs vertical between her eyebrows that wasn't there before. And some of the tips of her curls have faded to grey. Though she's still tiny. Still rake thin. And still unmistakably Joy Stapleton.

'Thank you for being here, Mrs Gleeson,' Bracken says.

'Oh, Sandra, please,' I reply, batting my hand at him.

'Okay... Sandra it is then. The court appreciates and thanks you for your time. Can you state your occupation – and if you don't mind, former occupation – for the record of the court, please?'

'Sure,' I say, repositioning my seating position. 'I work for Integration.'

'Well, you don't just work for Integration, do you?'

'No,' I say, laughing, until I realise this is really not the place,

nor the time for my snorty chuckle to be heard. 'I am the founding member of Integration. We are a non-profit organisation whose goals are to ensure immigrants and refugees transition into our societies as seamlessly as possible.'

'Very noble,' Bracken says, nodding. 'And before that?'

'Well before that I was a member of An Garda Siochana. For eight years. I was a uniformed Garda for four years, then an inspector for two years and a detective for the last two years before turning in my badge.'

'Mind telling the court why you turned in your badge?'

'Sure. I, eh... I didn't feel comfortable. My honest opinion is that the police force is somewhat controlled by what I call systemic fractures. I found, as an investigator, that I was forced to fit my investigations into a certain pattern that was already structured. So, often I found myself having to arrest somebody without true investigation and I felt... well... I felt as if I wasn't doing what I set out to do.'

'Which was?'

'Which was to play a role in society. That's why I wanted to be a policewoman as far back as I can remember. I thought I could help people in our society that way. But that's not what being a member of An Garda Siochana turned out to be.'

'That's interesting. We'll come back to that in a minute or two actually. But for the court, can you firstly detail a case you began investigating back in November of 2008?'

'Well, I assume you are talking about the Oscar and Reese Stapleton case?' *I say. We rehearsed that bit. Not that I'm in any way here just to please Gerd Bracken. Truth be known, I don't really like the man. He's a bit slimy. A bit full of himself. But we did talk through what he would ask of me during this trial and I agreed to go along with his script – as long as I was telling the truth. He just wanted to frame the truth in his own pattern. Which is fine by me. He knows what he's doing.*

'You assisted Lead Detective Ray De Brun on the Stapleton case, correct?'

'Yes, I did indeed,' *I reply.* 'But I should stress at this point, that although I am likely to point to some flaws in the investigative prac-

tices here in Ireland, I am not here to slander any persons, specifically. The people aren't the problem. The system they work in is the problem. For example, Detective Ray De Brun – as you chose to bring up his name – was a fine detective. And is a fine human being.'

I didn't rehearse that with Bracken. It actually takes him by surprise and he stalls, twitching his fingers. I didn't even plan to say it; it's just that he brought up Ray's name. And I don't wanna go shouting my head off about how flawed the system is and have everyone think I'm defaming Ray. I'm not. I actually like Ray.

'Okay, so you mentioned a flawed system, Sandra. Can you detail that for me?'

'Objection, Your Honour. That's a rather broad question,' the young lawyer on the opposite side of the room calls out.

I look up to Judge Delia who is sucking on her lips, stewing in thought. Her features are hard to read. The eyes behind her 1950s style retro glasses are oval and so dark that it looks as if her pupils are constantly dilated. And she has that cropped brown haircut most women in their sixties seem to have. Though, it's hard to put an age on Judge Delia with any accuracy, but she's got to be around the sixty mark, surely. Or perhaps the hair-do just adds a few years.

'Yes, be more specific in your line of questioning, Mr Bracken,' she eventually says.

'Of course, Your Honour,' Bracken replies, shuffling his frame back around to face me. 'Sandra, you said you felt you were part of a fractured system when you worked for the police force. Can you detail to me how you feel that fractured system played a role in the investigation into Joy Stapleton?'

'Oh, well.' I sit more upright, leaning my forearms onto the small shelf carved around the squared edges of the witness box. 'The Stapleton case, I guess, is a good example of the systemic issues we face with regards policing in this country, because the investigation focused on one suspect from the get-go and then fitted a case entirely around that suspect. Like I say – and I want to repeat this – I don't think the personnel who work in the force are to blame. They – we – we were just following a decades old system that can, in my humble* *opinion, lead even the best of detectives down the wrong path. My honest opinion is that the system gives investigators tunnel vision. And as I said, I don't blame the individuals, personally. I just believe a lot of detectives suffer with tunnel vision because, ultimately, they are led to believe that success in their line of work is measured by a successful prosecution. But that is so far wide of how success for a detective should be measured. Success for an investigator should be seeking the truth. Bottom line. But that's not what it is. Detectives are measured by the justice system based on whether or not they get a successful prosecution. Detectives are measured by the top end of the police force based on whether or not they get a successful prosecution. And they are measured by their line managers and peers on whether or not they get a successful prosecution. They're even measured by the public by that means too. And it must be said that there is a huge difference between striving to find a successful prosecution, as opposed to striving to find the truth.'*

I tap my tongue against my dry pallet, then look to the court assistant and motion a mock sipping to her. I was told there'd be a jug of water in the witness box but there isn't. She nods back at me, then turns and paces out a side door.

'Well, this, coming from an experienced member of the police force is really troubling. Are you saying Joy Stapleton was a suspect right from the get-go and that detectives were solely focused on getting her prosecuted for this crime?'

'Absolutely she was,' I say. 'And because of that, the whole investigation turned into a task of finding out what she did, rather than us being out there and exploring the entire truth of what happened to Oscar and Reese.'

'Can you give us examples of this?'

The court assistant walks back through the side door, holding a paper cup towards me. I mouth a 'thank you' to her as she hands it to me and then take a quick sip, just to wet my whistle.

'Well, detectives felt Joy was suspicious,' I say, 'but there was absolutely zero evidence to suggest she had anything to do with her sons going missing. Of course, because she was a mother who was, at times back then, uncontrollably grieving, investigators had to walk on eggshells around her. Personally, I would have had a preference for looking into other possibilities, cos as far as I was concerned Joy Stapleton was going nowhere. She wasn't getting away from us.'

'So, there were other leads?' Bracken asks.

'Well, in truth, we had nothing to go on. It was like Oscar and Reese just vanished into thin air. So, I wanted to explore all of the thin air. But our investigation seemed to solely narrow onto the grieving mother.'

'Okay, well, if you can give me a specific example of what you call narrowing the investigation...'

'Well, the last witness you had sitting here this morning – Mr Grimshaw... Him and his dog Bunny, right? Our bosses were aware Mr Grimshaw had helped detectives solve murder cases in the UK, so they called him over with his dog to sniff out the Stapleton home. I don't think this was a calculated or conscious deliberate step over the line. I think our bosses genuinely just felt, "How can we prove the mother did this? – let's get sniffer dogs in". So, they searched and searched for a dog handler who they knew had a history of assisting police forces with positive conclusions in this specific regard. They couldn't find one in Ireland, and eventually came to Mr Grimshaw in the UK. And, of course Grimshaw, through his sniffer dog, gave them exactly what they wanted. But truth be known, as you have found out in this court this morning, that is not scientific evidence at all. And I've never believed it to be.'

'Speculation, Your Honour,' the other lawyer yells out.

'Not your place to speculate, Mrs Gleeson,' the judge tells me. 'If you can just answer the direct question please.'

'Well, what I will say is, Bunny the dog's findings – if you want to call them that – weren't enough for an arrest anyway. I was very surprised that evidence was even allowed in the original trial, to be honest. We knew – or certainly I knew – Mr Grimshaw's credibility was lacking. It amazed me it was allowed into court... but that too, I guess, is a reflection of the court system fitting into a flawed system.'

'That is more speculation, Your Honour,' the lawyer says, this time slapping his hand to the desk in front of him.

'Mrs Gleeson.' The judge's eyes peer over her glasses at me.

'Your job here is not to speculate, but to answer direct questions. I will not remind you of that again.'

'Sorry,' I say. Then I turn back to Bracken, cringing a little inside. 'I guess what I mean is the dog coming in is a good example of an investigation following a system, rather than the investigation following the truth. Does that make sense?'

Bracken interlocks his fingers across his stomach.

'If you could explain that a little more clearly for the court, Sandra.'

'Well, instead of following evidence and letting the evidence lead detectives to a suspect, the detectives already had their suspect and then tried to create the evidence around her. Same with the CCTV footage.'

I take another sip of water, and as I do, I afford myself another quick glance at Joy. She's sitting as still as she can, her fingers forming a fallen steeple on the desk in front of her. She fascinates me. She really does. She's either one of the coldest killers in the history of our nation. Or she has lived one of the most unfortunate and saddest lives in the history of our nation. It doesn't get any more intriguing than that.

'Are you referring to the CCTV of the lady in the pink hooded top?'

'Yes,' I say, before taking another sip of water – though it doesn't seem to be doing anything for the cotton on my tongue. 'When the bodies of Oscar and Reese were found two years after they were reported missing, the investigation didn't turn into "How did these bodies get to this location?" It immediately turned into "How do we link Joy to this location?"'

What I'm saying is true. About four hours after the bodies had been confirmed as the two Stapleton boys, one detective at our station was rubbing his hands together with glee, shouting 'We're gonna nail her now.' I don't think any of the cops I worked with were nasty, or calculated, or manipulative, even. They were just following the system, without realising how fractured it truly was. Some people just never notice the obvious things that are staring them in the face.

'So, they were actively looking to link Joy to that scene?'

'Exactly. I calculated at the time – because I have been fascinated by this case and this is actually the case that really started to open my eyes into how the system operates – that officers must have viewed over five thousand hours of CCTV footage. There were two hundred and twenty-eight CCTV cameras at the bottom of the Dublin mountains that recorded footage that night. Some of which still had their footage stored digitally, most didn't. But we still managed to get five thousand hours of footage from different cameras. My problem was they weren't viewing five thousand hours looking for anything suspicious. They were specifically looking for Joy. They wanted to put her near the scene of where the bodies were found.'

'And then what?'

'Then they found those famous three seconds of footage... the footage we've all seen. Where a figure walks by a garden wearing a pink hoodie. And that was that. They felt they had their woman. We knew Joy had been wearing a pink hooded top the day before the boys were reported missing. But as you know, Mr Bracken, this footage is only three seconds long, and we see no face, just a figure in a pink hoodie. And, as was brought up in the original trial as an argument, there was no footage of the woman in the pink hoodie going up the mountain. Only coming down.'

'Sorry... They used three seconds out of five thousand hours as a reason to arrest Joy Stapleton?'

'They did.'

'So, in your expert opinion, detectives fit the whole investigation around their suspect, rather than allowing the investigation to lead them to a suspect, right?'

'Exactly, Mr Bracken. That is the fracture in the system.'

He spins on his heels and points one finger towards the ceiling.

'For the record, this is Sandra Gleeson – an assistant detective working on the investigation into the Oscar and Reese Stapleton case – admitting to us here, under oath, that the investigation was flawed and that my client was a suspect from the get-go. Sandra, the court thank you for your time.'

'Mrs Gleeson,' the other lawyer says, standing up. 'You interviewed for the position of Chief Superintendent in early 2011, correct?'

'That is correct,' I say, before reaching for my glass again. I thought I might get a little breather before cross examination, but it seems to have started before Bracken has even sat down.

'You didn't get that job, did you?'

'No. There was somebody more qualified than me for that position.'

'Seems odd then, that you left the police force nine months later. If you were gunning for a promotion, surely you weren't really that angered by 'the system' as you call it?'

'As I said, I had already made up my mind that the system was flawed.'

'Okay, but that didn't stop you still wanting to be part of that system, did it? You interviewed for a promotion. Are you sure you were not bitter about being overlooked for this position, subsequently left the force and have, ever since, been rather negative about your former bosses?'

I gasp, then slam the paper cup I'm holding onto the shelf in front of me.

'Sir, I left a sixty thousand euro a year job with a fantastic pension and security to earn no wage by running a charity that deals with helping people in society. I wasn't bitter. I was better. I wanted to help people.'

His face drops. Stick that in your pipe and smoke it, young man. You little shit. Trying to trap me. My opinion on the investigative procedures in this country have nothing to do with that Chief Superintendent's position. I never felt I was going to get that role, anyway. Stevie Wood was much more primed for it than I was. He was next in line. I only interviewed for it because that was part of the system too. You were expected to interview... expected to show an eagerness for climbing the ranks.

'You know what, Mrs Gleeson,' the lawyer says, shoving both of his hands into his trouser pockets. 'Let's just get some clarity on the testimony you've given here today, shall we? You are here to testify *that in your experience, as a police officer and investigator, the system in which investigators operate in is flawed, right? "Fractured" you called it specifically. You've even said today that you think the judicial system is fractured in some way. Now I'm not disagreeing with you. And I am sure you will find other members of An Garda Siochana and other employees in the judicial system who would agree with you also. But is such testimony really pertinent to this specific case? You happen to be a person who is critical of the system who also happened to work on the Stapleton case, right? So, Mr Bracken rounding you up to testify at this court case kind of gives off the impression that the Stapleton case, specifically, was fractured and that it led to the wrong person being arrested. But that is not what you are here to testify today, is it? You are only here to testify that the system in which you once worked, is, in your opinion, fractured, correct?'*

'That is correct, Sir,' I say. 'I am only here to testify that the system is flawed. Not whether or not I think Joy is innocent or guilty. This case — as far as I'm concerned — all comes down to whether or not you believe Joy Stapleton is the lady in that three-seconds of CCTV footage — or whether or not you believe it to be a crazy coincidence.'

'And do you think it's a crazy coincidence, Mrs Gleeson?'

'Objection.' Bracken stands as he shouts, scooting his chair back.

'Your Honour,' the other lawyer says, 'question is pertinent.'

Judge Delia squelches up her mouth then switches her stare from the lawyer to me. But not in time to see me stifle a gasp. I didn't think I'd be asked this directly. Bracken knew I wouldn't guarantee him a positive answer if he asked me on the stand if I thought Joy was guilty or innocent, because we discussed it and I told him I couldn't be certain that it's not Joy in that footage. But he also told me that Jonathan Ryan wouldn't ask this question either. Because it would be just too darn risky for him. If I say right now that, 'No, I don't think that's Joy Stapleton in that CCTV footage', then I'd blow this case wide open. But if I say I do think it's her, then my testimony here really would and should be regarded as redundant by the judge. I feel my bullishness slip away from me as I wait on her to make her mind up. I hope she doesn't make me answer that question.

'I'll allow it,' she says. 'I feel that question specifically pertinent to this witness given the testimony she has offered today. You may answer, Mrs Gleeson.'

I look over the rim of the paper cup at Joy as I gulp down the last of my water. She stares back at me, accompanying it with a sombre pursing of her lips. Jesus, I've obsessed about her face for years. Obsessed about this case. It was the case I cut my teeth on as a detective. The case that made me realise the whole system is flawed from top to bottom. I've read every word ever written about this case; have even read the transcripts of the original trial three times. There can't be many people – if anyone – who knows it in more depth than I do. Truth be known, there simply is no evidence that links Joy Stapleton to this crime. By the time the bodies were found, all forensic evidence had long since weathered away. This whole case comes down to those three seconds of CCTV footage – footage I haven't been able to stop thinking about for years. I've even dreamt about it. And in the dream, the hooded figure in the CCTV stops walking, then turns around to stare up to the CCTV camera to wave at me... And yet every time she does, the fecking face is always just a blur. Truth be known, I simply – like everybody else – can't know for certain if it is Joy under that hoodie. Though I have to say, I can see why people find the defence of "coincidence" difficult to swallow.

'Mrs Gleeson, would you like me to repeat the question?' the lawyer asks, growing in impatience as I continue to hide behind my paper cup. 'Do you or do you not think it is just a coincidence that somebody with the exact unique hoodie as Mrs Stapleton happened to be walking close to where her sons' bodies were found on the night we believe them to have been murdered?'

'I'm no expert on coincidences,' I say, taking the cup away from my mouth. 'I have no experience in coincidence. I do, however, have experience in investigative work. And I believe that the investigation that led to Joy Stapleton's arrest was flawed. That's all I'm prepared to testify.'

Joy wobbled herself into the canteen, now flanked – as she had been for the past two months – by only one officer, before pausing. None of her pals were at their usual bench. She glanced around and, sweeping the curls away from her face, placed her palm against her forehead, confused.

'They're all in the kitchen,' one of the elderly prisoners told her.

So, Joy removed her hand from her forehead, offered the back of the elderly woman's head a grateful nod and paced around the back of the counter until she swept open the double doors that led to the kitchen.

They were all gathered around a bench. It was Lizzie who looked up first.

'Oh no, she's here,' she said.

Then the whole group looked up from the bench to see Joy's confused expression heading towards them.

'Surprise!' they yelled in unison, stepping aside and showing Joy the half-iced cake that was slopped onto the bench.

'Congrats, sista,' Christy said, squeezing Joy's shoulder 'We're one year in today. You've come a long way, girl. I'm proud o' ya.'

They ate cake for breakfast, washed down with lukewarm tea, and then Joy sat in the television room with Christy, not only looking backwards about how far they'd come during their year inside together, but looking forwards, to their fight to get Joy's double-life sentence overturned.

It only took Christy to reveal that the visions she saw under that pink hoodie had brown hair, brown eyes and a pale face, before Joy was accusing Lavinia Kirwan of killing her boys. Though her best friend had long been on her radar as a suspect – especially after Lavinia had testified against Joy in the original trial;

saying that Joy was suffering mentally in the lead up to the boys' disappearance.

But to make absolutely sure, Joy made Christy go deeper into her visions, to see if a glint of green was in those eyes, like the glint Joy knew Lavinia had in hers; and to see if there was a tiny mole on the side of the figure's neck much like the one Lavinia had. Each time Christy went deeper into her vision, under pleas from Joy, she came back only further determining within Joy's mind that it was indeed her best friend who had murdered Oscar and Reese.

They began the 'Joy Stapleton is Innocent' campaign; a campaign that was supported by about one-third of Elm House, as well as, bizarrely, about one-third of the population outside of the prison's walls.

Although most were sympathetic to Joy's plight, the theory of Lavinia being the killer never really made it past the confines of the prison without being met by derision. Mostly because Lavinia had a rock-solid alibi for the night in question.

By this stage Joy was settling comfortably into prison life, if it weren't for the cold. For some reason she felt colder than the rest of the prisoners, and often wore two sweat tops to wander around the landings of Elm House. She was still being flanked by one prison officer, though most in the wing felt that was largely unnecessary as, by this stage, nobody wanted to harm Joy more so than they wanted to harm any of the other prisoners. Yes, there was a split between Nancy's Cohorts and Christy's Crazies, but physical attacks were pretty much non-existent in Elm House, save for the odd square-up in the games room when somebody felt the rules were being flaunted. Both factions had learned to live together, the only real tension coming when Nancy and Christy happened to confront each other. But they were both prison-wise and aware of their aging years. So, nothing untoward happened between them, bar a tense silence that would eventually be filled. Joy felt uncomfortable by the manner in which Nancy would stare her up and down and lick her lips when Christy wasn't around, but she had long since stopped feeling intimidated.

What didn't leave her, and she was beginning to realise never would for the rest of her life, was the monotony of prison. 'Boredom,' she had come to tell anyone who would listen, 'was the real price convicts paid for their crimes.'

Although the 'Joy is Innocent' campaign had filled many of her weeks and months with some sort of ambition, she was tired and impatient with the lack of progress the campaign was making.

Her lawyers had lauded the efforts of her supporters, but told Joy in no uncertain terms that the courts weren't going to move any quicker for her just because her campaign was earning the attention of the tabloid newspapers. She wasn't entitled to an appeal. And certainly wasn't guaranteed one.

'An appeal in your case would take so long, Joy, you'd be quicker finding new evidence that'd turn the screw on a retrial,' her lawyer told her. 'With the backing and support you have, you could pile the pressure on the system.'

And then he left, never to be seen by Joy again. His time was well and truly up on this case. He had worked with Joy from the early days of her arrest, and was kind, considerate and always professional as he guided her through her original trial. But ultimately, he lost, and she eventually lost him less than a year into her sentence because he just couldn't afford the years it would take to force an appeal through. He knew the system better than anyone; knew he'd be throwing away years of his promising career if he was to stay with this case. He said he'd do the best he could, but Joy hadn't seen nor heard from him for months and she began to realise it was up to her and Christy to get herself out of this mess. Besides, she was never convinced that lawyer truly felt she was innocent anyway. Not like Christy does.

So, with no husband coming to the prison to visit her, and no lawyer now filling her in on her legal rights, Joy only had one hope of a visit – albeit a distant hope, given her father's ill-health. But one day, about ten months in, when she was wiping down the tables in the canteen, Mathilda crept up behind her.

'You got a visitor today, Joy,' she said. 'It's your daddy.'

He looked aged, as if he was fading into a sepia photograph. But he smiled when he saw his tiny daughter walking towards him

– the first time she'd seen him genuinely smile since her mother had passed.

They spoke about her case, about her new-found theory that Lavinia may have played a part. Her father entertained the idea, but ultimately didn't seem positive that Joy was likely to turn this mess around. He swore as he held her stare that he believed her innocence, but the inconsistency in his breathing, coupled with the fact that he couldn't maintain his focus on what she was saying for very long, confirmed to Joy that he wasn't up for the fight. She knew she couldn't rely on him to help her.

'Do what you can, kid,' he said. Then he gave her another hug and hobbled his way over to the front desk where Joy watched him struggle to sit into a wheelchair before being pushed out of the prison by a stranger dressed in purple scrubs.

She was saddened to see her father in such ill-health, but a visit was a visit and she skipped her way back to Elm House, the promise of a smile on her lips. The smile, however, didn't last long, not with somebody lurking around the corner.

'You child-killing bitch,' Marian snarled at her. Marian was one of Nancy's cohorts – small but stocky; wide shoulders and thick arms. Joy backed up against the concrete wall and tried to steady her breathing as Marian inched her ugly mug nearer hers. 'You're lucky. If you didn't have Christy Jabefemi by your side most of the time, you'd be in a wheelchair much like I saw your daddy getting into one back at the visitor's hall.'

Then Marian snapped her teeth shut, just inches from Joy's face, and went on her way. The intimidation shook Joy, but by the time she got back to Elm House, everything seemed just as normal as it had been the day before: Christy's Crazies existing alongside Nancy's Cohorts.

She dropped by Christy's cell; not to inform her that she'd just been intimidated by Marian Crosby on the landing below them, but to chat – as if they hadn't spent the last eight months since Joy got out of isolation chatting pretty much every hour they were allowed out of their cells.

'They say a gal on Maple House took her life last night.'

'Really?' Joy asked, her mouth popping open.

'Yep. Used her bed sheets to tie the noose. Ya know, e'rtime I hear of a prisoner hanging, I immediately think they were murdered.'

'Murdered?'

'It's just so easy. I've heard it done befo'. Ya tie the noose, visit the prisoner when they asleep, put the noose around their neck and pull as hard as ya can. But ya gotta get that noose up the top o' the neck, not the bottom, not the middle. The very top. It's not a strangling. It's a hanging. Folk hang from here,' she said, positioning her hand around the edge of her jawline, 'not here,' she said, lowering to the centre of her neck.

'So, you think somebody killed her?'

'Oh, I don't know... I don't know what's going on in Maple House,' Christy said. 'I'm just sayin' e'rtime I hear of a hanging in prisons, I get a little suspish, ya know whaddam sayin'?'

'Who was she?'

'Chick called Audrey. Audrey Murray. Only twenty-eight, that's what I heard. She was in doin' two year for drug dealin'. Now why you wanna go kill yoself when you only in for a couple years?'

Joy shrugged.

'Maybe she didn't enjoy living in the outside world as much as she didn't like living in this inside world.'

'Or maybe, maybe she was just off her head... drugs can do that.'

'Wouldn't know,' Joy says, perching herself on the bed next to Christy.

'You too squeaky clean t'ever do drugs, Joy?'

Joy puffed out a laugh.

'Guess so.'

'Never sniffled a line o' coke ya whole life?'

Joy shook her curls.

'Weed. Ya smoked some dope, right?'

'Haven't actually. I took my first drag of a cigarette when I was fifteen and it choked me so much I swore I'd never smoke again... and I haven't. Wouldn't touch one. What about you?'

'Me?' Christy said, cackling that husky laugh of hers. 'Do I look like I do drugs?'

Joy stared into Christy's bloodshot eyes, then tilted her head slightly, like a puppy dog.

'Yes!'

Christy fell back on to the bed, cackling.

'Yo right. Yo right. I do a lot of drugs outside,' she said, sitting back up. 'Meth. Girl, I love and hate me some meth in equal measure.'

'Meth.' Joy shivered. 'Why?'

'Transforms you. It transforms me anyway. I transform from feeling suicidal just like Audrey Murray, Lord Jesus rest her soul, to making me feel like I can't get enough o' this life.'

'Really? Like an antidepressant?' Joy asked.

Christy put her arm around Joy and squeezed her.

'S'more than that. It's like an alternative world. A world that makes me feel closer to Jesus.'

She intrigued Joy by regaling her greatest hits of misde-meanours she had experienced since she first discovered the effects of methamphetamine some fifteen years prior. And why, whilst she loves being under the influence of the drug, she hates the come down, and constantly has to battle in her mind between living the high of the chemicals coursing through her veins against the low of the aftermath. A big negative, Christy informed Joy, of constantly chasing the high was the fact that it was expensive. And that's why Christy became a thief. She needed money to fund her habit. Which is what kept landing her ass back inside Mountjoy Prison. But while Christy was surviving well inside by using the legal substitute for meth, Desoxyn – which she had administered each day by a medic – she knew that as soon as she was a free woman again, the first thing she'd do was rob somebody so that she could afford the buzz of the real thing.

'I normally suffer in prison. Even with the Desoxyn they give me in here,' Christy said. 'But you, girl, havin' you in here with me, you really helping me survive. Hey... I guess you ma new drug.'

They both cackled; Joy by now having adopted the almost

uniformed prison cackle that she found most intimidating in other prisoners when she first arrived.

And it was at the loudest of Joy's laughing, through eyes that were watering, that she saw him appear in the cell's doorway.

'Aidan!' she squealed.

∴

Delia brings a balled fist to her mouth and yawns into it.

Trials have always been exhausting for her. Not physically, of course – all she does is sit, whether at the trial itself or back here in her dimly lit office. Her exhaustion is purely mental. She once read that there are so many variables to consider when examining a trial of any magnitude, that the muscle strain required to consider them all is the equivalent, to the brain, of running a marathon.

What Delia finds most exhausting of all when judging is the required batting away of her gut. 'Instinct is most annoying for a judge,' she has often repeated over the years. She has had to train herself to not allow her thinking to be clouded in any way by her gut. And yet despite twenty years as a judge – thirty-three years in the judicial system wholly – she still hasn't mastered it.

She uses a technique she read about in a book that details decision-making, called *Mind Fuck*. It involves her scrutinizing every minute detail of a witness's testimony or piece of evidence and then filtering it all into two separate pockets within her brain; one pocket for details of the trial that affect her emotionally. And the other pocket for parts of the trial that fit within proper legal parameters.

The main reason she was yawning into her fist was down to the fact that Sandra Gleeson's testimony was straining this filtering process. Delia definitely noted a slice of solace in the former detective who had spent just over ninety minutes on the stand that afternoon. She could empathise with Sandra when she was complaining of working within the restraints of a fractured system. And because of that, her gut kept screaming that this was a credible witness and must be taken seriously.

After Delia had re-awoken her tired, old computer – following her usual routine of staring around her desk, soaking in the smile of her husband as he wrapped his arm around Callum – the first sentence she typed into her notes was, 'I believe Sandra Gleeson.' But Delia also believed that statement, strong as it looked typed at the top of a blank Word document, held no real significance when considered inside the legal parameters of the system in which she worked. It made absolutely no difference whether or not she believed the witness, because belief without proof is almost akin to redundant in judicial terms. It never matters what a judge or a jury believe, it only matters what can be proven to them.

'What did Sandra Gleeson's testimony prove?' Delia mutters to herself, while dipping her chin into her neck so she can stare down the length of her robe. Delia often does this; speaks to herself, during a deliberation. She believes her outer voice controls her inner voice, as if it refrains her from going outside the lines of her filtering process.

She pauses, and then begins to slowly tip-tap her fingernail against the mouse before she shoots back upright and begins to type.

She proved that when searching for CCTV footage, the investigators were ONLY looking for Joy.

She sits back in her chair and sighs, swiping her glasses up from the bridge of her nose and combing them back into her hair.

'She said there was over five thousand hours' worth of footage searched in the aftermath of the bodies being found... wow!' Delia says to herself. Then she presses the balls of her palms into her eyes and swings ever so subtly from side to side in her chair. 'Five thousand hours....'

This was eye-opening for Delia, even though, right this second, she had her eyes closed. The fact that five thousand hours' worth of CCTV footage had been viewed by investigators was never raised during the original trial. In fact, all that was ever spoken about during that original trial were three seconds out of those five thousand hours. Three measly seconds that end before you can even whisper the question, *'Is that Joy Stapleton?'* to yourself. Three seconds that only show the back of a woman in a pink hoodie walking by a lone, large bungalow owned by a paranoid couple who had a camera installed that peers out onto their modest front lawn. Investigators combed the whole area at the foot of the Dublin mountains looking for CCTV footage – from main roads and private companies – in the aftermath of the boys' bodies being found. One police officer noticed a residential camera during a round of routine questioning and footage from the night in question was requested from the owners of the bungalow. Everything had been stored digitally and so the police received the night-long footage almost immediately.

'Three seconds out of five thousand,' Delia says, sitting back upright. She stretches her fingers, all the while staring around her desk in further thought, filing away her gut instinct as best she could. She likes Sandra Gleeson. Trusts Sandra Gleeson. Can empathise with Sandra Gleeson. But she has to keep reminding herself that none of that matters.

'If they were only looking for Joy in all of that footage,' she whispers, 'then what did they miss?'

She washes a hand over her face, then slaps that same hand to the top of her desk.

'C'mon, Delia,' she says to herself. 'Think!'

Her mind wanders to Gerd Bracken; only because it would fascinate her to know what he would have made of Sandra Gleeson's testimony. He probably doesn't realise how much of an impact her time on the stand has had on the judge. He'll likely have thought Sandra did a good job for him, and that it certainly opened up a crack of doubt. But there's no way he'd have imagined Judge Delia would be so conflicted by what his witness had to say.

Jonathan Ryan, Delia feels, will probably be thinking Sandra's testimony didn't hurt him as he had likely feared it would. Yes, she raised doubt on the legitimacy of the original investigation. But he'll be secretly buoyed by the fact that he held firm in his cross examination. He went balls-out, shocking everybody in the courtroom by asking whether or not she felt the woman in the CCTV footage was or wasn't Joy Stapleton.

But Sandra, to her credit, held firm – and gave as good a non-answer as she possibly could. The way Sandra tackled that question only reaffirmed to Delia that Sandra was both a worthy and a trustworthy witness. She was willing to criticise the manner in which the police scrutinized all of the CCTV footage. But she wasn't willing to criticise the footage itself.

'Everything comes down to those three seconds,' Delia mutters to herself. Though what she was saying wasn't much of a revelation to her. Even when she answered Eddie Taunton's question in that interview all those years ago, Delia had said exactly that.

'The whole entire trial, when you consider it fully, really came down to the CCTV footage,' she had said in the most formal way possible, all suited for her interview in a John Rocha single breasted jacket, complimented by a frilled blouse that bustled together at the collar to form a bow. 'As you know, Mr Taunton, coincident cases are largely problematic for a judge and jury. But when all is taken into consideration, such as the fact that the pink hooded top in the footage has distinguishable features and is the only one believed to be owned by anyone in Ireland. When you consider the fact that this footage was recorded the night before the boys were reported missing, in a neighbourhood not too far from where the bodies were eventually found. And when you consider that nobody ever came forward to say "That was me in that footage. You can mark me out of your enquiries." Taking all of these *coincidences* into consideration, Mr Taunton, I didn't feel the defence could rely on coincidence as their argument.'

'So, in your professional opinion, the jury got the Stapleton case right?' Taunton asked her.

'I'm certain they did, Sir.'

She couldn't have envisaged, of course, that interview answer would eventually lead to her presiding over the retrial of Joy Stapleton some eight years later.

She begins to tap her finger nail against her mouse again, running through her head whether or not she would answer that question the same way if she were asked it in an interview today; and was beginning to admit to herself that Sandra Gleeson's testimony this afternoon would probably halt her from being so confident in her initial judgement.

She wiggles her mouse, to locate the icon on her screen, then drags it to a folder on her desktop. The computer pauses before flashing an image of a neatly mowed garden at night onto the screen. As white digits tick away in the bottom right corner, a figure walks through the shot, shielded to the waist by a small garden wall – a tiny figure, head down and smothered by a pink hood.

Delia pauses the footage with the figure in the centre of the shot, then inches her nose closer to the screen. She examines the red band around the waist of the hooded top and what appears to be a red string bouncing up from the woman's chest; the exact same trimmings that are on Joy Stapleton's unique hooded top.

A loud ping distracts her from her thoughts, and then a box begins to flash in the top corner of her screen.

An email. From a sender whose address she isn't quite familiar with.

She drags her icon towards the box and clicks on it. And then the computer groans before it flashes another video image on to the screen. Delia presses at the play button and stares at the footage, her eyes widening.

'Oh my... oh my... Oh my fucking God!' she screams. Unusual for Delia. She can't stand swearing. Can never understand why anybody would ever have any use for it, not when there is an infinite amount of words they could use. Her breathing grows in sharpness. Then she stands up and swipes a heavy slap towards the screen of her computer monitor, knocking over her cups of pens and her framed photograph. The frame skids across the desk and falls to the floor. She can hear the glass of the frame smash over the strange grunting sound huffing from her computer's speakers. 'Who the fuck?' Delia says, stretching for her mouse, so she can switch the video off. 'Who the fuck sent me this?'

She bends down, snatches at the smashed photo frame and then immediately brings her thumb to her mouth.

'Mother fuc—' she just about stops herself from swearing again by filling her mouth with her thumb. She sucks on it frantically, then removes it and shakes her entire hand in the air, spraying blood to the floor.

'Judge McCormick.' Knuckles rattle lightly at her door.

'Yes, Aisling?' Delia calls out, before twisting her wrist and looking at her watch.

'You're due back in court now.'

'Yes, thank you. Thank you, Aisling. Coming now,' she says, gripping her thumb tight with her other hand.

'Who the fuck sent me that video?' she whispers.

'Sorry?'

'Oh, don't mind me,' she shouts back to Aisling before she strides towards the door and snatches it open, finding her assistant's eyes furrowed on the other side of it. 'I was talking to myself again.'

'Judge McCormick, are you okay?' Aisling asks.

Delia offers her assistant a fake smile.

'Course I am. Though you couldn't, eh... you couldn't fetch me a plaster, could you? Cut myself on some glass.' She holds her thumb up.

'Ouch... eh... I'm not quite sure where we keep plasters, but I'll take a look in the canteen. There might be a first aid box there. Meanwhile...' Aisling stands aside and waves her hand up the hallway, in the direction of the courtrooms.

'Yes. Yes!' Delia says, nodding her head before she begins to stride forward as fast as she can, kicking her robe with each foot as she goes. She drops the fake smile when she turns onto the next corridor, and as soon as she does, she begins to feel her head spinning. And her stomach. She can't be certain she's not going to vomit. She wants to pause. Wants to catch her breath. But she knows she's already late.

'Who the fuck sent me that?' she murmurs to herself. 'Eddie Taunton. Can't be... can it?'

She brings her hand to her forehead, her gaze fixed to the blurred black and white tiled flooring of the court's corridors as she paces. Though she does look up in time to see the court clerk dressed in all black at the end of the corridor open a door and nod inside it. And before she reaches the clerk to offer another fake smile, Delia hears a voice bellow from behind that door.

'All rise.'

The courtroom is packed again; everybody on their feet to welcome the decision-maker – the only person with any power over the fate of Joy Stapleton. Though Delia is beginning to wonder if she has any power at all now as she sits into her high-chair. Her head is still spinning when the court clerk makes a coughing sound, prompting Delia to shake herself from her daze.

'Sorry,' she mutters. Then she stares down at the courtroom, glancing at Joy first, then at Bracken. She offers Jonathan Ryan an almost-friendly nose twitch. Then she flicks her eyes around the room in search of Eddie Taunton. He's not here.

'Mother fucker,' she whispers to herself.

'Sorry, Your Honour?' a court clerk says.

'No... No, I'm sorry. Eh...' She rifles through the paperwork on her desk, before clawing a sheet out from the middle, smudging the top corner of it with a thumbprint of blood. Her hands begin to shake as she holds the sheet. So, she places it back down to the desk in front of her, her hands now hidden from the gallery. 'Mr Bracken, can you, eh...' she fake coughs and burps at the same time; vomit bubbling in the pit of stomach, 'Call your next witness, please.'

'My pleasure, Your Honour,' Bracken says standing up, 'I call to the stand, Monsieur Mathieu Dupont.'

2,371 days ago...

'Joy!' Mathilda shouted.

Joy jumped, holding a palm to her chest, then swivelled.

'Sorry, Mathilda,' she replied. 'I know... I'm supposed to be at school. I'm heading there now.'

'Nope. You're not. You're coming with me.'

'Where?'

'Never mind where. You're coming with me.'

'But I'm about five minutes late for school. I was just having a chat with—'

'Now!' Mathilda said. She didn't roar it. Didn't raise her voice. But her tone cut through. And so, Joy creased her face at Emilie – the prisoner she had been in conversation with – then left her to it to follow Mathilda's rattling keys down the steel steps of Elm House before turning right.

'This isn't the way to school.'

'I told you... you're not going to school.'

'But won't I miss class?'

'You didn't seem that concerned when you were just hanging out at the back of the kitchen with Emilie.'

Joy held her eyes closed and sighed.

She had enrolled in school. Again. After she had spent the first four months of her sentence in isolation following her attack, she decided to do a course when all of the options of how to spend her time on a regular wing were offered to her. The menu wasn't that detailed, in truth. Each prisoner had two basic options: work around the prison, or do a course in the education halls at the far end of the prison. The working options didn't appeal. Joy had never worked in a kitchen before, and even when she was a house-wife and a mother of two, the oven did most of the cooking for her. Gardening wasn't to her liking either. Nor was the washing and cleaning or laundry rooms. So, she decided upon a course in creative writing at the educational facility. Her lack of confidence let her down, however, and after three months she felt she had nothing to offer the class and that was that: she wanted out. She pleaded with the Governor that if he let her out of her course early, she'd do any job at all around the prison, that she didn't mind which one. So, he placed her in the laundry room – the least favoured role generally among the prisoners. Her disdain for that job, which was really only for three hours a day, became evident much quicker than her disdain for producing creative writing did, but her frustrations didn't matter one jot. She would serve in the laundry room for a full year before the Governor would agree to let her choose another means by which to spend her afternoons. So, when that time eventually came around, she chose school again, rather than work. This time a course in Healthy Living was the one she opted for. Not because she was desperate to lose the puppy weight she had gained during her first eighteen months inside, but because that was the course Christy was doing, and they wanted to spend as much time with each other as they possibly could. She'd only started the course a couple of weeks ago, and here she was about to miss the lesson on ripe vegetables because Mathilda was leading her around a maze of landings and through a dozen gates before they ended up deep into the bowels of the prison.

'Never been down here before,' Joy said looking around herself. 'Where we going?'

'I've been told to take you down here cos you got a visitor.'

'A visitor? Me? Down here? Why?'

'That's a helluva lot of questions within one breath, Joy,' Mathilda said. Then her keys stopped jangling, and she spun on her heels. 'Ye gotta wear these.' Mathilda unclipped a pair of handcuffs from her waist belt.

Joy clenched both fists and held her arms out, all the while staring at the yellow door they had stopped outside.

'Who's in there?' she asked.

Mathilda shrugged. Then she turned away from Joy and banged at the yellow door.

'Sir, she's here.'

The door opened and the Governor's large face appeared. He nodded solemnly at Joy and then stood aside. And as he did, Joy saw the piercing blue eyes of her husband for the first time in way too long. Her breathing immediately quickened and her heart thudded. The last time a prison officer told her she had a surprise visit she ended up sitting across from Conor Quinn – a young up and coming lawyer who convinced her he could land her a retrial. She was initially buoyed by his positivity. But after six meetings in the space of five months she was beginning to get irritated, rather than excited, by his visits. It seemed he rarely had an update for her when he did show up, and she was beginning to form an eerie impression that he was meeting with her because he had a crush on her. He wasn't the only one. Joy Stapleton had dozens of admirers, a lot of whom would write to her regularly; to detail their sexual desires. On her first Valentine's Day in prison, Joy Stapleton received over one-hundred cards from strangers. She was actually a little peeved when, on her second Valentine's Day, in the February just gone, that number had halved. Conor Quinn reminded her of the creepy men who wrote to her regularly. She felt he was content to just be associated with her – to spend time with Ireland's most infamous criminal. She told him the last time she met him that he shouldn't come back until he had made concrete progress towards a retrial. And as a result, she hadn't heard from him for a while and was beginning to realise the inevitable – she truly was going to spend the rest of her life in this godforsaken place. Though that slow realisation didn't depress her as much as she feared it would. She was beginning to feel that she was now a better fit in prison than she would be for the outside world. She wasn't even sure where she would fit in out there anymore. In the real world she'd stand out as the most notorious killer in the whole of the country. In here, she's just another criminal. She barely stands out at all. Not anymore. Not after the furore of her first arriving in Elm House. Though she was beginning to wonder if that furore would spark up again, certainly now that Stella had been brought back to Elm House. It's not as if Stella's arrival was a big shock – she didn't turn up sitting at a desk without warning like her husband just had.

The Governor and some of the prison officers had spoken to Joy about Stella's likely return. Joy had told them she held no ill-feeling toward her fellow prisoner and that she wouldn't have a problem if Stella came back to Elm House. But that wasn't true at all. She *did* have a problem with it. A huge problem. Because she was in fear of Stella; in fear of having her face smashed against one of the dining room tables again.

'You sure you're okay with this?' Aidan asked, reading that Joy wasn't as comfortable as she had been letting on when Stella finally returned to the wing.

'I'll be fine,' Joy said to Aidan. 'I've got you, right?'

Aidan smiled at her. As he found himself doing regularly. He'd been back in Elm House just over six months now and spent most of his working hours either pacing the landing outside Joy's cell. Or – when her door finally buzzed open in the mornings – accompanying her to and from the dining room. They shared a similar sense of humour and there was, undoubtedly, a spark between them that didn't go unnoticed. The talk amongst prisoners was that they were riding each other. But they weren't. Even if Joy was often daydreaming about it.

'What are you doing here?' was the first thing that popped out of her mouth. Hardly welcoming; certainly not considering she had waited over a year and a half to see those blue eyes.

'I, eh... I,' Shay stuttered.

Then the Governor held a hand in front of Joy's chest as she walked through the yellow door to greet her husband.

'Uh-huh,' the Governor said. 'No touching.' He sat Joy in the seat opposite Shay and chained the cuffs she was already wearing to a metal loop under the desk.

'Why are we... why are we here?' Joy asked the Governor while looking around herself.

The Governor stood back upright, all six foot eight inches of him, then clasped his shovel-sized hands together.

'Mr Stapleton contacted me personally about visiting you a couple of weeks ago because he feared his celebrity status would cause somewhat a fuss in the visitor's hall. So, we, eh, we discussed the possibility of him having a private meeting with you and... well, here we are...'

Joy continued to look around herself. The room they were in was no bigger than her cell. And it was swallowed up by two white desks; one of which they were both sitting across from each other at, their faces no more than three feet apart.

The Governor kissed his own lips, then stepped his heavy frame outside and pulled the door tight behind him, though Joy could tell he didn't move from that spot, because she couldn't hear the familiar sweeping of shoes off the concrete floor. She had learned most of the sounds of the prison by now.

Though it was a silence she was hearing as she stared at her husband. Joy wanted so much to be able to move her hands across the desk so she could take his hands in hers. But she wasn't sure how he would react to that.

'Thank you,' she whispered, instead.

He contorted his face by squelching up his mouth, then he reached over and lightly grazed her elbow.

'I'm sorry it's taken so long... I just... I, eh...'

It was unlike Shay to not finish his sentences; to be uncertain of what he was trying to say. She only knew him to be the confident football star she had met and fallen in love with. She stared into his eyes, noticing they weren't quite as aqua as they once were. The stress of losing his two sons, coupled with his wife being sent down for two life sentences had clearly turned those blue eyes grey. He looked jaded. Aged. Far from the pinup he had once been.

'You don't need to explain yourself,' Joy whispered again, because she was aware of the ears just outside the door. It was likely, she felt, that both Mathilda and the Governor were prying. Though she couldn't blame them. The whole nation would love to be a fly on the wall for this meeting. 'I'm glad to see you... even if...' She lifted her arms as high as she could, which wasn't very high at all, before the cuffs clanked against the bottom of the desk.

'Joy,' Shay said, as straight as he could, 'I've had the same questions rolling around in my head for years now...' She unclenched her jaw, and inched herself closer to him. 'Hundreds of fucking questions... thousands even. And... oh, I don't know... I just don't know. I guess I've figured after all this time that this whole nightmare really only boils down to one question. And the only person who knows the answer to that question is you. So here I am... an innocent, broken man asking you to answer one question for me, so that the thousands of questions that fly around my head will finally shut the fuck up. Then maybe... just maybe...'

'Maybe you might get some closure.'

'Closure?' he said out of the corner of his mouth. 'Sleep. Let's start with some sleep. Fuck sake, I haven't had a full night's sleep since the day our boys went missing... I had so many questions that day alone. But the story just kept getting worse and worse...'

'I understand,' Joy said, sniffling up her nose, 'I don't sleep either.'

Shay exhaled a stuttering breath, letting it release in grunting stages, while he bounced his knee incessantly up and down under the desk.

'Well, we are not sleeping for different reasons,' he said. 'The reasons I can't sleep is because I want an answer to a question that you know the answer to... so please, don't compare your lack of sleep to mine.'

Joy swallowed hard. When she walked into this pokey office, she wondered in which tone Shay would speak to her. And even though she had tried to give him her best puppy dog eyes and to paint on her genuine empathy for him, she was aware she had already taken a miss-step, and as a result was getting the curt, abrupt Shay. She didn't know what to say to him. Or even how to say it.

'Sorry,' she whispered. 'This isn't about me. I've missed you. I've missed you so much.' Shay swayed his jaw from side-to-side. 'Have you missed me, Shay?'

'Jesus,' he snapped, raising his voice, 'how the hell am I supposed to know the answer to that? There are a thousand questions forming a queue in my head that are way ahead of that one.'

'Shhh,' Joy hissed over the desk at her husband, 'they're outside, listening.'

Shay held his eyes closed with annoyance, then got to his feet.

'I shouldn't have come... I should have just—'

'Don't go. Please don't go,' Joy begged, squeezing her palms together, the chains clanging against the desk. 'I'll shut up. I won't talk, unless it's to answer that one question you have. Please. Sit down. Talk to me, Shay.'

He pressed his hands against his hips, then, after a pause, relented, sitting back down and producing another long sigh.

'Okay... okay, just get to it, Shay,' he said to himself, rubbing at his face.

He had stayed out of the limelight ever since Joy was arrested, despite multiple pleas for interviews. He had turned down invites from *The Late Late Show* on no fewer than eight occasions and had rejected without too much consideration, a one-million euro advance to write his memoirs by a giant of a publishing company. That wasn't the only publishing deal he had been offered, but it was certainly the most lucrative one. The million-euro offer didn't register much interest though. Money meant nothing to him. Life, it seemed, meant nothing to him. Not anymore. He was too confused and pained to think about anything other than his own confusion and pain.

'When I'm trying to sleep at night,' he spat out, releasing his hands from his face, 'all I hear is that phone call you made to the police, reporting our boys missing. Just your voice on repeat, saying the same thing over and over again. And all that goes on in the fore-front of my mind as you are saying these words over and over again is me thinking, *is she acting?*'

'I'm not acting.'

'Shhh,' Shay hissed. 'You said you wouldn't talk.' He steadied his breathing. 'I mean, I can hear it... I can hear the panic in your voice. I hear the panic every time you shout, *'My two sons have been taken!'* I hear it so loud. But I keep asking myself, 'Is she acting panicked? Or is she *genuinely* panicked? Do I even know the woman I was married to at all?' Joy opened her mouth, then relented, her eyes filling with tears. 'But surely you couldn't have been acting for all those years afterwards; not when we were out looking for the boys; not when we started the campaign to find them; not after their bodies were found, right? I mean you just can't have been acting all these years...'

'Is that your question, Shay because, no, I wasn't act—'

'No,' he said, 'that isn't my question. But then again, I seemed to be the last one to know, didn't I? So maybe it's just me. Maybe I didn't know the woman I had married after all. I was the last person to twig that the police were looking at you the whole time. But even when I finally realised they were, and when I got over the shock of it, I still believed you. Because I couldn't believe you had anything to do with killing our boys. That doesn't make any sense.'

'Of course it doesn't,' Joy whispered.

Shay held up his index finger, silencing her again.

'But none of it makes any sense. And then... and then they showed me that CCTV footage.' Joy looked down at the desk, shaking her curls subtly from side to side. 'And I'm pretty sure the first time I saw it, yeah, I recognised that hoodie, but I didn't immediately think, 'that is Joy'. Though it's hard for me to know exactly what I thought the first time I saw it... But what I can tell you, Joy, is that every time I watch that footage now... I see you. Every time. Every damn time I watch it, I see your face under that hood.'

'Shay, you can't believe—'

'Shhh,' Shay hissed again, his cheeks now streaming with tears, his arms stiff by his side. 'I'm just telling you what I think I see, Joy.' He began to sob. 'Not what I know. But I guess, all these questions that fly around my head, about the phone call to the police, about the CCTV footage, about you calling it a coincidence, about the dozens of theories I've read about... they're all nonsense, aren't they? Because no matter what way I think about this, it all comes back to one thing for me. It all comes back to those three seconds of CCTV footage, where a girl wearing a hoodie only you could possibly be wearing walks down a road just a few hundred yards away from where our boys were found.'

Joy leaned closer, placing her forearms on the desk, her chains rattling.

'Let me answer your question, Shay.'

He sniffled up his nose, then wiped a hand over his face, mopping up the wet.

'You always say that it's just a coincidence somebody was wearing that same top; it's no coincidence, is it, Joy? I want you to look me straight in the eye and tell me the absolute truth... You owe me the truth. Is that you in that CCTV footage?'

'No,' she said without hesitating. 'And you have to believe me, Shay. You *have* to believe me.'

He blinked at her, through his tears. Then he stood abruptly, scooting the chair he was sat on towards the back wall.

'Okay...' he said, shrugging his shoulders, 'that is all I came here to ask... so, I, eh... I'm...' he tailed off his muttering as he pulled open the yellow door, exposing both the Governor and Mathilda outside.

'No. Shay,' Joy called out. 'Please.' Shay paused in the door frame, his hand still on the handle of the door, and stared back at his wife, his face blotchy and swollen. 'If you came here to ask me one question... then can you please, *please,* allow me one question of my own... please?'

She gently pressed her thumb into the corners of her eyes, to mop up her tears. Then she was certain she noticed Shay nod, even though he didn't.

'Thank you,' she said, 'all I want to know, Shay, is whether or not you believe me. That's all I want to know. It's all I *need* to know.'

She held her lips tightly closed as she tried to study the muscles in his face. But none of them moved.

'What do you mean believe you?' he spat out, before gulping back more tears. 'Believe you about what in particular? Do I believe you killed our boys?... I genuinely don't know. Do I believe that is you in that CCTV footage?... I genuinely. Don't. Know. I don't know anything. *Anything!*' He punched the yellow door, then he paced out of the pokey office and across the concrete landing.

∴

Delia is so taken by how handsome Mathieu Dupont is, with his jet-black hair, jet-black eyebrows and perfectly chiselled chin smothered in stubble, that his looks seem to have almost diluted her panic attack.

'Mr Dupont, can you state your occupation for the court please?' Bracken asks as soon as the witness has sat.

'Of course, eh,' he says, his French accent thick. 'I, eh... am the PDG – or as you say in Ireland, CEO – of a company we call Provenir.'

'And Provenir is a multi-million euro company that specialises in innovative video engineering, correct?'

'Objection, Your Honour,' Jonathan Ryan shouts. 'What does the value of the witness's company have to do with the relevancy of this trial?'

'Rephrase the question,' Delia says without hesitating, releasing her sweaty hands from her own grip. She stares at her thumb, then lightly squeezes at it, creating a fresh bubble of blood.

'Okay, so Provenir is a successful company, shall we say, that specialises in innovative video engineering, correct?' Bracken asks.

'That is eh... correct. Among other things,' Dupont replies.

'Okay, and isn't it a fact that your company Provenir assisted Pixar on two of their blockbuster Hollywood movies, yes?'

'Oui... yes, we did. We assisted with some communication through email to some of the production company's researchers. We didn't get to go to Hollywood. There was no set.' Dupont laughs. 'We were in communication with Pixar on some specific difficulties they had about perception. That was it. I think it was five emails back and forward... that was it.'

'But your company got a mention in the credits of the movies, correct?'

'Yes.' Dupont laughs again. A husky laugh that sounds as if he might have already smoked a full box of cigarettes this morning.

'You were also a lecturer in Nice, correct – at Nice Sophia Antipolis University?'

'That is correct. Yes. Over the course of maybe eight years.'

'Closer to ten, according to the University itself, Mr Dupont. Nine years and seven months to be precise.'

Dupont laughs his husky smoker's laugh again.

'Was it almost ten years? Wow-wow-wee-wa,' he says. 'My, eh... memory is not so great.'

Bracken smiles back at his witness, showing his veneers. But even he must know that he doesn't come anywhere close to having the best smile in this courtroom. Not today.

Delia gulps, then lightly burps as a pocket of air jumps itself up her throat. She brings her hand to her mouth, then looks about herself, hoping the stenographer didn't hear her almost throw up.

'So, you are a specialist in innovative engineering, and you lectured on this subject for nigh on a decade at a prestigious university in northern France, Mr Dupont. That's very impressive. Thank you for taking the time out of your busy schedule to be with us at this trial today.' Dupont nods back. 'Let me ask you,' Bracken continues, 'upon hearing of the Joy Stapleton case for the very first time when, I believe, a student brought you an analysis of the CCTV footage for his end-of-year assignment, you began to look into the case yourself, correct?'

'I thought it was a very, *very* interesting case, yes.'

'You used your innovative software to try to discover if the woman in that footage could possibly have been Joy Stapleton, correct?'

'That is correct. Well, I first started looking at it with my student – his name is Eric Dupont... no relation.' He smiles a vertical dimple into his stubbled cheek. 'Then I brought it into our studio to take a closer look... eh... intrigued, is the best word to describe it.'

'You were confident you could tell the exact height of the person in that footage... wouldn't that be fair to suggest?'

'Well eh... Mr Bracken,' he says, his accent thickening, 'what I would say is that I felt I could do my best with my best technology to determine the height of the person in the footage.'

'And in brief terms for the court, can you detail how you could do that?'

'Sure I, eh... we – my company, Provenir – developed 3D model software that is able to read persons from still images and determine the exact height of that person.'

'So, that mightn't sound impressive to the courts, because measuring somebody from a photograph or a still seems a little easy...' Bracken holds his hands in front of himself and puffs a laugh. 'But can you tell the court how intricate the measurements must be to determine exact height?'

'Yes. It is not so easy. Because we, each of us, hold so many different heights. Just because my doctor measures me at six foot, three, it does not mean that I am always six foot, three. In fact, I most likely never am six foot, three. Or rarely. I really only am six foot, three when somebody says, Monsieur Dupont, can you stand against that wall so I can measure you? And I think that has only happened to me maybe four or five times in my life. So, most likely and more often than not, I am not six foot, three, even though it is my official height. We all slouch, hunch, bend, lean, pivot... all these things. And, for example, an everyday average height throughout any given day can be up to two whole inches lower than a person's official registered height.'

Delia lightly burps, only this time she envelops it so well that she is certain the stenographer couldn't have heard her. Then the door to her right sweeps open and Aisling walks in, nodding to the judge. She hands her a plaster before sneaking back out in silence. The judge stares up at Bracken as she unpeels the plaster and begins to curl it around her thumb. Then she nods at him, signalling that he should continue.

'So, you took the still of the figure from the CCTV footage, Mr Dupont, then built a 3D model of her and measured her exact height. Is that correct?'

'That is correct, yes.'

'And can you now reveal to the court what the exact height the person is in that footage?'

'One hundred and fifty-four point seven, one five centimetres. Which in your money here in Ireland is exactly five foot, and three quarters of one inch.'

'Five foot, and three quarters of an inch,' Bracken says, nodding his head. 'The defendant here today, Joy Stapleton, Mr Dupont, according to her prison records is five foot, two inches in height. Your finding is that the figure in the CCTV footage is one whole inch and a further quarter inch smaller than that, yes?'

'Yes.'

'That might sound like a tiny measurement to many in this courtroom today, but in your line of work, that's a gulf... correct?'

'What I can say, Mr Bracken, with absolute certainty is that the figure in the CCTV is definitely not five foot, two inches.'

A light gasp is heard at the back of the court and Bracken pauses to allow the effect of it to float through the room.

'And this software you use to determine your exact findings, Mr Dupont, what's it called?'

'Oh... Sonix17, we are not very creative with names,' Dupont says, laughing again, exposing his vertical dimple. Delia almost laughs with him, but in trying to stifle it, she awakens another frog in her throat.

'And Sonix17 was built when?' Bracken continues.

'2017, as the name suggests. I told you we were not very creative with names.'

'2017? Very recently. So, it is fair to say that this technology did not exist in 2012... when Joy Stapleton's original trial took place, correct?'

'Course not, no,' Dupont says, shaking his head.

Delia knew that question was asked just for her benefit – to underline to her that this was brand new information being brought into the legal argument. A retrial can only really be granted if new evidence emerges. This expert's testimony, with new-age technology that couldn't have been used during the original trial, coupled with the fact that Bunny the dog had, since the original trial, been labelled a fraud, was the brand new evidence the defendant was bringing to this court. Delia had known these were the likely trump cards of the defence. But she didn't realised the new technology would be delivered to her in such a convincing and specific manner.

'That is all, Your Honour,' Bracken says, nodding up at Delia. She purses her lips back at him, then squints to the back rows of the gallery. There's still no sign of Taunton. So, she flicks her gaze to her son, then has to hold her eyes closed with frustration to allow the image in the video to wash through her thoughts. She holds her hand firmer to her mouth in anticipation of another burp. But none comes.

'Your Honour, may I?' Jonathan Ryan calls out from his desk.

'Of course, Mr Ryan.'

Ryan rises to his feet, a mysterious smug grin on the corner of his lips. Delia had noted the maturity in his performances during the opening two days of this retrial. This is the third trial she's presided over cases that he has attempted to prosecute. And he seemed, in her eyes, to be getting more assured and more confident each time he appeared in front of her.

'Mr Dupont, thank you for being with us here today,' Ryan says. 'I have found your testimony most interesting, I must say. I also find it wildly inaccurate and I will detail exactly why that is in one moment. But before I do that,' Ryan strides into the middle of the courtroom floor, 'can I just have something clarified, please? When Mr Bracken was questioning you earlier, he suggested your company, Provenir, was a specialist in video engineering. You answered him by saying "among other things". It is the "other things",' Ryan curls his fingers to denote quote marks, 'that your company *really* specialises in, isn't it? You don't specialise in detailing the height of figures from CCTV footage, correct?'

Dupont laughs again.

'Of course not. We would not be so successful with such a business model.'

'So, what your company really is successful at is developing perceptive-space software for smart phone app manufacturers, correct?'

'Eh... yes. When you say specialise, that is what we really specialise in. That is what makes our company successful. Correct. Working with app developers is pretty much our entire business.'

'Yes. And can I just confirm that when Mr Bracken says you were a lecturer at the University in Nice for ten years. That's not ten years full-time, right? A few times a year you would give lectures on video engineering at the university.'

'Yes. It was three times a year. Each October, January and April.'

'So, thirty lectures in total?'

Dupont laughs.

'It must be... yes.'

'So let me get this straight, Mr Dupont... when Mr Bracken introduces you to the court as somebody who not only specialises in determining the height of somebody through a CCTV still and somebody who has lectured extensively on the subject, that's quite a hyperbolic description, is it not?'

'Hyper...'

'Hyperbolic. An exaggeration?'

'Well, that was Mr Bracken's description,' Dupont sucks the dimple into his cheek again. 'Not mine. I do not consider myself a lecturer. I never have. I liked passing my expertise to students and would have done more hours in the university, but time would not allow, of course.'

'Yes. Well, Mr Bracken has a tendency to be hyperbolic when

he feels a witness requires it,' Ryan says, darting a quick glance to the judge.

Delia picks up her gavel and thumps it twice to her desk.

'Mr Ryan,' she yells out. 'I am surprised.' Her eyes grow wide as she stares down at Ryan.

'Sorry, Your Honour,' he says, holding up his two hands and then turning back to the witness. 'Mr Dupont, have you ever met the defendant, Mrs Joy Stapleton?'

'No, no,' Dupont says, shaking his head before signalling to the defendant as if anybody in the courtroom needed her pointed out. 'Today is my first day to see her.'

'So, you, through your software, were able to determine the exact height of a woman you have never met?'

'Well, that is not true. I was not looking to determine if or if not the figure in the footage was Mrs Stapleton. I was just trying to determine the height of the woman in the footage.'

'And you came up with five foot, and three quarters of an inch?'

'Yes.'

'And why do you think that couldn't be Mrs Stapleton?'

'Well... as I said, I was not looking for Mrs Stapleton. I was looking for the exact height of the figure in the footage only.'

'But you testified here today that, and I quote "I can confirm that the figure is not five foot, two." Yes?'

'I did.'

'Where did the figure of five foot, two come from?'

'Well... it came from Mrs Stapleton's prison records, no?'

'Ahhh,' Ryan says. And as he does, Delia gulps, swallowing the threat of another burp. 'Mr Dupont you are a man of exact measurement, are you not?'

'I am. Yes. I guess.'

'Well, do you honestly believe that the measurements taken, probably quite swiftly inside a cold prison medical room with an old stadiometer would in any way be scientifically precise?'

'I did not say that the record of the prison measurement is correct.'

'No, you didn't. Which is why I called your testimony wildly inaccurate at the beginning of my cross examination, Mr Dupont. You may have been measuring against an inaccurate record. We, the prosecution team, tried to retrieve exact measurements of the defendant. We were denied. You admitted under oath here today that this is the first time you have ever seen Mrs Stapleton in the flesh, correct?'

'It is still correct, yes.'

'So, I take it you've never measured her either, right?'

Dupont shakes his head and rubs his fingers across the stubble of his chin.

'No. I have not measured Mrs Stapleton. I live between Nice and Paris. Yesterday was my first time in Dublin in ten years.'

'Because Mr Bracken invited you to be part of this trial... to get you up here to label you successful at this and that, just so your testimony would sound impressive. But if your testimony is all about accuracy, then it fails somewhat if you are comparing to a measurement recorded in a cold prison room by a dodgy stadiometer, does it not?'

'I am not here to—'

'It's okay, Mr Dupont. You don't have to answer that. Because I can tell you that the prison record of Joy Stapleton is not the only record of her height. When Mrs Stapleton was measured by a Doctor Mishia Rasaad in the Coombe Hospital in May 2004, pregnant with her first son, she was measured at five foot, two and a quarter inches. Not five foot, and one quarter inch. When she was measured for a health check-up, five months after giving birth, she was more specifically measured at five foot, one and one-tenth. Then on arrival in prison she was measured at five foot, two, which as you know was marked in a diary. Quite a discrepancy in all those numbers, Mr Dupont, wouldn't you agree? What did Mr Bracken call it earlier, measurements of that ilk are like a gulf to you, right?'

'That doesn't prove the woman in the footage is Mrs Stapleton. None of those measurements you just mentioned are five foot and three quarters of an inch as my software suggests the woman in the CCTV is.'

'No, but what it does suggest, Mr Dupont, is that the measurements you came here to testify against are inaccurate. Wildly inaccurate. Thank you, Your Honour.'

'We thank the witness,' Delia calls out. Then she stands, leaving Dupont looking perplexed that his testimony ended so abruptly and so inconclusively. 'Court dismissed,' Delia follows up with. And as she does, she spins on her heels and dashes down the steps and out the side door as if she's on a mission. The bright white lights of the modern corridor don't help to stem her spinning head. So, she pulls at the neck of her robe, whipping it up over her head and scrunching it up into a ball in her hands as she begins to take sharper breaths.

Then she abruptly halts her power walk, brings the scrunched-up robe to her mouth and vomits into it.

2,275 days ago…

'This way,' Joy said to Carol.

And so Carol followed her. Down the steel steps, across the concrete landing, then into the large space all of the noise seemed to be emanating from.

'Thank you,' Carol shouted over the chatter.

'Don't worry about the noise; all that screeching you hear in prison, it's nothing. Ain't no cats being strangled or hens a-cackling – that's genuinely just the noise of three hundred of us women talking over each other. Loud bunch, aren't we?'

Carol tried to smile, but it came off more like a grimace.

'I, eh… I thought I could ask you because… well… because you're a familiar face, I guess.'

Joy pursed her lips at the new prisoner. She looked just as young and petrified as Joy had been when she'd first arrived in Elm House.

'How long have you been in here now?' Carol asked, as Joy handed her a tray.

'Just coming up to two years.'

'Two years… jeez, is it that long? Can't imagine two years in here… let alone two lifetimes… oh, sorry,' Carol said, holding her hand over her open mouth.

'Don't worry about it. How long a stretch you got?'

'Three months.'

'Three months? For what?'

Carol looked down at the oversized flipflops she was wearing.

'Well… well, it's a bit embarrassing. I tried to skim from my boss. I was running his accounts. Just took a few quid here and there. I didn't think he'd notice. If I fancied a new pair of shoes and I knew I couldn't afford them… I'd just… y'know.'

'Three months for a pair of shoes? Judge musta hated you.'

'Well… it wasn't just one pair of shoes, if you know what I

mean. I didn't have a clue how much I'd spent... not until the police came to the office one day. Thirty-six grand I'd spent on myself over the course of eighteen months... Almost double me wages.'

She turned down the corners of her mouth. But Joy was too busy standing on her tip-toes to stare over the kitchen counter to bother listening to Carol's justifications for her crime.

'So, you normally have a choice of three cereals; today it's porridge, Rice Krispies or Corn Flakes. They're not the real deal... cheap knock off versions. But they're alright with a splash of milk. Oh yeah, and then you can have two slices of toast.'

'Ah... okay... this isn't so bad, I guess. I think I'll go for the, eh... Rice Krisp... no, feck it, the Corn Flakes today and I'll—' she looked around. But Joy was gone.

After deciding against cereals, Joy had jumped ahead of the queue and grabbed two slices of buttered toast before heading off to the bench populated by Christy's Crazies.

'Who that bitch?' Christy asked her.

'A nobody. Carol something or other... I was thinking of recruiting her over to our side, but she's only in for three months. Larceny. She's not worth it to us. She'll be gone before we know it.'

They each stared at Carol, all silently taking an in-breath as Nancy Trott sidled up to her, placing a hand to her shoulder.

'See... now she like that kinda gal, does Nancy. Small. Pretty. She love you,' she said to Joy. 'You just lucky I got to you first, sista. We hadn't been in that van together on our first day here, you be gettin' penetrated by those fat, chubby fingers o' hers all night long.'

The gang of Crazies cackled and guffawed at what Christy had just said, even though they well believed her account to be accurate. They weren't sure which one of Nancy's Cohorts Nancy was fingering or being fingered by regularly, probably all of them, but they all knew they would rather be a member of the perceived crazy gang than Nancy's gang – even if it did mean they had to regularly read passages from a bible they knew to be bullshit. It made much more sense to them to pretend to believe in God than be finger raped.

'Okay... okay... let's settle,' Christy said, grabbing the two prisoners next to her by the hand. 'Our Lord Jesus, we thank you for the blessing of these foods you provide for us today and each and every day. May you walk with us and guide us as we continue our journey. We thank you, oh Lord. Amen.'

Then she let go of their hands as the whole bench muttered an 'Amen' in unison, and everybody picked up either a large spoon or a slice of toast and silently got stuck into their breakfasts.

It was during that rather noisy period, when the screeching first strikes up in earnest as the whole wing is finishing breakfast, that Stella hobbled by their table. She stared at them, as she usually does, menacingly, but she wasn't intimidating. Not anymore. Though every time Joy laid eyes on her, she could feel the blunt force to the bridge of her nose, even though that attack had, by now, occurred almost two years ago.

'Ye know, I was thinkin' bout that bitch in ma sleep last night,' Christy said. 'I had a vision. She ain't long for this world. That's what ma vision told me.'

And then all of Christy's Crazies got up from their bench, brought their bowls and plates to the counter and headed back to their cells where they would spend the next hour alone while the prison officers took over the dining room to have breakfast themselves.

At 9:30 a.m., the cells reopened, and then it was off to either work, or school, depending on which road you had chosen. Joy was enjoying the Healthy Foods course she was studying by now, even though she had received a poor grade on her most recent assignment. It wasn't necessarily the course content she was enjoying while she was cooked up in the small education room at the back end of the prison, it was Christy's company. They were two peas in a pod; rarely separated when the cell doors were open.

Joy and Christy would talk openly about Joy's plight; about the fight of an innocent mother spending two life sentences behind bars for the most heinous crime imaginable. The Joy Stapleton is Innocent campaign was going strong; certainly outside the prison. It had snowballed somewhat by social media, though mainstream media rarely covered the cause. They did, when the Joy is Innocent campaign was first founded. But when Joy and Christy started shouting from within the confines of the prison that they had a theory about Joy's former best friend Lavinia Kirwan being the mystery woman in the unique pink hooded top, the cause took a dip in reputation. Lavinia had a solid alibi for the night in question. The woman in the pink hoodie simply couldn't have been her. That fact didn't stop Christy and Joy growing their theory, though. And they would often sit on the bed inside one of their cells and cook up more analysis of Lavinia's possible involvement. But in truth, nobody was listening to them. And especially not Shay. Since his visit five months ago, Joy had heard nothing from her husband. The only update she had been given on his life came via one of the tabloid newspapers, which detailed a story suggesting Shay's hours at his job had been reduced and that he'd been demoted. The newspaper speculated his health had been an issue in the demotion; that he was suffering from constant waves of depression. She thought about writing to him, reaching out after she'd read that story. But despite sitting down with a blank sheet of paper and a pen, she managed no words.

2,274 days ago...

It wasn't long after the doors had clicked open, as they do first thing every morning, that the first shriek was heard. It was piercing. And Joy knew immediately that something serious had happened. Then Mathilda and Aidan raced up and down the landings of Elm House and began shuffling prisoners back into their cells, while yelling for lockdown.

'What is it, what's happened?' Joy asked Aidan as he raced towards her.

He looked around himself, his face paler than normal.

'We, eh... we just found Stella Cantwell in her cell. She was hanging.'

Joy held a hand to her mouth, then stepped back into her cell to perch herself on her mattress while Aidan locked the door from the outside.

It didn't take long for the doors to click back open, because it wasn't the prison staff's first rodeo in terms of cleaning up a suicide mess. Though it was the first time a hanging had happened in Elm House for many a year.

Aidan was still pale when Joy bumped into him on her way to visit Christy's cell.

'You okay?' Joy asked him. But he either didn't hear or didn't want to hear her. He just strolled on by as she rattled her knuckles against Christy's cell door.

'What the fuck?!' she shouted when she saw Christy's yellow stained teeth grimacing at her.

'I told you, I told you, Joy. She not long for this world and then within half a day, Our Lord Jesus Christ took her from us.'

'Christy,' Joy said, her eyes heavy. 'Did you murder Stella?'

Christy's bloodshot eyes almost popped out of her head.

'What you talkin' bout, girl? I ain't no killer.'

'But... but...' Joy held her palms out. She was dumbstruck.

When all of Christy's Crazies had gathered around the worn sofa in the games room, they couldn't hide their awe of their leader.

'I can't believe God communicates with you directly,' one of them said. 'And just so randomly like that. God comes to you in your dreams to tell you Stella is not long for this world and then next night she does it... she kills herself.'

Joy was the only one who didn't laud Christy's gift. It simply couldn't be that she could tell the future. Not like that. Though Joy didn't say anything. She needed to pretend she believed in Christy. After all, it was Christy's gift that had exonerated her in the eyes of most of the prisoners who resided in Elm House. Going against the grain now would only mean she was arguing against her own innocence.

She did question Christy when they were alone, asking her where she had been the evening previous; though she did it in a very subtle manner. Then she realised, as did the other Crazies who might, like Joy, be sceptical, that Christy couldn't have had anything to do with Stella's hanging. She had a solid alibi; was doing a medical in the health room during the time in question and was escorted to and from that medical by Mathilda before she was locked back up in her cell for the night.

'Oh my God,' one of the Crazies said to Joy, 'Stella really did kill herself. She killed herself right after Christy had seen it in her vision. This girl is the real deal. The real deal.'

Joy found herself shaking, even though Stella had handed down the only beating she had ever received her whole life. Her hands were covering her face and slightly quivering when Aidan walked into her cell later that afternoon.

'What a day!' he said, his face still pale. 'You okay?'

'Just a bit of shock is all,' she said before getting to her feet.

'I'm a little bit shocked meself,' Aidan said. 'I mean, I didn't get on with Stella or anything, she just kept herself to herself... but I never thought in a million years she'd go and top herself. She just didn't seem the kind. She... I dunno... I guess I feel guilty. I should have known she was depressed. She's on my wing. My landing.'

Joy inched closer to him and could smell the never-changing scent of Lynx on his neck.

'You don't need to beat yourself up, Aidan. Don't be silly. We never see the most obvious things that are right in front of us. Human nature isn't it?' Joy said.

'You sure you're gonna be alright? You seem a little shaken yourself. Can I get you anything? Want me to see if I can get you a warm mug of coffee?'

Without hesitating, and with her emotions bubbling, Joy inched even closer, then looped both arms around the back of Aidan's neck before she leaned upwards to press her lips against his.

'Hey,' he said, baulking backwards and wiping at his mouth. 'What the hell are you playing at?'

∴

Delia pulls out the long drawer from the bottom of the stack of tall library shelves in her dimly lit office and removes a fresh robe.

She had ordered Aisling, as she was approaching her office all hot and bothered, to arrange a clean-up of the corridor that leads to the side entrance of the main courtroom.

'There's something funny along the tiles, there,' she shouted into Aisling's pokey office. 'As if somebody got sick or something. See to it that it's mopped up as soon as possible, won't you, my dear?'

She struggles to get her robe over her head, not helped by the fact that her glasses have been combed back into her hair. But when she eventually tugs it down and flattens it at the knees, she takes a seat at her desk. She doesn't necessarily need to don a new robe as court is over for the day, but she intends on working on the trial at her computer and always likes to be dressed for the occasion. Though she knows working on the trial won't be the first thing she does when she reawakens her computer.

She hovers her hand over her mouse, then wiggles at it frantically, bringing the screen to life. She doesn't want to watch it again. But feels she needs to see the whole video through, just in case there is a personal message or instruction at the end of it. All she'd seen of it so far was about six seconds before she'd slapped a hand at her computer monitor. And the video goes on for a full two and a half minutes.

She lowers the volume on her monitor, then covers a hand over her eyes before tapping at her mouse. A sound of repeated rustling, then a groan, cackles from her speakers.

Delia slightly widens the gaps between her fingers and turns her eyes inwards so that the image on the screen blurs somewhat and she doesn't have to take the full impact of it. The rustling continues, as another groan, this one more high-pitched, is followed by an elongated panting. Then the video abruptly stops.

'That's it?' she says, wiggling her mouse. She clicks back into the email, and rechecks to confirm that there is no message accompanying it. Just an email address in the sent bar and the video in the attachments.

She pauses her fingers, plastered thumb and all, over her keyboard, then lets out an audible sigh as she begins to type.

Who is this? What do you want from me?

She shakes her head and then pokes one finger at the mouse, sending off her two questions before she has time to stop herself.

She couldn't think of how else she could have conceivably replied to that email, even though her next move was constantly floating through her mind in between the silences of Mathieu Dupont's testimony.

Her stomach has stopped producing bile – her burping and vomiting all done – and her hands aren't shaking anywhere near as prominently as they were inside the court room. The time she spent in the women's' toilets, splashing her face with water, helped recede her panicking somewhat. But she keeps wringing her sweating hands as she stares at her email list, waiting on a reply to drop into her inbox. But her screen just shines back at her, unblinking.

'Feck it,' she mutters to herself. Then she clicks her email account off the screen and opens the Word document she had been working from.

She types 'Mathieu Dupont' underneath the minimal amount of notes she has taken so far, then taps her fingernail repeatedly against the mouse in contemplation before typing the word 'interesting' next to the name.

'Mathieu Dupont,' she mutters to herself. She imagines his face, the vertical dimple covered in stubble, the dark eyebrows framing his deep-set eyes. 'Well... he was definitely manufactured by Bracken, but certainly legitimate nonetheless,' she says. And then she types the word 'legitimate' next to the word 'interesting.'

'One hundred and fifty... what was it again?' she says, tip-tapping her fingernails against the mouse before she swiftly swipes at the receiver of her desk phone.

'Aisling,' she says, 'can you get me a copy of Mathieu Dupont's testimony, please? I, eh... didn't take many notes during the trial today, for some reason, and I need to know the exact height his 3D software measured the figure in the CCTV footage.'

'One hundred and fifty-four point seven, one five centimetres,' Aisling says without hesitating. 'I am literally reading through the transcripts myself now. I'll print you off a copy and bring them into you as soon as I can.'

'Thank you,' Delia says. Then she places the receiver back down and proceeds to type.

$$154.715 \; cm = five', \; \frac{3}{4}"$$

'Joy has never been measured at that height. Lots of different heights, yes. Likely because of her great big mop of curls. But never five foot and three quarters of an inch.' Delia holds a fist under her chin as she swivels left and right in her chair. Then she hears footsteps and a familiar one-knuckle rap at her door. Her stomach immediately turns itself over before she can shout 'Come in, Callum.'

Her son's eyes squint at her as he enters.

'Were you okay in court today, Mum?' he asks. 'You looked a little... distracted.'

She shakes her head back at him and puffs out a short snort of laughter.

'I'm fine, dear,' she replies.

'Distracted by the hunk in the witness box, huh?' he says, plonking himself into the seat opposite and giggling.

'Bit of a cliché, don't you think? Tall, dark, handsome, thick French accent, all wrapped up in a skinny designer suit,' she suggests.

'Well, if that's what cliché is, let cliché rain down on me any day of the week. And twice on Sundays.'

Callum giggles again, then stops abruptly when he notices his mother stare down at her lap, her face still, her fist to her mouth – just as she had been through most of Dupont's testimony.

'Mum... seriously, what's up with you?'

Delia shakes her head.

'Was interesting testimony, don't ya think?' she says, swallowing back the bile.

'Certainly was. Though I think Jonathan Ryan crossed well... did his best to undermine Dupont's credibility.'

'Did he, though? Did he really undermine him?' she asks.

'Made his testimony pretty darn unconvincing, seeing as he hadn't even measured the suspect herself.'

'Still... all-in-all, his testim—'

Delia stops as her speakers ping, and a flashing box appears in the top corner of her screen. Without hesitating, she drags her icon towards it and clicks at her mouse.

Return a Guilty verdict and this footage will stay between us.
Deliver not guilty... then this goes everywhere.

'Mother fuck—' she mutters before stopping herself.

'Mum!' Callum says, his brow dipping. 'What is wrong with you today?'

Light footsteps followed by a knock at the door distracts them.

'In you come, Aisling,' Delia calls out.

Aisling enters, offering a friendly smile to Callum.

'Transcripts,' she says, handing a small pile of papers across the desk to her boss. 'Fascinating reading. Considerable testimony today, huh?'

'What? You think so too?' Callum says. 'You sure you girls weren't just swayed by that neat stubble... or was it the dimple?'

'Weren't you?' Aisling says. 'Pretty much a turning point in the case in my humble opinion.'

'Nah,' Callum says. 'The turning point, if it's ever going to come, will come tomorrow. Shay Stapleton takes the stand first thing in the morning, right? If anybody has come up with answers to this mystery over the years it must be him. Poor man must have obsessed about this case non-stop for the twelve years since his boys first went missing.'

'We'll see,' Aisling says, before she sweeps out the door, dragging it shut behind her.

'I mean, I get that Dupont came with new technology, but really? I thought Jonathan Ryan handled him well,' Callum says as he watches his mother rifle through the paperwork.

'You seem to be transfixed on how Ryan handled him,' Delia says, without looking up. 'But the gem of his testimony lies in the answers he gave to Bracken's questions. This is... this is...' Delia holds her fist to her mouth again and burps loudly into it. Then she bends down and drags the metal bin from under her desk closer to her feet.

'Mum, Mum,' Callum cries, standing up and chicaning himself around the desk. He hunkers down beside his bent-over mother and rubs at her back. And as he does so, glass crunches beneath his feet.

'What the hell?' He bends down to pick up the smashed photo frame and stares at it. 'Oh, it's the one of you, Dad and me,' he says. 'When did you break this... *how* did you break this?' He leans in closer to his mum, gripping her in a one-armed embrace. 'What's wrong, Mum? Tell me. You can tell me.'

He places the photo frame back on the desk, a large V-shape of glass missing from the centre of it, and then purrs a sorrowful look towards his mother. Delia sucks up the dribbles that are threatening to run on to her top lip before she pats her son's shoulder repeatedly.

'I know I can tell you anything, son,' she says, rubbing the ball of one of her palms into her eye. 'But you are the one person I can't show this to.'

'Show?' Callum asks, his voice all high-pitched.

'Forget it,' Delia says, waving him away.

'Show me what?... Mum?... Mum?'

Delia leans forward, her two elbows on her desk, her hands slapped to her cheeks.

'Callum... I... we...' She drops both forearms down onto the desk, then sits back in her chair and begins to wiggle her mouse. 'We're being blackmailed.' She opens up her emails, then reaches out to her computer monitor and tilts it ever so slightly, so that it's more face on with her son. 'I don't know what to do... who to...' she says, almost sobbing. Then she reaches for her mouse again, clicks on the video link and baulks backwards, wrapping her arms around her head.

Callum inches his nose closer to the screen, and realises the torso on it belongs to him; his penis throbbing, his knuckles wrapped tight around it. He watches himself tugging and grunting. Tugging and grunting.

'Holy fucking shit!' he says, turning to his mother. 'Holy fucking shit. That's my computer, recording me. My computer! Somebody hacked into my computer. They must have accessed my camera and...' He covers his mouth with his hand, then stands backwards against the wall of Delia's office. 'Who the fuck sent you that?' he asks.

Delia removes her arms from her head, then clicks at her mouse, bringing up the last email she was sent.

Return a Guilty verdict and this footage will stay between us. Deliver not guilty... then this goes everywhere.

'Eddie fucking Taunton,' Callum says. 'Didn't you say he wanted a guilty verdict? Mother fucker had somebody hack into my computer, triggered my camera while I was watching porn and... and... well... The dirty, fat, perverted bastard.'

'Callum, please!'

Delia holds her fingertips to her temple, her stare glaring down at the small pebbles of glass glistening beneath her feet.

'Well... y'know what... it's not that bad. It's not that bad,' Callum says, kneeling down beside his mother's chair and staring up at her. He grabs both of her hands. '*Yes*, you are being blackmailed. *Yes*, somebody hacked into my computer and... yes, it seems we're in trouble. But we're not. Not at all. All you have to do is return a guilty verdict. Then this is all over and that video can... go away. Just get on with the trial as if everything is normal... then at the end of it just deliver your guilty verdict.'

'Even if Joy is innocent?' Delia asks.

'Mum... you don't... no. You don't think she's innocent, do you? You've never thought she was innocent...' Callum places a hand either side of his mother's face and stares up into her eyes. 'Mum, seriously, talk to me... you don't think she's innocent now... do you?'

'I *am* innocent,' Joy said, her hands on her hips, one eyebrow arched to mirror Debbie's glare. 'The only reason I'm in this kip is because of that pink hoodie, and that is not my pink hoodie in that CCTV footage.'

'It could only have been fuckin' you,' Debbie snarled.

'You don't know what you're talking about!'

Debbie stepped closer to Joy, and Joy's heart thudded. Debbie Hart was a new inmate at Elm House, but she had already made her presence felt. She was loud and brash and certainly stocky – as wide as she was tall. Her greying hair was all shaven on one side and she had a swirling tattoo on the side of her neck that looked as if it had been designed by a four-year-old. But thankfully, for Joy as well as the other smaller girls in Elm House, Debbie wouldn't be hanging around for too long. Two months. Max. Inside on a GBH charge. Which is why Joy's heart was thudding right this minute. Because she knew all too well that Debbie could handle herself. Yet, despite her fear, Joy still couldn't stand there and listen to a prisoner insist she was guilty of killing her sons. Not to her face. So, she plucked up enough courage to take a step closer to Debbie and held her breath.

'You're a fuckin' child killer,' Debbie snarled.

'I am no child kill—'

Before Joy had finished her retort, Debbie shoved her, and the other prisoners gathered around them to watch the fight in as close proximity as they possibly could.

'That's enough!' a voice boomed.

And as it did, the crowd parted to allow Christy to walk through.

Joy was leaning on her forearms on the concrete floor, Debbie hunched over her, her fist balled.

Christy stepped towards them and offered Joy a hand while curling her top lip at Debbie.

'You wanna pick on someone, pick on someone yo own size. Wanna piece of me, bitch?'

Debbie stared into Christy's bloodshot eyes, contemplating. Then she broke her stare to glance at Joy before grunting and storming back down the grated landing and towards her cell at the far end of Elm House.

'What was all that about?' Christy asked. And as almost everybody in the crowd tried to explain that Debbie had approached Joy for a fight, Joy sulked away, chicaning through the crowd until she found herself back in her own cell. Alone. And crying – sobbing as heavily as she had done the first night she had arrived.

It wasn't long until Christy had come to her rescue, perched, as she had done countless times over the past two and a half years, on the edge of Joy's bed, consoling her with words of wisdom that were filled with profanities and verses from the bible that weren't.

'You very emotional, sista... you wanna tell me why yo face look like Niagara Falls... and don't say it's cos that Debbie Hart bitch be intimidatin' you. I know you stronger than that.'

Joy sniffed up her tears.

'Fuck Debbie Hart,' Joy said. 'She doesn't mean anything to me. Besides, she's gonna be outta here in a matter of weeks. I would've fought her, though. I was willing to stand up for myself, even if she did hand me a beating. I'm not gonna just stand there and have somebody call me a child killer to my face.'

Christy dabbed at Joy's eyes with the sleeve of her sweat top.

'Then tell me, what else got you all emotional?'

'I dunno,' Joy said, lying back onto her bed, her legs hanging over the side. 'It's loadsa different things but most of all... I guess... I mean... I don't know what to tell you, cos I'm embarrassed about it... but a few months back I tried to... I tried to kiss Aidan.'

'Kiss him?' Christy's red eyes widened, and she held a hand to her mouth.

'I mean... I was a bit... I don't know. He was just standing there one day, and I was vulnerable and alone and sad. And I just threw my arms around him and... and...'

'Ah!' Christy said, 'That's why that boy ain't been around us much these days, huh? He keepin' his distance from you, ain't he? That's why you haven't been yourself.'

Joy answered by sobbing. So, Christy lay beside her, to hold her in a tight embrace and whisper into her ear, life lessons filled with profanity and bible verses that weren't.

'Ah, good. I got the two of you together,' Mathilda said, interrupting their moment. 'Stapleton, you're coming with me. Jabefemi, you've an appointment in the Governor's office.'

'The Governor's office... wot I do?' Christy asked.

Mathilda shrugged her shoulders.

'How t'hell would I know? Just get your lanky ass up there. Meanwhile, Stapleton, step outside with me.'

'She didn't start anything,' Christy said. 'Debbie came over to her, pushed her to the ground and then I stepped in and put a stop to it.'

'I don't know what you're talking about, Jabefemi,' Mathilda said. 'And I don't care either. Stapleton, c'mon, let's go.'

Mathilda led Joy down the steel staircase, across the landing of Elm House and deeper into the bowels of the prison. It had been pretty much close to a year since she was last in this vicinity; when she was being led to a surprise meeting with her husband.

'Here y'go,' Mathilda said, stopping outside the exact same yellow door Joy was certain they had stopped outside that time last year.

'It's not... it's not Shay again, is it?' she asked. And then without saying anything, Mathilda gingerly pushed open the yellow door to show Joy the greying face of her husband.

'I gotta put these on first,' Mathilda said, whipping a pair of cuffs from her waistband.

'Well, well, to what do I owe this pleasure?' Joy said as she sat across from her husband, chained once again to a loop under the desk. She stared at him, noticing that some of the blue had returned to his eyes. 'You look good, Shay. How's the outside world treating you?'

'Eh...' he said, leaning forward on the table, 'I, eh... well, I'm doing good. Better. How about you?'

'Same as you. Better. I'm getting used to it, aren't I? But I guess I may as well. Ain't nobody coming to rescue me, are they? I had to get rid of my last lawyer. Think the creepy prick fancied me or something. He'd turn up all smiles and compliments, but he never did anything. For eighteen months he tried to work around things so he could get me a retrial, but... I'm not sure he was doing anything at all to be honest.'

She shrugged her shoulders, causing her cuffs to clank.

'So, who's representing you now?'

'I haven't got anybody. Don't see the point. I'm gonna be here the rest of my life and I guess I've just had to come to terms with it.'

Shay thinned his lips at his wife, then he reached a hand across the table and placed it on top of hers. It was the first time they'd touched since the week before Joy's original trial – just over two and a half years ago.

'I, eh... I didn't actually come here to talk about this place.' He looked around himself. 'I came here to ask for a divorce.' Joy was surprised that she was surprised. She had expected this request as soon as she was found guilty, yet Shay had never so much as raised the topic. 'I, eh... I met somebody else. Jennifer. Jennifer Stevenson. She's a vet.'

Joy held her eyes closed.

'How old?'

'How... sorry? Your first question is how old is my fiancée?'

'Fiancée?' Joy threw her arms to the air, but the chains clanked and dragged them back to the desk, causing an echoing racket. Though the shooting pain in her wrists wasn't as severe as the throbbing pangs in her heart.

'I had to move on. Course I had to move on. I, eh... I met her last Christmas, at a charity function and we... we hit it off. I asked her a couple of weeks ago to marry me and she said 'Yes'. So, I, eh...'

'So, you've come to see me to ask me to sign a piece of paper that'll free you up to marry her?'

'Well...' Shay shifted himself uneasily in his chair, 'I don't have any papers with me. I am just here to tell you – face to face – that I'm filing for divorce. I'm sorry. I'm so sorr—'

'You don't need to apologise,' Joy said, cutting her husband short. 'When you have the papers, send them in and I'll sign 'em. Shay... congratulations. I'm glad you're happier. Your eyes have turned blue again. Mathilda!' she shouted, 'I'm good now. You can take me back to the cell.'

Mathilda pushed the yellow door slightly open and peered through the crack.

'You have fifty-five more minutes, you two. Might as well make the most of it.'

Joy sighed, then stared across the cramped desk to look into the eyes she once thought she'd be spending a lifetime getting lost in.

They didn't talk about much, aside from a quick catch-up, before Shay eventually left. Joy relented and then exaggerated; telling him she was having a hard time of it with the bullies in the prison; that in fact just before he had come to visit her, she had been beaten up. He could well believe her, what with her face swollen from all of the crying she had done earlier.

'So, there we have it, after all these years, Shay Stapleton finally gonna divorce your ass,' Mathilda said as she led Joy back around the maze of landings.

'Mathilda,' Joy said, stopping. 'Shut the fuck up and stop listening into my visitations.' Then she stomped herself all the way back to her cell, like a fourteen-year-old who'd been sent to bed early for misbehaving. But she only stayed in her cell for a matter of minutes; too emotionally drained to be in her own company. She knew what she needed; the calming Texan/Nigerian drawl of her best friend. Her only true friend. The only person who could right her wrongs; who could stop her mind from travelling to the darkest of places. The only person who truly believed she was innocent.

She paced across the landing and pushed at Christy's cell door, but it wouldn't budge.

'Christy. Christy, you in there?' she said as she slapped her open palms against the door. 'I need you. I need you. You're not gonna believe this. Shay wants a divorce. Mother fucker's getting married again... Christy? Christy?'

She hunkered down, to stare through the boxed gap in the centre of Christy's cell door. But the cell looked vacant.

'She's gone,' Aidan's voice echoed. Joy, stunned, spun around and looked up to see him standing on the landing above her, leaning over the rail. 'Governor came to her about an hour ago, told her her time was up. She's a free woman now, Joy. Christy's already back on the streets.'

1,977 days ago...

Linda rubbed at Joy's legs, but it didn't seem to be having the calming effect she was aiming for. Joy was still stretched out on her mattress sobbing, just as she had been for almost the entirety of the past twenty-four hours.

'We'll get through this. We can take everything Christy taught us and just continue to learn from it through the rest of our time here,' Linda said.

Joy gulped, then wiped at her nose with her sleeve, causing a streak of snot to stretch across her cheek. She didn't notice. And Linda felt it best left unsaid, given the sombre circumstances.

'S'all right for you to say, Linda. You've only got a couple of years left. I'm gonna be here the rest of me life. I can't do it... I can't do it without Christy. Besides...'

Linda continued to rub along Joy's short legs.

'Besides what?'

'Christy getting out isn't the only reason I'm in this state.'

'Huh?'

'Shay.'

'Shay... your husband? What about him?'

'He came to see me yesterday. He's met someone else – asked her to marry him.'

Linda rubbed even more fervently, while producing a sympathetic purr.

'I know you've loved that man so much, Joy. But aren't you better off detaching from him once and for all? You talk so much about what he thinks; what he does and doesn't believe. Maybe, just maybe this could be a fresh start for you.'

Joy sobbed again. Then she sat up in her bed and rested the cheek with the streak of snot stretched across it onto Linda's shoulder.

'I wish I could be more positive like you are, Linda Wood. It's just... uuuuugh... two body blows in the space of one hour yesterday. First, Shay asking me for a divorce. And then I come back to tell Christy and she's just... she's gone. Pfftt. Out of my life like that... forever. But ye know what seems to be hurting the most?'

'What's that, baby?' Linda said, now rubbing in circles at the small of Joy's lower back.

'I spent the guts of an hour with Shay yesterday. Mother fucker never once mentioned our boys. He never mentioned the case at all. All this time has passed... and all this drama has passed... and ye know what? The most painful and frustrating part for me in all of this is that I've simply never, *ever*, truly known what's been going on inside my husband's head.'

SHAY STAPLETON

Nine autographs I signed between getting out of the car and reaching the front doors of the Criminal Courts. I counted as I was signing. Only because I was miffed. Though I often am when I sign an autograph these days – not quite sure if I'm more famous for being a footballer or for being Joy Stapleton's husband.

There used to be a time I'd love to be asked for my autograph. In fact, I'd often walk up and down Grafton Street in my spare time just so Dubliners would recognise me and ask me to sign a slip of paper for them while they told me where they were when I side-footed home the winning goal in the 2005 Leinster final. But now I do the total opposite of that. I stay indoors. So that I can stay out of sight of the general public as much as I possibly can.

I'm only out today for her. For Joy. Her torture has been going on way too long. Though so, too, has mine. I guess I'm just hopeful this trial will go some way to diluting my torture. I came here to let the judge know that I feel, after all this time, that Joy is innocent; that she isn't responsible for the fact that our two boys' skeletons were found in wasteland up in the Dublin mountains. But the truth is, as it's always been, I really don't know what to fucking believe. All I can hope for at this stage is that if Joy is to be set free, then so too might I. I know that's selfish. But I need it. I need the freedom. I need to be able to breathe fresh air again.

Nobody in this world feels more guilty about Oscar and Reese's murders than I do. I wasn't there for them when they needed me most. Guilt riddles me. It eats at me. And it has done ever since I received that phone call from Joy – screaming at me that our boys had been taken.

My best friend Steve pats me on the back as Gerd Bracken calls out my name, and as I stand, my ears are immediately enveloped by humming. I feel a slight sense of dizziness, almost vertigo-like, as if the red carpet wants me to lean towards it. But I make my way up the three steps to the witness box, without falling; avoiding eye contact with Joy as I sidle by. Though as I sit into the leather cushioned witness box, after I've been swiftly sworn in, I allow myself a glance at her. So many years have passed since I last saw that face. She looks as if she's aged. But haven't we all? Her eyes glance upwards to meet mine, but I immediately blink away. Last time Joy laid her eyes on me, I was, dare I say it, still handsome. Now I just see an old man staring back at me every time I look in a mirror. Like proper old. I'm only thirty-eight, but I see a fifty-eight-year-old in my reflection. I actually remember, distinctly, just waking up one morning and noticing I had two extra chins. As if they just appeared overnight. And the blue in my eyes, which I used to be complimented on constantly, has turned grey... a bit like my hair. A bit like my skin. I'm just grey all over these days. Grey and chubby. A bit like the cloud that constantly floats above me.

'Mr Stapleton,' Bracken says, appearing in front of me with his hands clasped against his belly. 'I and the court sincerely thank you for being here today. Can you start by stating your profession for the court, please?'

'Eh... well, I work in public relations for Jameson Hotels.'

'But it's fair to say the population of this country would know you in another capacity...'

'Yes, as the man whose two sons were murdered.' Before Bracken can react, I hold my hands up. 'Sorry. Yes. Of course. I, ehm... was also a member of the Dublin football squad from 2002 up until... well, 2009. I stopped playing when Oscar and Reese went missing, then came back eighteen months later and played a couple more games, but my heart just wasn't...'

'It's understandable, Mr Stapleton. You were, it is fair to say, a well-known sports star in the mid part of the noughties, correct?'

'Correct.'

'You crossed paths with Joy Lansbury as she was then in December of 2002. You guys had Reese just shy of one year later. In May of 2006 you got married. Then in March 2007, Oscar was born. Four Stapletons living in a beautiful four-bedroom semi-detached home in Rathfarnham... correct?'

'Correct.'

'How would you describe your family life in those days... the days before your boys were first reported missing back in November of 2008?'

I shift uneasily in the witness box, my fingers drumming on my lap.

'Well... I would describe it as normal.'

'Happy?'

'Objection, Your Honour, Mr Bracken is putting words into the witness's mouth,' the lawyer on the other side of the room calls out.

'He's only asking a question, Mr Ryan,' the judge says.

I look at her and then she looks at me. And nods.

'I would say happy, yes.' I sniffle up some tears that are threatening to fall. I promised myself I wouldn't cry. Though I knew I couldn't guarantee that promise. I reach inside my suit breast pocket and take out the photograph of Oscar and Reese, just to squeeze it in the hope that it will gift me some strength. I stare at this photograph every day. Truth is, I often spend hours just staring at it. Their two little faces smiling back at me. It's so odd. It seems it's all I've got left of them. One flash of a camera. A moment in time captured forever; a moment I will never get tired of staring at.

'Although you were a footballer at the height of the sport – and I'm sure most will know you scored in a Leinster final in 2005 – you still worked for Jameson Hotels, correct?'

'Yes.'

'GAA stars are, of course, not paid for their efforts. They need full-time work for their livelihoods. And you travelled for work, yes?'

'Yes. I had to stay in a lot of our sister hotels in different counties regularly... that was part of my job.'

'Yet despite the amount of travelling you did, you were utterly faithful to your wife and children and couldn't wait to get home to them each time you travelled, correct?'

I clear my throat, and lean closer to the microphone.

'Mr Bracken, I will say under oath, that I was always faithful to my wife and boys. I never once committed adultery. I always wanted to come home to them. Yes.'

That's not entirely true. I didn't always want to come home to them. I have to admit, I liked the solitude working in the hotel industry offered me. That's why the guilt riddles me. I was in a bloody hotel doing absolutely nothin', when my boys were taken. I should've been home. I should've been a better father. A better husband. And I guess that when Joy and I first started dating I was seeing other girls at the same time. It was part and parcel of being a sports star. Girls would offer themselves up to me. But once Joy fell pregnant for the first time, I didn't dare look at another woman. In fact, I stopped socialising altogether so that the temptation of other women would die. And it did. I never cheated on my family. Other than to pretend to them that I really missed them while I was being pampered in a five-star hotel.

'And you knew Joy Stapleton better than anyone? You lived with her for five whole years and you shared some amazing memories, correct?'

'Those five years were the best five years of my life. We had two children. We got married. We honeymooned in South Africa. We travelled to different countries on many different holidays. We were... we were two young people in their early twenties very much in love and very much looking forward.'

A tear threatens to race out of my eye, so I pinch the photo of Reese and Oscar tighter.

'In 2008, may I ask you, Mr Stapleton, did you notice any change in your wife's behaviour?'

I shake my head.

'You must verbally answer the question, Mr Stapleton,' the judge says, looking down at me. The judge seems firm, but fair. Though I've noticed her out of the corner of my eye every now and then get distracted by somebody sitting at the back of the gallery. Her eyes seem to flicker there every now and then.

'Oh... sorry. I, eh... no! I've been asked this question I don't know how many times over the years. I've even asked myself it. Did Joy murder the boys because she was suffering with postnatal depression, or some mental health condition? Truth be known, Joy was the same Joy she had always been to me. I am just here to tell the truth, Mr Bracken... as you well know. I have to say, hand on heart,' I push the photo of the boys to my chest, 'I didn't notice any behavioural differences in Joy before... before...'

A squeaky sob pulses from the back of my throat and forces its way out through my mouth. I sound like a puppy dog who's just has his tail trod on. And then my dam breaks, and tears begin to race down both of my cheeks.

'It's okay, I can give you time to—'

'No,' I sob, pressing the ball of my hand into my eyes. 'Let's keep going.'

'Well, eh... what I was going to ask next, Shay, is... because of the fact that you never witnessed any behavioural differences in Joy, you have never been convinced by the verdict of the original trial, have you?'

I sigh out what probably sounds like a laugh, though it's a laugh hiccoughed through snot and tears. This is one of two big questions Bracken rehearsed with me. I just need to remember what my answer is supposed to be, which is not easy when dozens of people are sat in a gallery gawking at my swollen face.

'No. The original trial, for me, had too many holes in it. I've never been convinced by anything in this case. It's just been... it's just been...'

I wipe my entire hand across my face as another sob throws itself up from the back of my throat, then I look back up at Bracken.

'Take your time, Mr Stapleton,' he says. He has been so nice to me, has Bracken. But I'm not sure I've ever made my mind up about him. He begged me to testify when the retrial was granted; begged me to get on the stand and state for the record – once and for all – that I didn't believe Joy killed Oscar and Reese. I agreed. Not because I'm certain. But because I just want this whole thing over and done with. It's consumed my life. It has ruined my life. I can't move on... I just can't. I hope Joy being set free will help free me too. I know that is so damn selfish. But I'm half-way through my life right now. I'm going to be dead in about forty years. I just need... I just need... to move on. I need to turn the grey cloud that hovers above my head into a white one. And that can only happen when people finally stop asking me about Joy. If she gets out... maybe, just maybe I can move on. My whole existence has just been so static for over a decade now. So insignificant. And numbing. As if I can't get my life into another gear. I got engaged once. About four years ago to a beautiful Galway girl called Jennifer. She's adorable. In every way. We met, fell in love, got engaged and then... and then I left her. Because... because I just couldn't move on. Some other lucky bastard is engaged to her now.

'So, let me ask you this more specifically,' Bracken says. 'Have you ever been convinced of Joy's involvement in the murder of your two sons?'

I swipe my sleeve across my face, mopping up the last of the tears, then steady myself by gripping the shelfed edges of the witness box, the photograph now resting on my lap; my boys smiling up at me.

'Sorry,' I say, composing myself. 'No. I've never been convinced of Joy's involvement in Oscar and Reese's murders.'

There... I finally got out the sentence Bracken and I rehearsed. A sentence that I'm sure will be splashed all over tomorrow's newspapers. I only said that sentence because it's true. I am not, nor ever have been, convinced of her guilt. There were times, especially during the first trial, that I was growing in certainty that she did it. Then holes would appear in theories and it just became impossible to have any definitive opinion, let alone proof. I've literally never known what to believe since the day my boys went missing. But

even if she is guilty; even if she did flip one day and did the unthink-
able – under the stress of raising two young boys all on her own
while her husband was away being pampered – then I'm as much to
blame as she is.

I allow myself another glance at her and, this time, she meets my
eye immediately, as if she was waiting to catch my eyes darting
towards hers.

'Mr Stapleton,' Bracken says, approaching the witness box and
forcing me to blink away from Joy. 'May I say that, under the
circumstances, it is very brave of you to not only be here, but to
testify under the strains of such unimaginable emotion. I cannot
fathom your experiences. It is heroic for you to be here today to tell
your truth; for the one person who knew Joy more than anyone else
to say under oath that you have never been convinced of her involve-
ment in your sons' murders. I used to watch you in Croke Park, Sir.
Was a big fan. Am a big fan. You were always a hero to so many
people. But you have never been so heroic as you have been here
today. I thank you. The courts thank you.'

Bracken stretches his hand towards me and I take it and shake
it. I've never seen that done in a courtroom before. I'm still feeling a
little shocked that his questioning has come to a sudden halt, when
the lawyer on the opposite side of the room is striding towards me,
unbuttoning his blazer.

'Mr Stapleton,' he says, 'you have just testified here that you
have never been convinced your wife is guilty of your sons' murders,
yes?'

I cough. Then nod my head.

'Mr Stapleton, you must verbally answer for the record of the
court,' the judge reminds me.

'Yes. That is what I have just testified,' I say, taking the picture
of the boys from my lap and pressing it to my chest again.

'So, let me get this straight. You are a loving husband, who has
just lost his two sons. Then their bodies are found two years later,
and soon after that your wife is arrested and sent to prison for two
life sentences for those murders. Yet you have never been convinced
of her guilt?'

I nod my head a little, while whispering, 'Yes.'

'That is some tragedy. Not only have you lost your sons. But your wife... As Mr Bracken said, that must be unimaginable. Now, can you tell me, Mr Stapleton – and I would like to state for the record that you very much have always had my sympathies and my sympathies remain with you as I ask these questions, but – can you tell me why in all of the eight years your wife has spent in Mountjoy Prison, and given that you have never been convinced of her guilt, you have only ever visited her on two occasions?'

I squeeze the photograph as firmly to my heart as I possibly can.

'Well... in the same way that I've never been convinced of Joy's guilt, I've also never been convinced either way. You have to understand... I know as much as anybody knows about this case. And nobody seems to know the truth.'

'Ah... so, Mr Stapleton,' the lawyer says as he takes a step closer to me. 'Not only are you testifying that you aren't convinced of Joy's guilt, but you are also not convinced of her claims of innocence, yes?'

I open my mouth, but nothing comes out. Not before the tears do. I snort and wash my hands over my face again. What a question to be asked. Though it's not as if I didn't know it was coming. We knew it would. Bracken had told me I would be asked if I was convinced of Joy's innocence after testifying to him that I wasn't convinced of her guilt.

'I am more convinced of her innocence,' I say, just as we had rehearsed, 'because I knew Joy better than anybody. And I am quite certain she is not a killer.'

It stuns the lawyer a little bit. His chin tilts upwards and his eyes squint. He didn't think I'd answer that so emphatically. But I did. Because it was what Bracken had manufactured. And I was fine with it. Because I just want this nightmare to end.

'Well,' the lawyer says, still a little taken aback, 'you say you knew Joy well enough and of course you wouldn't have married a woman or started a family with a woman you believed was capable of murder... but given that you were away travelling so much for

work, is it possible that you didn't notice your wife transforming into a killer?'

'Objection!' Bracken stands up.

'Fair question,' the lawyer says, turning to judge Delia.

I stare at the judge... and wait...

'You may answer,' she says to me.

I look back at the lawyer, through new tears that have just snuck up on me.

'If you are suggesting she may have suffered some mental health problems to an extent that she would kill our two sons, then I am already on record as saying I don't believe that to be the case. I testified ten minutes ago to Mr Bracken that I did not witness Joy suffering any depression after our boys were born. She was happy. We were happy.'

The lawyer looks about himself, and as he does I turn the photo of my boys' smiling faces towards me and stifle a smile back at them. Though all I manage to do is blink more tears down my cheeks.

'Mr Stapleton, I cannot possibly comprehend the amount of emotion you must be feeling. But I must do my job properly... so forgive me. But you are here today testifying that you do not believe, after all these years, that your wife is guilty of this crime, yet you have only visited her two times in eight years. And we also know that the second time you visited her was to seek a divorce... wasn't it? Because you had just got engaged to another woman, correct?'

My chins quiver.

'Please,' I sob. 'Please... can you not just let me move on? I came here to say what I had to say so I could move on... please.'

∴

Delia remains upright in her highchair, her two arms folded and resting onto the desk, her lips ever so slightly pouted. She had learned, many years ago, how to refrain from showing emotion inside the courtroom. A turning out of her lips is about as much as she has ever skirted the lines of what is deemed appropriate for a trial judge. Though she is holding up well, especially in comparison to those in the gallery; some of whom are dabbing at their eyes, most of whom haven't bothered and have decided, instead, to just allow the tears to flood down their cheeks.

'Mr Stapleton,' she says, intervening, 'the question is pertinent. Given that you have come here to testify, I would like you to answer it. If you need more time, I am happy to adjourn the court and allow you to—'

'I'll answer the question,' he says, sitting more upright and sniffling up his nose. Delia's lips pout even further and her brow dips, heavy with empathy. 'Yes, I was engaged to Jennifer a few years ago. I met her at a charity do one Christmas, we hit it off... we were going to restaurants on dates. I was finally getting back out there. Living myself a life. Then after I asked her to marry me and the media got wind of the story, they started to follow us about. They wanted a picture of Jennifer's ring, and me and her all cosy or something... I don't know. But it frightened me. It made me want to stay home and I started to suffer with more grief and... and... eventually, I just told Jennifer that she needed to move on. That is the truth of it all. I don't understand what this has to do with the trial. Yes, I once asked Joy for a divorce, but I never went through with it. There was no divorce.'

Jonathan Ryan coughs, unsure whether his line of questioning is working. He wanted to display Shay as somebody who couldn't possibly have thought Joy was innocent all these years, not when he had only visited her twice and had since got engaged to another women. But the witness's raw and emotive responses seem to only have endeared him more to the gallery.

'Okay, Mr Stapleton,' Ryan relents, 'I just want to ask you three more questions, to re-establish some points, then you are free to leave. Firstly, you say you are not convinced of your wife's guilt in this case, but you have only visited her twice in prison in the past eight years, correct?'

'Yes, I've already confirmed that.'

'Okay, Mr Stapleton, we are just re-establishing some points. Secondly, you got engaged to another woman in 2016, correct?'

'Yes,' Shay says, before allowing a frustrated sigh to blow through his lips.

'And whilst you are not convinced of your wife's guilt, you are also not convinced by her innocence, yes?'

Shay shrugs his shoulders.

'I guess so,' he says.

And then Ryan turns to Delia and nods at her before returning to his desk.

'Mr Stapleton,' Delia says sombrely, just as the witness is getting to his feet, 'I don't often break protocol in the court, but feel it's warranted to add an extra thank you to the one already offered up by Mr Bracken. Your time is really appreciated.'

Delia was genuinely moved by Shay Stapleton's testimony, not because he got so emotional discussing the unfathomable murder of his two young sons, but because he was willing to support his wife after all these years. Delia knew next to nothing about sports, but even she could tell why Shay had been such an outstanding athlete for his county. He was strong. He was brave. And he was undoubtedly loyal. But as he was stepping down from the witness box, Delia was trying to filter through her mind whether or not Shay being all those things truly counted towards her judgement.

As the witness walks his sizeable frame down the aisle of the court, Delia's eyes burn again towards the bushy v-shaped eyebrows in the back row.

She waits until Shay, in total silence, sweeps open the double doors and disappears out of them before she twists her wrist towards her face.

'It's just gone one p.m.,' she calls out. 'We will take nigh on ninety minutes for lunch. Court will reconvene at 2:30 p.m. precisely.'

She hammers down her gavel once and then stands abruptly, her eyes fixed once again on those eyebrows.

Eddie squints back at her, then rises to his feet as a sea of heads pass him to rush towards the same double doors Shay Stapleton had exited just moments ago.

'Edward Taunton!' Delia calls out as his eyebrows get lost in the crowd.

There is no answer to her call as those attempting to exit swivel their heads back and forth from the judge to the double doors.

'Eddie!' Callum, standing on the other side of the courtroom, shouts. The crowd stop in unison, and stare. But Callum just waves them on, and as they finally disperse through the double doors, Eddie's obese frame comes into view, his hands in his pockets, his tiny eyes squinting under the arch of his bushy eyebrows.

'I need to have a discussion with you in my office. Now!'

'I, eh... I need to—'

'Now!' Delia shouts.

Then she takes the three steps down from her highchair and storms out the side entrance of the courtroom. She whips off her robe as she paces down the corridor; the emotional gut-wrench she had felt during Shay's touching testimony well and truly replaced by a fierce doggedness.

When she snatches open her office door, she tosses her

bunched up robe to one side and wiggles at the mouse of her computer as she sits into her leather chair.

'How the hell am I going to deal with this?' she says to herself as she waits on her monitor to blink back to life.

She stifles a yawn, only because she is so mastered in the art of doing so that it has become her usual yawning practice. She's spent twenty-five years as a criminal judge, overseeing many, many a dour hour of needless interactions in the midst of trials, and has therefore grown accustomed to mastering the stifling of a yawn. She *is* tired, but not just mentally today. She hadn't slept last night. Not much, anyway. She kept tossing and turning in her bed, the images of her son masturbating flashing in front of her eyes every time she tried to concentrate on the specifics of the retrial. Then Eddie's eyebrows would make their way into her thoughts and her fists would form into a tense ball under her duvet. She gazes around her desk, while waiting on the screen to blink to life, and looks at her son's proud smirk in the cracked photo frame, then the monitor hums and the screen blinks on at the same moment footsteps make their way to her door. She anticipates a knock, but none comes. The door just sweeps open.

'Where is he?' Callum says.

'You beat him to it.'

'Mother fucker better get here.'

'Callum McCormick, mind your language.' Delia snaps at her son as if he's a teenager again.

'How you going to approach this, Mum?'

'Oh, good afternoon, Mr Taunton,' Aisling calls out from the hallway, before heavy footsteps thud closer and knuckles rattle ominously against the door.

'Come in, Eddie,' Delia shouts.

He walks in, stares at Delia, then at Callum, before he ever so slowly glances around the dimly lit office.

'You need to talk?' he says.

'Sit down, Eddie,' Delia orders.

Eddie puffs out a snigger, then shuffles around Callum and takes a seat opposite the judge.

'I thought Shay's testimony was very touching—'

'Shut up, Eddie. And listen to me.'

'Excuse *me*, Delia,' he protests, sitting upright and pointing his finger. But Delia slaps her hand to her desk, causing another thin shard of glass to fall from the cracked photo frame.

'*You* are listening to *me* now,' Delia says. She leans more forward in her chair, mirroring Eddie, her eyes wide over the rim of her glasses. 'Tell me about the video.'

'The vid…. What? The CCTV footage of Joy?'

'Wise up,' Callum says from behind Eddie. 'And grow up. You know what my mother is talking about.'

Eddie stares over his shoulder at Callum, then fills his cheeks with air before slowly exhaling through tightly pursed lips, producing a rasping sound.

'Shay Stapleton's testimony, whilst tragic and touching, was largely a nonsense, right… you know that…'

'We're not talking about Shay Stapleton, Eddie. We're talking about the video,' Callum says.

'Calm down, little boy,' Eddie replies, turning in the chair again to eyeball Callum. Delia keeps her eyes wide. Then Eddie turns to her and continues. 'He's just a grieving father who's never been allowed to grieve. And now he's just happy for his wife or ex-wife or whatever she is to him to be free… regardless of whether or not he thinks she had anything to do with it. He's been asked about his sons and his wife every day for twelve years. The man is sick of it. He's testifying so Joy can get out of prison, because he thinks it may end his pain, too. Yes, his testimony was touching. Yes, his testimony was emotional. Heck, I almost cried. He used to be a hero of mine, y'know? I used to cheer him on from the Hogan Stand. But you don't need to view his testimony in any way other than testimony from a grief-stricken father who is not a professional in any line of investigative work. Nor judicial work. You – Delia – are one of the best trial lawyers this country has produced. You know that. You know you can't let the emotions of a grieving father change your mind. Joy Stapleton did this.'

'The reason we called you here was not to discuss Joy Stapleton—'

'Calm down, Callum,' Delia says, dropping the curtness in her tone. 'Keep talking, Eddie.'

'Well, what more do you want me to say? This retrial has offered up tidbits of interesting anecdotes, but nothing should change your mind on this, Delia. You need to protect the original verdict. It's as simple as that.'

'And that's why you sent me a video of my son in a private moment? To blackmail me into protecting the original verdict?'

'Have you any idea what a not guilty verdict would do for the whole judicial arm of our nation? The whole house would come crumbling down. They'd totally drain the swamp. A not guilty verdict here would be detrimental not only for the judicial system, but our nation as a whole.' Delia gets to her feet and begins to pace the small square of floor to the side of her desk. 'C'mon Delia... You know Bunny the dog had fuck all to do with the guilty verdict in the original trial anyway. So, it shouldn't have anything to do with this retrial. We have Joy, for crying out loud, on camera walking away from the scene of where her boys' bodies were dumped.'

'That's not what Mathieu Dupont's testimony suggested. The height of the person in that footage doesn't compute to Joy.'

'That's bullshit testimony, Delia. Dupont is a fit-to-type witness. You know it. I know it. Anybody who knows law knows it. Gerd Bracken wanted to find somebody who could throw doubt on the figure in that footage and he found it in Dupont. He had to get to France before he could find somebody who *might* pour cold water on the fact that that is – without doubt – Joy Stapleton in that CCTV footage. This trial doesn't come down to coincidence, Delia. You told me that yourself years ago. Joy Stapleton is guilty. I don't care what fit-to-type testimony the court has heard over the past week. Besides... you've only heard the defence arguments so far. You can't let your head get swayed. What you have to do here is simple. Protect the original verdict. And let's all move on from this.'

'Drain the swamp? You think this whole place is a swamp just because you yourself happen to be a sloth? Don't lump me and all the other great judges in these courts in with the likes of you, Eddie. You think I'm dirty? You think I play dirty? Don't you dare...' She continues to pace the small square of floorboards. 'Y'know, I was lying in bed last night wondering why you picked on Callum. And you know what I realised? It's because you could get nothing on me, isn't it? You would have worked trying to find dirt on me so you could blackmail me into delivering a guilty verdict, but you found nothing... right? You looked at my exemplary work record... nothing dirty in that. You would have hacked into my computer as you did Callum's. No dirt in that. So, you had to turn to my son. And even then, you got nothing. What? An innocent man masturbating? Think about it. That's the worst you could find on *me*... The fact that my son masturbates? You think that's a sin? I masturbate too... we all masturbate, Eddie.'

'Mum!'

'Sorry, Callum,' Delia says without looking at her son.

Callum audibly shivers.

Eddie remains seated, the two McCormicks gazing down at him, as his grin turns into a chuckle.

'Delia, if you don't mind sitting. Please,' he says trying to compose himself. A silence settles between them before Delia finally relents and takes the seat opposite him. 'We're a country of what... ninety-nine years of age? Our judiciary system is much younger than that. It was only born in 1961, for crying out loud. It's a baby. It's younger than you and I... And it's vulnerable. You know it's vulnerable.'

'It's only vulnerable because you've been running it for over twenty years.'

'Delia, please,' Eddie says as Callum begins to pace back and forward behind him.

'It's true, Eddie. The system's a mess because you allowed it to become a mess on your watch.'

'That is ridiculous to suggest,' Eddie snaps back. 'This nation is growing at such a rapid rate that it is nigh on impossible for any sector to grow with it. We do the best we can here in the—'

'Is bribing the judge of the biggest retrial in the system's history "doing the best you can", Eddie?'

Eddie snorts.

'If Joy Stapleton is to be acquitted, everything falls down. Have you any idea what the newspapers are speculating her pay-out will be if she gets out?'

'I don't read the newspapers, Eddie.'

'Fifty million.'

'That's why I don't read the newspapers, Eddie. They're full of shit.'

'It will collapse us. The nation would lose total faith in the judicial system. Heads will roll. A whole review will be done. It will regress the whole progress the judicial system has made over the years. We'd be set back a hundred paces.'

'You keep saying that, Eddie. What you seem to be missing is the fact that you are willing to keep an innocent mother behind bars for the rest of her life just because you want to protect a system you have failed.'

'She's not fucking innocent, Delia! Listen to me. You know she's not. You told me that before.'

'I am looking at this trial—'

'Yeah, yeah... with a fresh pair of eyes. I get it. But that's what's worrying me. The evidence this retrial was granted on is bullshit. We can't afford to lose this one. That's her... that is Joy Stapleton in that CCTV footage. It's no coincidence. Just do the right thing, Delia. Let this whole mess go away. For everybody involved. All you have to do is protect the original verdict.'

Callum stops pacing, and places the tips of his fingers onto Delia's desk.

'Eddie's right, Mum,' he says.

1,806 days ago...

Joy was pretending – not just to everyone around her, but to herself too – that she was finding solace in the responsibilities she and Linda had undertaken in the wake of Christy's release. They had tried, hard, over the past two and a half months, to ensure Christy's Crazies were maintained as a functional and, more importantly, peaceful group within Elm House. They followed pretty much the same routine they always had done when Christy was around; they assembled at the same bench for breakfast as soon as the cell doors clicked open – to begin their day with prayer, even though Joy wasn't sure any members left in the group actually believed in God anymore. Then they'd laze around the worn sofa at the back of the games room after work or school, catching up on prison gossip, by often exaggerating stories they'd heard about prisoners in the other Houses. Or sometimes the Crazies would all sit together in the TV room, watching reruns of old British quiz shows and giggling along because their attempts at answers were often so terribly wide of the mark. Their days pretty much ticked by in much the same way as they had when Christy was there, only this time the group lacked leadership, no matter how hard Joy and Linda had tried to take a reign on affairs. Neither of them had the gravitas Christy had; they certainly didn't have her presence, nor her voice. Two softly spoken south Dublin accents couldn't compare to a brash and husky Texan/Nigerian drawl. And so, despite Joy and Linda's efforts, all the twenty or so members of the Crazies did on a daily basis was follow each other around in packs like lost penguins during the seven hours they weren't locked inside their cells.

Though despite the Crazies' lack of direction, they still managed to remain peaceful and unharmed, even though Joy kept repeating that a grey cloud was hanging over them. Nancy Trott had been sent to isolation not long after Christy was released ten weeks ago having been caught with three mobile phones in her cell, and would be due back on the wing any coming day.

Joy had pretty much curled up on her mattress for the first fortnight in the wake of the double blow that was Christy's release and Shay's request for a divorce. Though slowly but surely, she crawled herself back to her feet. And because Linda had such willingness to have a companion whilst in prison, she pushed Joy to get off her bed and try to take a rein on the Crazies.

Aside from the grey Nancy-shaped cloud that was hanging over her, Joy was starting to gain some semblance of prison normality. Though images of her husband bedding a younger, hotter model sometimes tainted her thoughts.

She was literally thinking of Shay while flicking her way through the previous day's copy of the *Irish Daily Star* when he stared right back at her. Her mouth popped open. And she had to stand to soak him all in. A headshot of him was placed below a headline that read:

Stapleton ends engagement

She whizzed through the story, sucked in by the quotes from a 'close family friend' who suggested Shay had gotten cold feet not long after asking young veterinarian Jennifer Stevenson to marry him because he was so overcome with a heavy and nauseating sense of disloyalty to his sons.

'That's why he hasn't sent in the divorce papers,' Joy whispered to herself, 'he doesn't need a divorce anymore.'

'Huh?' Linda asked, overhearing her friend's mumbling.

Joy looked at her, then sucked in her cheeks and turned the newspaper around so Linda could see it.

'I feel so sorry for him,' Joy said, almost sobbing as she sat back down on the worn sofa next to Linda. 'Almost as sorry as I feel for myself. Neither of us deserved this mess of a life we got. We were so happy... honestly Linda – the two of us really were so happy.'

Linda threw an arm around Joy and they both sat in silence, Shay's aged face staring back at them from the newspaper, until the mumbling of voices behind them began to rise in volume. Then a screeching and a howling sounded.

Joy and Linda both turned to look over their shoulder at the gathering crowd, and when the crowd parted, there she stood. Nancy Trott. High-fiving members of her cohorts with a grin stretched wide across her face.

'Bollocks!' Joy whispered out of the side of her mouth.

1,805 days ago...

'Not hungry?' Linda asked.

Joy shrugged her shoulders, then played around with her spoon, patting it down repeatedly to crush her Corn Flakes.

'Nope.'

'What's wrong?'

'Been dreading her coming back,' Joy said nodding over to the bench in the middle of the dining room to where Nancy had her cohorts in fits of giggles.

'We've just got to keep our heads down like we always have. We don't need to talk to them or do anything with them. Same as always. Besides, that bitch isn't going to cause any drama is she? She's only just back from isolation... she won't wanna be going back there again.'

Joy sighed, then pushed her bowl away.

She liked Linda. A lot. Linda was one of the Crazies most awed by Christy's visions. And because Christy had a vision that Oscar and Reese weren't killed by their mother, it meant Linda truly believed in Joy's innocence. But she didn't admire Linda. Not the way she wanted to admire a best friend. Not the way she admired Christy, even though she thought her bat-shit crazy. And certainly not how she once admired Lavinia. Lavinia could be bitchy and judgemental, but she never allowed anybody to control her. Linda was weak in comparison to the types of women Joy liked to be around. And she knew all too well that if Nancy started something, there would be fuck all her new best buddy could do about it.

'Okay, listen up,' boomed a voice.

Joy looked up to see Nancy stepping onto the table she had been sat at, before she began to clatter a wooden spoon against one of the kitchen's soup pots.

'Get down from there,' Aidan cut in, ordering Nancy with a wave of his hand.

She grinned at the prison officer, then took one step down so she was standing on the bench she had just been sitting on, and not the table top.

'Ah... I see you've grown some balls over the weeks I've been away, Aidan. Heard you got yourself a promotion, too.' Then she clanged the soup pot again with the wooden spoon before she began to shout. 'Girls. I am calling a truce in Elm House. There is no need for there to be separate groups among us. We are all one. All in this shithole together. So, let's get through it together, yes?'

A chorus of 'yeses' erupted from around Nancy, but the Crazies table at the far end of the dining room remained mostly subdued, save for some mumbling.

'For the past three years, we've had two separate factions on this wing. That ends today!' Hurrahs and applauses rippled around Nancy. 'Some of you only have a couple of months to serve, some of you a couple of years... some of you gonna be here the rest of your lives.' Joy looked up through her curls at Nancy, assuming she was talking not only about her, but to her. But Nancy barely looked her way. 'Wherever you are in your sentence, whatever time you have left to serve, you are going to serve it in a peaceful wing. No more Nancy's Cohorts. No more Christie's Crazies... not now that Queen Crazy herself is no longer with us. We are Elm House. That's the only group name we need. Though having said that, every group needs a leader. And while I believe in democracy, I also believe in power. So, ladies – and gentleman,' she said, eyeballing Aidan with a grin as he stood looking helplessly up at her, his hands on his hips, 'I will be the leader of prisoners in Elm House and I promise to represent each and every prisoner in here equally. I will represent the guilty, the innocent, the thieves, the murderers.' Joy glanced at Nancy again. But Nancy still hadn't looked her way. 'Don't matter who you are or how you got here. We are all in this together, and we will all get through this together. But...' she said, before pausing and sucking on her lips, 'I can't do it alone. I can't keep track of ninety women all by myself... so I need me a deputy.' The hurrahs roared from the benches around Nancy, lasting so long she had to calm them down with a wave of her hands. 'Now, I've had a long time cooked up in an isolation cell to think about this. And I know who my deputy should be.' The raucous chanting around Nancy died, and there seemed to be a synchronized sucking in of breaths. 'So, without further ado, I give to you, Elm House, your new deputy leader. The one. The only. Missus Joy Stapleton.'

This time, when Joy looked up through her curls, Nancy wasn't only staring at her, but pointing her wooden spoon at her. Then Nancy started to clank the spoon against the soup pot again, generating louder cheering from those all flanked around her that created such a raucous noise that Aidan had no choice but to squeeze at the button of the walkie talkie on his shoulder and frantically ask for assistance.

'Judge Delia, you're due back in court now – it's two-thirty.'

Delia rises to her feet and stabs a finger at the standby button of her computer monitor, all in a bit of a fluster, knocking over the already-smashed photo of her family again.

'Coming, Aisling,' she calls out.

She picks up the photo, rests it on the table, then sweeps away teeny glass shards from her desk with her hand before eyeballing the two men standing opposite her.

'Protect the verdict, Delia,' Eddie grunts.

She doesn't respond. Instead, she spins around, pulls at the bottom drawer under her library shelves and takes out a fresh robe.

'Mum, we need to sit down and talk this through,' Callum says as she yanks the robe over her head where it gets caught on her glasses that she had, once again, forgotten she'd combed back into her hair.

'In case you haven't bloody noticed, Callum,' Delia whisper-shouts through the robe, 'I'm in the middle of one of the biggest trials in the history of these courts.' She frees herself, by yanking the robe fully down, revealing her face again. 'I have to sit down and listen to everybody. The witnesses. The lawyers. And now you want me to sit down and listen to you, Callum. And you Eddie.

Over what... stupid bloody blackmail games? How dare you. How fucking dare you, Eddie Taunton.'

She swipes her door open, startling Aisling, and begins to pace down the corridor.

'Mum, Mum,' Callum calls, racing until he catches up with her just as she's turning on to the long corridor.

'He's right. We're all in a mess,' he says. 'And you're the only one who can clean the mess up. You can't let that video get out. It'll ruin my career. I'll be seen as a serious contender in the courts.'

Delia keeps pacing, saying nothing, her breathing heavy. She notices the young woman dressed in black up ahead open the courtroom side door and nod into it. Then the call goes up.

'All rise.'

'Mum, please.'

Delia stops, grabs her son by the collar of his shirt and pins him against the wall.

'Shut up, Callum,' she says. 'I have a trial to judge.'

She stares into his eyes before releasing her grip. Then she turns around and smiles at the young woman dressed in black before she paces into the courtroom and up the three steps that lead to her highchair.

Courtrooms are normally silent, save for the hum of the air conditioning machines. But there certainly seems to be a stretched sense of eeriness in this courtroom today. Maybe it's because the trial is at the half-way mark and minds are working overtime – soaking in the entirety of the defence's arguments. Though the eeriness is most likely down to the impact of Shay Stapleton's testimony this morning. It had cast a huge wave of emotion right through the room. And it doesn't seem as if that wave has fully receded. Not yet anyway.

Delia gulps when she finds the correct hymn sheet she is supposed to be singing from and when she pulls the page out from the middle of her pile and stares at the name on it, she lightly gasps. She hadn't realised such contrasting testimony would follow Shay Stapleton's. Had she been paying more attention to the trial, instead of getting caught up in Eddie Taunton's games, she likely wouldn't have allowed the next witness. Not today. Because whatever emotional wave Shay had tsunamied over this courtroom this morning was about to come right back the other way.

'Mr Ryan,' Delia calls out. 'The trial turns to the evidence the prosecution will argue. Can you please call your first witness?'

'Of course, thank you,' Ryan says, standing and straightening the knot of his tie. 'Your Honour, we call Lavinia Kirwan to the stand.'

The back doors of the courtroom sweep open and in the large doorframe, silhouetted, stands a tiny figure. Lavinia can't be much taller than Joy, if at all. But she's not 'all hair' like Joy is. Her hair, fine and mousy brown in colour, is swept back into a tight bun.

Delia notices as the witness walks up the aisle that she doesn't once acknowledge the defendant. Lavinia stares straight ahead as she is sworn in. Then she sits her boney frame into the oversized square witness box and tilts the microphone lower.

'Ms Kirwan, thank you for taking the time to be with us here today,' Jonathan Ryan says. 'You met Joy Stapleton when you were... how old?'

'We were four, I guess. First year of primary school.'

'And you are now aged... if you don't mind me asking?'

'Thirty-six... I just turned thirty-six earlier this week as it happens.'

'Well... many happy returns, Ms Kirwan. So... even with my bad maths, that tells me you have known Mrs Stapleton for thirty-two years, correct?'

'Even with my bad maths, I believe you are correct, Mr Ryan, yes.'

'Okay. So, you have known her much longer than Shay Stapleton has known her, right?'

'Your Honour,' Mr Bracken shouts, scooting himself to his feet. 'This is not a competition between witnesses.'

'I agree. No need,' Delia says turning to Jonathan Ryan. She knew what he was getting at; knew he just wanted to point out that this testimony was just as worthy, if not more so, as the emotional heart-tugging testimony offered up by the defendant's husband this morning.

'Okay... well thirty-two years, nonetheless. And you were best friends all that time?'

'Yeah. I mean everybody in primary school was best friends so I'm not sure I had one best friend at that stage. But by the time we got to secondary school, me and Joy used to walk with each other to and from school every day and we became really close. We shared most of our teen years in each other's bedrooms listening to boybands.'

'So, you know her as much as anybody, it's fair to say.'

'I would say so, yes,' Lavinia replies.

'Well then, let me ask this question: do you believe the jurors in the original trial in which Joy Stapleton was convicted for the murder of her two sons, Reese and Oscar Stapleton, got their verdict correct?'

'Objection,' Bracken calls.

'Ma'am,' Ryan says, 'I am not asking an independent witness. I am asking the opinion of a witness who we have just proven has known the defendant for over three decades.'

'Not allowed, Mr Ryan. Be careful with your line of questioning,' Delia says.

Ryan stares back at the judge, his eyebrow creased. She knows she's already been harsher with him than she has been with Bracken through this trial. But that's because it's justified. Bracken is better at skirting around the legalities of what is and what isn't appropriate when it comes to lines of questioning. Ryan's turn of phrases in trying to get his witness's points across aren't quite as subtle or mastered. She understands what he is trying to do; open up by having Lavinia explain how close she and Joy were, then hitting the judge with the whopping gut-punch that Lavinia has believed all along that her best friend is guilty of these murders. But he'll have to go about it another way.

'Okay, well, let me put it to you this way, Ms Kirwan... Since Reese and Oscar Stapleton were reported missing, you have gone on record to say you felt Joy was acting differently to how she normally acts, is that correct?'

'Yes, it is.'

'Can you elaborate?'

'There wasn't any standout moments where I thought, "Wow, Joy is losing it." I don't have absolute proof. It's just small things. Things that maybe only a best friend would notice. She was off schedule in different ways. She used to obsess about time... she'd never be late, would Joy. But in the months leading up to Oscar and Reese going missing, she just always seemed to be late. She'd never turn up to anything on time. And she got more forgetful.'

Joy lets an audible sigh erupt from the back of her throat. The only time she's made a peep throughout the entirety of this retrial. And it stuns the court into a silence.

LAVINIA KIRWAN

He nods at the judge, then readjusts his standing position to face me again.

'Okay, well, let me put it to you this way, Ms Kirwan... Since Reese and Oscar Stapleton were reported missing, you have gone on record to say you felt Joy was acting differently to how she normally acts, is that correct?'

'Yes, it is,' I reply, without hesitating. Just as we'd rehearsed.

'Can you elaborate?'

I sit more upright.

'There wasn't any standout moments where I thought, Wow, Joy is losing it,' I say. 'I don't have absolute proof. It's just small things. Things that maybe only a best friend would notice. She was off schedule. In different ways. She used to obsess about time... she'd never be late, would Joy. But in the months leading up to Oscar and Reese going missing, she just always seemed to be late. She'd never turn up to anything on time. And she got more forgetful.'

There's a beat of silence before she gasps. Loudly. Like, loudly enough for everybody in the courtroom to hear. It makes me instantly snap a stare at her – the first time I've seen those eyes in over a decade. She's aged. Definitely. Her skin is a lot paler – almost like milk. And her hands look really wrinkled. Much more wrinkled than mine. I might even be prettier than she is now. If we went out to some pub or club tonight, maybe I'd be the one who got all the attention.

The court has stayed silent since her gasp. I don't really react but to stare at her. I'm not going to let that murderous bitch intimidate me while I'm up here. Typical Joy though. Trying to steal the limelight from me.

'Okay,' the judge calls out. 'Mrs Stapleton, if you could refrain from making any noises.'

Then the judge nods back at Jonathan Ryan and he readjusts his feet to face me again.

'Can you give the court any specifics on Joy Stapleton getting more forgetful and not being herself in the lead up to Oscar and Reese being reported missing?'

'There was one time that I was supposed to meet her and the two boys in Dundrum shopping centre. We were supposed to meet at one p.m., so we could have lunch together. She didn't get there till gone two... about ten past two. I ate alone. Other times she would phone me and then we'd be on the call for a few minutes and when I asked why she'd rung, she'd say she'd forgotten. I could tell her mind was going a bit... a bit different. She was tired all the time.'

'Tired?'

'Yes. She wasn't getting much sleep. She'd do all the night feeds. Shay was rarely there and on the rare occasion he was, it was still all left up to her. I think Shay's idea of having kids was old-school and traditional. He thought his role as a father was to genuinely just assume that the mother did everything.'

'Objection,' Bracken shouts.

'It's pertinent,' the judge says, staring down at me again. I can understand why Bracken objected to that; I'm not here to testify about Shay's parental abilities, and he's not the one on trial. I don't hold anything against him. Never have. So, he wasn't a great husband or a father... big deal. Neither was my father. But that never turned my mother into a killer. Truth is, I never really got close with Shay. I would have liked to, and in fact I actually fancied him long before Joy happened to bump into him in town one night, but he was the type of guy who didn't really hang out with his girlfriend's best *friends; the type who wouldn't even make the effort to. He was a lad's lad. As most sports stars are. He'd spend his time either hanging out with his teammates or being away in some plush hotel for work. Sure, if he rarely had the time for his wife and kids, how could he ever have had the time for his wife's best friend?*

'So,' Jonathan Ryan says. 'She was tired?'

'Yes. And apart from her not getting a great amount of sleep due to the night feeds or whatever, Oscar in particular was high-maintenance for Joy, even in the daytime. He needed constant attention. It drained her.'

Hell, Oscar used to drain me. And I only had to see him a couple of hours a week. He was just one of those annoying little boys with one of those high-pitched voices that would never stop asking question after question after question. He'd even ask questions he already knew the answers to, just to get attention. But I can't say that out loud. Course I can't. Ye can't speak ill of the dead. Especially not the young dead.

'Thank you for being so honest,' Ryan says. 'Now, to move on slightly... when Oscar and Reese were reported missing, you helped out with combing the streets in search of the boys, correct?'

'That is correct.'

'By this stage, you didn't suspect Mrs Stapleton, right?'

'No. I didn't. I genuinely believed her. I thought someone had taken them – that they'd been snatched. I prayed every day and every night for them to come home safely. It didn't cross my mind at all that they were dead, lying in a ditch in the Dublin mountains.'

'So, when did you become suspicious that your best friend was involved?'

'It was dawning on me as time went on... but when the bodies were found, I immediately said to my brother, "I bet she did it. I'm sure she did it." Then a while later the CCTV footage was made public and as soon as I saw it... and I mean this from the bottom of my heart... as soon as I saw that footage, I pointed at the screen and said, 'That's her! That's Joy!'

The courtroom falls eerily silent. Just as Jonathan Ryan had told me it would after I'd said that line. I'm not saying it for effect or anything like that. I'm saying it because it's true. I know Joy. I know that's her in that CCTV footage.

'Well, that is very powerful testimony, Ms Kirwan, indeed. Before I let you go though, there is something else I must ask. About five years ago, your name came up as a possible suspect in this case, correct?'

I offer a light snigger into the microphone.

'Yes.'

'By whom?'

'Joy. From prison. I'm not quite sure where her head was at then, I hadn't seen her in years. I just remember seeing it online somewhere, that Joy was trying to scream from prison that I was the woman under the pink hood all along.'

'Now, the defendant has chosen not to testify at her own retrial here, so she can't answer this herself, but do you know where she got that theory from?'

'I had my lawyer look into it, to try to get some answers. Apparently, Joy was making this noise through the Joy is Innocent campaign from within the prison. But when my lawyers spoke to some people, they couldn't get much info on where her theory originated from. Apparently one of prisoners just dreamt it up or something and tried to convince Joy of it. It all came out of nowhere.'

'And of course, this theory proves Mrs Stapleton was not making any sense, right?'

'Yeah. This is more proof that she's not of sound mind. The police did look at me in the days after Oscar and Reese went missing; they looked into all of us. Of course they did. But I was at the cinema the night they went missing. I was on a date with a bloke called Andy Harkness, and we had drinks afterwards... So...'

'So, the police ruled you out?'

'They did indeed. They checked everything, and in fact I rechecked everything after Joy started making stuff up about me from prison. On the night Joy killed and buried Oscar and Reese in the mountains, and when she was caught on those three seconds of CCTV footage, I, myself, was caught on a CCTV camera going into the cinema, and coming out of the cinema two hours later. Then *there is more footage of me walking up Parnell Street and then going into Murray's pub on O'Connell Street at 10:45 p.m. and leaving at just gone one-thirty a.m.–my whole night is accounted for.'*

'Thank you so much for your time, Ms Kirwan,' Jonathan Ryan says. Then he makes his way back to his desk and offers me an approval of my performance by winking at me subtly.

'Mr Bracken,' the judge calls out. And suddenly Bracken is on his feet before I can even take a sip of water to compose myself.

'Ms Kirwan, can you state for the record what your occupation is?'

'Mine?'

Bracken nods his head, showing me his bright-white veneers. The cheesy prick.

'Eh... well right now I work in a shop, as a shop assistant, I guess. Before that I worked in a bookies. I worked as a cleaner. I was also a receptionist in Fullams Accountancy once.'

'Ah... so lots of different career paths, yes?'

'You could say that, yes.'

'Yet despite your many careers, you were never a detective, right?'

I tut.

'No.'

'So, you don't know Joy is guilty with any degree of certainty, do you?'

'I know it was her.'

'Well, let me stop you there, Ms Kirwan. Are you saying you knew Joy was capable of murdering her two sons?'

'No. I'm not saying I knew beforehand. Of course not.'

'Exactly. So, you didn't know she was going to do it in the same way that you don't know in the aftermath. What definitive proof do you have to suggest Joy Stapleton is guilty? Any forensic evidence this court doesn't know about? Any eye witnesses the court have yet to hear from who saw the crime?'

'No.'

'No. So, you can't know with a degree of certainty that Joy was involved in these murders at all, can you?'

I take a sip of my water. And as I do, I take in the state of his leathery orange skin as he stands staring up at me from just below the witness box. Jonathan Ryan told me Bracken would lay it on thick with me. I just didn't know he'd look so smug while doin' it.

'I know in the way only a best friend would know.'

'Hardly definitive proof of murder is it?' he replies, the grin still on his face. 'Okay, so let's move on slightly. I need to ask you this question, Ms Kirwan – and I guess the answer is in the title I just called you – you are not married, have never married, is that correct?'

I silently tut again.

'I don't see what this has to do with anything.'

'Answer the question, Ms Kirwan,' the judge says, kinda bluntly at me.

'Eh... no. I have never married.'

'Never had any children? Never been a mother?'

Ah. I see where he's going. I cough into my fist, then take another sip of water.

'No. I haven't been married and have never had any children... So?'

'So, you have no first-hand experience of the ailments you accuse Mrs Stapleton of having after she had given birth to two boys, have you?'

'Ailments?'

'You suggested here today that Mrs Stapleton was suffering with some mental health fragilities in the weeks leading up to Oscar and Reese Stapleton being reported missing, yes?'

'Yes. And?'

'And, I am asking if you have any first-hand experiences of these post-partem mental health fragilities you accuse her of having?'

'Well, obviously not if I've never had kids.' *I tut. And because I do it loudly, I look up at the judge to see if she is going to snap at me. She frowns over her glasses, then diverts her eyes back to Bracken.*

'Do you have any academic qualifications in post-partem depressions, Ms Kirwan?'

I huff silently though my nose. I knew the cross-examination would end up as an examination of me. But I'm not the one on trial here. She is. She's the murderer. All I'm guilty of is not reporting to Shay that she was acting all strange before she killed her boys... before it was too late.

'*No, of course I've no qualifications in post-partem depression.*'

'*Right. So, you have no first-hand experience, and no qualifications in post-partem depression. And you have no qualifications in detective work. Yet, despite all that, you think you are capable of solving the country's biggest ever crime, yes?*'

'*I know Joy better than anyone!*'

'*Really? Did you ever live with Joy?*'

'*No.*'

'*Ever marry her?*'

'*Course not.*'

'*Ever carry her children?*'

'*Objection!*'

'*No need, Your Honour, I'm done,*' Bracken says. *The tangerine-coloured cunt. I could strangle him. I see what he's doing. Trying to suggest Shay knew Joy better than I did and that means his testimony should hold stronger than mine. Gerd Bracken should be ashamed of himself. Defending her. Making it out as if she's innocent. She's a fucking murderer. There's no doubt about it in my mind whatsoever... and there shouldn't be a doubt in anyone's mind. That is Joy in that CCTV footage. There is no such thing as a fucking coincidence in this case.*

1,625 days ago...

Aidan told Joy, in confidence, that the Governor had mentioned in passing that he wouldn't have sanctioned Christy Jabefemi's release the year previous had he known it would cause such a dramatic turn in Elm House. Her presence had ensured a somewhat peaceful ambience on the wing; extraordinary given that some of the most notorious inmates in the country were incarcerated there. Although Christy was a bat-shit crazy meth head in the eyes of almost all of the staff, they were aware that her athletic physique and bulbous bloodshot eyes made her an intimidating prospect for the other inmates. Even Nancy Trott.

'I told him it was getting out of hand on the wing now, but there's not much he can do – resources are stretched,' Aidan said.

'It's not that bad here, is it?' Joy shrugged, unable to look him in the eye.

She was glad that Aidan was back confiding in her. He had steered away from his friendly banter with Joy ever since she took it too far and tried to kiss him. But whilst she appreciated his rekindled support, she didn't want him coming this close to her. Not because she may feel an urge to kiss him again, but because Nancy had warned her to stay well away.

'I know you fancy the pants off him, but he's one of them, d'ya hear me?' Nancy had said to her numerous times over the past months. 'I know how these guys operate... been around the block too many times. They pretend to be all pally-pally with you so they can get you to open up, then they're sneaking back to the Gov and spewing everything you said. Aidan doesn't like you, Joy. Not the way you like him. Besides, he likes dick. Not pussy. S'what I heard anyway. If he comes up to you to talk, just keep your mouth shut and walk away.'

Aidan wasn't the only person Nancy had tried to turn Joy against.

'She was a junkie clown,' she had said of Christy. 'You thought she was protecting you all in here, she wasn't. She was deluded. Is back out on the streets now high as a kite, I hear. Bitch could never be trusted. Somehow you fell for her shit. Hell, I even saw you doing prayers with her. And the talk is she was only getting close with you so she could sell a story on you when she got out.'

Joy didn't have the inclination, nor the energy to ask Nancy why, if that was the case, Christy hadn't yet sold her story, despite being out for over a year. So, she just silently sighed instead. Which was becoming a regular tic for Joy. Her energy levels were low; lower than ever. She was fatigued by her role as Nancy's second-in-command. And as a result, she became insular, and mute; doing more listening than she did talking because Nancy's orders were so plentiful and exhausting. So, rather than arguing or even talking back, Joy just nodded along and did as she was told.

Nancy would hold court first thing in the morning, inside the dining-room, ensuring all prisoners sat together and not in cliques. Then she'd bang on the soup pot with her wooden spoon, call everybody's attention and introduce new prisoners or rattle off a eulogy or two about those who had just been released. The contents of what Nancy would talk about, openly in the dining room to every prisoner as well as the prison officers on duty, seemed genuinely caring and inclusive. But Joy knew better than anybody by now that that was all just a front. All Nancy was doing by coming across as the caring leader of the wing was getting everybody onside, so that they wouldn't rat her out.

Nancy had been smuggling in valuable prison assets; from sweets to mobile phones. She'd come up with the plan when bored out of her head in isolation at the start of the year. An associate of hers in the outside world had come into contact with one of the screws on another wing whom she had a hold over. He was bringing the phones and treats into the prison and then placing them into a marked laundry basket which one of the prisoners would eventually wheel to Joy's cell. Joy would then be tasked with distributing the goods to prisoners who had already paid Nancy in advance. It was a terribly dangerous game for Joy to get involved in, especially as she could have been housing anything up to a thousand euros worth of phones at any one time, but she had no choice in the matter. It was to her advantage that the screws in Elm House would never have thought of Joy getting involved in such affairs and that she would never be considered suspicious. Though that had actually been a part of Nancy's plan all along – getting goody-goody Joy Stapleton involved as her distributor. That way they'd never get caught.

'What the fuck were you doing talking to him?' Nancy asked, appearing in Joy's cell doorway.

'I, eh... he, eh... he just came to talk to me... that's all. I can hardly kick him out of my cell.'

'What did he want to talk to you about?'

Joy shook her curls.

'Nothing really. He just said I look tired and that...'

'And what?'

'And that if I was having any trouble that I should come talk to him.'

Nancy stepped towards Joy, pressing her fat tits against her.

'I've told you before. Don't—'

'Talk to Aidan. I know. I get it, Nancy. It's just... what can I do when he comes to my cell?'

Joy shrugged her shoulders and then Nancy snarled up the corner of her lips before spinning on her heels.

'Okay, come in, Tina,' she whispered.

Tina appeared, the cold sores on her lips looking nastier than ever, pushing a laundry basket into Joy's cell.

'Not more phones,' Joy said, almost sighing. 'I just got rid of six for you on Monday.'

'Relax,' Nancy said, placing a hand to the back of Joy's neck.

'We've been providing the whole fucking prison with phones for six months now, everybody's practically got one. Orders are drying up. Besides,' she said, squeezing at Joy's neck, 'the phones were only a trial run.'

'Trial run. Trial run for what?'

Then Nancy nodded at Tina and Tina removed the dirty laundry sheets from the top of the basket.

'Oh, for fuck sake,' Joy said. 'What is that?'

'Meth,' Nancy whispered. 'The purest meth available on Dublin's streets right now. Well... *was* available on Dublin's streets. Cos we've just done the cops a great turn by taking it off the streets. And now it's gonna be your job, Joy, to hold it here in your cell, before you distribute it to the prisoners on my orders. This,' she said, slapping her hands to both of Joy's cheeks, 'is gonna make us a lot of money.'

'*You* a lot of money,' Joy said, 'I don't see a cent.'

Nancy grinned.

'No... *us* a lot of money. Only your share pays for your protection, doesn't it?' Then she slapped Joy on both cheeks again, only harder this time, before she turned on her heels.

'Now, find a good hiding place for that stuff somewhere in here. And don't get fuckin' caught with it.'

1,624 days ago...

Joy had delivered two small bags to a prisoner from Maple House while she was out in the yard after lunch. But the majority of the meth was still taped to the underside of the toilet bowl in the corner of her cell.

She wasn't overly stressed about it – it may as well be meth as phones. If she was caught, there was very little that could be done about it, aside from the goods being confiscated. Joy was serving two life sentences after all... what were they gonna do? Add an extra couple of months for drug possession?

'How long ya inside now, Joy?' Tina asked, showing her gummy teeth.

'Four years in September.'

'Jeez, is it that long, love? Fuck, I remember your trial. Was in the papers and all over the news for weeks... months.'

'Years!' Joy said, unmoving, still staring at the concrete floor of the TV room, which was all she seemed to really do when mixing with the other inmates these days.

'No offence. And I know we aren't really supposed to question prisoners on whether or not they're guilty, cos it's what's-the-word...?'

'Prison code,' one of the prisoners offered up.

'Yeah... it's code. But I have to say, I didn't know what to believe in your case, Joy. It was a real did-she, didn't-she, ye know what I mean?' Those sitting around nodded their heads, but they didn't offer their opinion. 'I thought you did it, I have to say... but now that I've met you in here. I'm not so sure. You seem too quiet to be a killer.'

'Thought killers normally were quiet,' one of the elderly women said.

'Suppose,' Tina replied, shrugging her shoulders. 'Anyway, what's going on with your appeal... haven't seen you shouting about your innocence in a long time. Weren't you saying it was yer old best mate or somethin' that killed your boys? That's gone all quiet...'

'She's stopped with the Joy is Innocent campaign, haven't you?' Nancy said, joining the group. Joy slowly nodded her head while still staring at the concrete floor. 'Okay... I need you, Joy. C'mon with me.'

Like the sheep she had morphed into, Joy followed Nancy out of the TV room and down the narrow landing that led to the laundry room at the back of Elm House.

She wondered, as she walked, how she had allowed Nancy to distract her from the Joy is Innocent campaign. While that candle was still burning on social media channels and in pockets of the outside world, Joy had pretty much given up the ghost. Nancy had tried to convince her that the lawyers were only looking out for themselves; that there was no chance of Joy's sentence ever being overturned, simply because the justice system wouldn't allow it. They couldn't allow it. It would make them look inept.

'You're fucked no matter what you do,' Nancy had told her

repeatedly. 'They ain't never gonna acquit you, it'd bring the whole system down. There'd be outrage around the whole country if they thought an innocent young mother had been put behind bars for killing her own kids. You just keep focused on spending your time in here and forget about those scum lawyers, ya hear me?'

So intimidated by Nancy, Joy had even begun to turn down meetings with her lawyers and resigned herself to being inside for the rest of her life.

'What's this?' Joy whispered after Nancy had led her behind the tumble dryers. Barbara and Rosemary were sat on the ground, their backs against the wall, their knees up by their ears.

'This is... this is introduction class,' Nancy replied.

'Introduction... an introduction to who?'

'Mr Crystal.'

'Huh?' Joy replied. What are you talking...'

She tailed off her sentence because she noticed Barbara was crunching tiny crystals into rizla papers that were resting on her crotch.

Joy shook her curls.

'No. I can't. I'm not—'

'Oh yes you are, girl,' Nancy said, gripping Joy by the back of the neck and squeezing hard.

When the meth joint had been rolled, Nancy took it from Rosemary and held it in front of Joy's face.

'I, eh... I don't even know what to—'

'It's just like smoking a cigarette, Joy. You'll be fine. If you're gonna be shifting this for me, you need to know what it's all about.'

Then Nancy took a lighter from her trouser pocket and sparked it.

❖

Callum sits in the corner of Delia's office, his back against the wall, his arms hugging his bent knees.

'You can't deny that was convincing,' he says.

'Callum, for goodness sake – can you just, please, go home?'

'I'm just saying... that was convincing testimony, that's all.'

'I don't need telling what is and what isn't convincing testimony, Callum.' Delia is pacing from side to side on the small square of carpet to the right of her desk.

'Shay's testimony was all emotion, Lavinia delivered much more analytical proof—'

'Shut up, Callum!' Delia shouts, holding a flat palm to her forehead. 'I don't need you to analyse the witnesses in a trial only *I* am presiding over. And I don't need your input on a trial only *I* am experienced enough to judge.'

Callum scrambles himself to his feet and dusts down his numb bum.

'I'm only trying to help. This is more than just a trial. Lavinia said that was definitely Joy in that CCTV footage. And nobody knows Joy better.'

'Not even her husband?'

'Mum... women know women best. You think a sports guy like

Shay Stapleton could read the signs of some sort of post partem depression? Or do you think a woman could do that better?'

Delia shakes her head while holding her hands to her hips.

'Callum, let me just point out that, right now this moment, you are in the midst of explaining to me how women work. Let that sink into your mind. What's the phrase... mansplaining... yes. You are mansplaining women to a woman.' Callum holds his eyes closed, then releases a long, slow sigh. 'This is my trial, Callum. You need to take yourself out of it.'

'I'm right in it. My bloody whole career is on the line.'

Delia swipes her coat from the standing rack to the side of her office door.

'You sound like a petulant little boy,' she says as she throws her arms into the sleeves.

Callum just stands there, staring at his mother, his eyes heavy, his hair all tossed from the countless times he has run his fingers through it.

'Do you not understand how much this would damage me?' he says. 'I can't believe you are even contemplating listening to the evidence of this trial... just protect the original verdict, Mum. She's guilty. Stop playing games.'

'Callum, when you calm down, come home and have some tea. Perhaps go for a long walk, get some fresh air before you decide to come home though, huh?'

Delia pulls her office door open, but she doesn't get much further, not without her son's fingers gripping her shoulder.

'Mum. I want to be just like you. I want to be a judge. I want to preside over the biggest trials these courts have to offer. If I don't get to be you when I'm older, my career will mean nothing to me. My life will mean nothing to me. I've been working up to being a trial judge... hell, *you've* been working me up to being a trial judge ever since I was a teenager. It's been all laid out for me. A Law degree from Trinity College. A job guaranteed at Wincott & Abbott before I'd even graduated. I am still the youngest ever board member of the Law Society. I've been walking the corridors of these courts for almost twenty years. I've always been taking the roads that lead to one of these offices. But I'm not going to get here if there is a video on the fucking internet of me pulling the fuckin' mickey off myself!'

Delia stares over the rim of her glasses at her son. Then she removes his hand from her shoulder and lets it drop.

'Like I said, Callum... when you calm down, come home and have some tea.'

Delia opens and closes another cupboard and moves on to the next one before slamming that one shut too. Then she sweeps her slippers back to the fridge. Back to where she started.

She shrugs her shoulders, grabs at the bruised apple from the top shelf and takes a large bite from it. Then she chicanes herself around her island, lifts a bottle of Massolino Parussi Barola from her cubed kitchen shelving unit, as well as a long-stem glass, and potters herself down her narrow hallway and into her living room.

It's an unusual living room. No TV. Instead, in each corner, stands floor-to-ceiling library shelves, filled with books of all sorts; from law manuals and non-fiction psychology, to classical works of fiction going as far back as Aristotle. The shelves reach all the way up to the eleven-foot high ceilings of her Georgian home and come with a sliding ladder. The room is always fully lit and is decorated, in its entirety, in the subtlest of pastel colours – the total opposite of her office in the courts, where it may seem to some visitors as if she is rationing electricity.

She rests the bottle and glass – with the apple gripped between her teeth – on to the drinks tray to the side of her large fireplace, then wrestles with the corkscrew until the cork releases with a pop. And just as she's about to pour herself a well-earned glass, the key crunches in the front door. She pauses, her eyes squinting, her mouth pursed... until the scent of Black Bean sauce wafts towards her.

'Thought you might be banging around in the kitchen looking for something to eat,' Callum says, holding a bulging white plastic bag aloft as he stands in the door frame of the living room.

He winks, then disappears into the kitchen where he makes a

racket of himself, before arriving back into the living room with two trays.

Delia stifles a smirk, then she sits on to her floral-patterned couch, and allows Callum to remove the small cartons of food from his plastic bag before placing them on to her tray for her.

'So, you took my advice... you came home for some tea after you'd calmed down?' she says.

Callum snorts out a laugh before racing back into the kitchen. When he returns, he hands his mother a knife and fork before sitting down himself and taking a tray to his lap.

'How calm am I supposed to be when you are being black-mailed by a video of me masturbating?' he says. Delia cocks her head as she shovels a forkful of rice into her mouth. 'But yeah... I'm a little calmer. I, eh... had heard about this sort of thing before. Guys being hacked and caught masturbating when their own laptop camera records them. An old client of mine had told me about it a while back. He's put me in touch with a private investigator who might have a few answers for us.' Callum raises his eyebrows, then in the silence that follows, picks up a forkful of rice himself and shovels it into his mouth.

'Yes. Well... although I have a trial to judge, I want you to know that I am sympathetic to the plight you – *we* – find ourselves in. But no matter what, I will be judging this trial fairly. How we deal with Eddie Taunton is a separate matter entirely. But I have to judge this trial as I see it in that court room, Callum.'

Callum washes a hand over his face.

'She's guilty, Mum. You know she is. You told me before that you've always felt she was guilty.'

'Callum, in case you haven't noticed, there is a fresh trial on-going with fresh evidence.'

'The fresh evidence is bullshit, Mum. You know it. I know it. Shay Stapleton's testimony was nothing more than that of a broken man who just wants this entire nightmare over and done with. Mathieu Dupont is a fit-to-type witness who didn't even get his measurements right. And Bunny the Dog... I mean, c'mon... This trial was granted on the basis of new evidence... well, we've all heard the new evidence and it's nonsense, Mum. All you have to do is protect the original verdict. Deliver guilty. And we can all move on.'

Delia sighs her nostrils into her glass of wine as she takes a sip, fogging it up.

'Your father would be ashamed listening to you now, Callum McCormick.'

'My father would beat the shit out of Eddie Taunton, that's what he'd do.'

Delia scoffs.

'Your father never hit a man his whole life.'

'Well... he would have sorted this mess out in some way.'

Delia heaves a heavy breath, then takes the tray from her lap and places it on the couch next to her; her appetite waning.

'I'm not sure you know your father as much as you think you do, Callum. He was a superhero alright. But only in the sense that he was a fine trial lawyer. One of the best ever.'

'He'd certainly have found Lavinia Kirwan's testimony interesting today, that's for sure,' Callum says.

Delia picks up her glass of wine and takes another sip.

'It was powerful testimony... nobody could deny that. But I'm not going to be deliberating this trial with you, Callum. Not after everything that's happened. We have to remove ourselves from this. Our fate must be separate from the fate of Joy Stapleton.'

'But, Mum—' Callum gets distracted by his phone vibrating in his pocket. He reaches for it, stares at the screen, then stabs at the green button.

'Hello,' he says. 'Callum McCormick speaking.'

His eyes squint as he listens to the voice on the other end of the line, then he places a hand over the receiver.

'It's the private eye I was telling you about,' he whispers.

1,477 days ago…

Joy no longer moved when her cell door clicked open first thing in the mornings. She didn't have the energy. It'd take her an age to roll over on her mattress before she'd eventually mope herself to her feet. And by the time she'd drag herself into the dining room, all of the best cereals would have been eaten up and only the deformed slices of toast were left. But she'd munch on a crust or two while swigging a glass of water, then head back to her cell to curl into a ball atop her mattress again. Mornings had turned grey for her. It was only in the evenings when she would come alive – because that's when she'd share a joint with Nancy.

She'd been taking an almost daily hit of meth for nigh on six months; only failing to get her high when Nancy's source couldn't follow through with delivering into the prison. Though it was rare when that happened. The majority of the ninety prisoners in Elm House were getting involved and were, like Joy, often walking around like zombies; jaded and fatigued. The screws had picked up on the eerie change in ambience on the wing, but it was pretty much impossible for them to put their finger on why, simply because each and every person under the influence of meth experiences different symptoms; different highs and different lows. Whereas Nancy was chatty and talkative, Tina sat there quiet, with a huge grin stretched across her face. And whereas Claire would go on a spring clean, helping with all sorts of maintenance around the wing, Linda liked to lie on her bed and get lost in a book. Joy, well, she would float around the landings of the wing, sometimes checking in with Nancy to laugh at her jokes; sometimes annoying Linda by asking what her book was about. She liked the evenings, did Joy; liked the airy sensation her mind would float into as soon as she sucked an inhale of meth to the back of her throat. But the mornings – the hangovers – they were tough for her to handle. Her head would be heavy, and her posture would

175

slouch. And she couldn't care to summon up enough energy to engage with any of her fellow inmates. Nor any of the prison officers. She and Aidan had long since been buddies. He would drop by to talk to her, but not as frequently as he used to do. Joy certainly felt safer when he was with her, but there was always the nagging feeling that Nancy would catch them talking and then have to deal with Joy later by slapping her or kicking at her shins.

'Where you off to?' Mathilda asked as Joy was slouching her way back to her cell, munching on the last of her crusts.

'Just gonna lie back down,' Joy said. 'Is that a crime?'

'It's not a crime,' Mathilda said, 'but that's not where you're going.'

'Huh?' Joy creased her brow into a vertical wrinkle; though she was starting to do that so often that the crease was becoming a permanent fixture.

'You've got a visitor. He's been here bright and early, demanding he talk to you. He's up in the Governor's office right now. Been told to bring you to him.'

'Who is he?' Mathilda shrugged. 'S'not my husband, is it?'

Mathilda shrugged again.

'I've told you all I know. Now, come on, follow me.'

'I'm, eh... really not feeling up for a visitor. I've got a splitting headache and I—'

Mathilda scoffed and scowled.

'I'm not asking you. I'm ordering you. Now come on, we're heading to the Governor's office. And may I just say, Joy, if you don't mind, but,' she sniffed up her nose, 'you look and smell like shit.'

Joy looked down at herself, taking in the stained tracksuit bottoms she hadn't bothered to wash for months, even though she was literally working in the laundry room five days a week. Then she heaved out a depressing sigh, before pacing after Mathilda. She knew she looked like shit; knew she was wasting her life by feeling so shitty for the first half of every day, then high as a kite for the second half. But she couldn't help herself. The gravitas of meth was, as it is for most, too alluring. Once she'd felt the high of the drug for the very first time, she couldn't help but keep coming back for more. They all did. Nancy let slip to Joy once that she was taking in over five grand a month; all distributed through outside channels. If the prisoner couldn't have somebody on the outside transfer money into Nancy's account for them, then they simply didn't get their fix. Though some desperate inmates would do Nancy the odd finger favour every now and then, just to get their high. But only the ones she fancied. Joy was told her fix of the drug in the evenings was payment enough for her distribution of the drug. Though she really didn't care. Money was insignificant to her. She was never going to experience the outside world again. Whereas Nancy, despite being inside for attempted murder, would have a chance of parole at some stage... whenever that time would come.

Joy would spend some mornings, with her head and heart heavy, wishing Nancy would disappear one day, just like Christy had. But that day never seemed to come around. And it didn't look as if it was going to come around any day soon. Not with the multiple misdemeanours Nancy kept getting picked up for in prison.

It wasn't all bad. Some of the times she spent with Nancy could be fun. They had a smart phone hidden at the back of the laundry room and would spend their time, while taking their hit of meth, doubled up in laughter while watching random YouTube videos.

When they first realised they could access the prison's Wi-Fi, they spent their time watching epic fail clips; giggling away at models tripping over on catwalks, or toddlers getting hit on the head with footballs. As inevitably happens when granted access to the internet, their searches eventually took them down the rabbit hole everybody ends up going down. It was Nancy who had suggested it. She was horny – one of her side effects of meth. And Joy agreed. Because she was suffering the same side effect. They'd giggle along as they watched middle-aged men with over-sized cocks fuck young women with bald pussies until they returned to their cells to bring themselves to their own climaxes.

But one night Nancy didn't want to wait until she got back to her cell.

She shuffled herself out of her tracksuit bottoms and pulled down her stained knickers, revealing a fiery-red bush. Then she began to play with herself while Joy giggled along, high as a kite. The night after that, Nancy didn't bother to do the work herself; instead, she grabbed Joy's hand and pushed it against her pubic bone, then began to roll it around in a circular motion. Joy held her eyes closed, while still grinning from her high, and only really reacted when Nancy curled one of her fingers against Joy's and slowly began to enter it into herself.

'No. No. No. It's beyond a joke now,' Joy said, whipping her hand away.

Nancy raised an eyebrow.

'Bitch. You wanna keep getting your fix of this,' she said, the joint pinched between her lips, 'then you need to play this little game with me. C'mon... when's the last time you had an orgasm at the hands of somebody else, huh?'

Nancy took the joint from her mouth and leaned forward to press her lips against Joy's.

'No,' Joy said, shaking her head, 'no kissing. I'm not gay. I don't wanna kiss.'

'Okay, okay,' Nancy said. 'No kissing.'

Then she gently took Joy's hand again, pressed it down to her groin and gingerly – *very* gingerly – curled her finger against Joy's until the tip of Joy's finger flexed inside her.

'Ye know where the office is from here, don'tcha?' Mathilda asked. Joy didn't bother to answer. Instead, she continued to the end of the landing, slodging like a grumpy teenager, until she eventually turned into the Governor's office.

But sitting there, at the Governor's large desk, wasn't the Governor himself. This man was, like the Governor, middle-aged, but he dressed entirely differently. He was wearing a pinstriped navy suit and a super shiny pair of brown leather shoes. He uncrossed his legs, grinned a smug smile at Joy and then got to his feet.

'Am I pleased to see you,' he said. He held his hand out for her to shake, but she was too taken by his leathery orange face that she failed to notice. So, she just frowned while he awkwardly put his hand back into his suit trouser pocket.

'Who are you?' she asked.

'My name is Gerd Bracken,' he said.

∴

Delia brushes down the creases on the front of her robe before pulling at her office door.

'Morning,' she calls to Aisling.

'Morning, Judge Delia,' Aisling replies. 'Another big day today, huh?'

'Oh, aren't they all? I've just been going through my notes and there's going to be written statements offered to the court today, as well as a key piece of evidence. Can you collect them all for me and have them back in my office by the time I return? I'll need to analyse that paperwork as soon as I'm done in the courtroom.'

Aisling smiles, then nods her head.

'Course I will.'

Delia mouths a 'thank you' to her assistant while squeezing the side of her shoulder, then she paces down the corridor. When she turns the corner, the young woman dressed in all black greets her from afar with a shy wave. Then she opens up the court's side door and nods into it before a bellow of 'all rise' is shouted.

Delia doesn't have to stare over the rim of her glasses to know the gallery is already packed as she climbs the three steps to her highchair, because she can already tell by the rumbling and mumbling. There seems to be a buzz circulating the room. She can never really predict what ambience is going to be present in a courtroom on any given day. Though she was well aware that yesterday's contrasting testimonies from Shay Stapleton and Lavinia Kirwan must have played havoc with everybody's opinions. They had certainly played havoc with hers. That and the fact that everybody knows this entire case all comes down to the coincidence of somebody walking near the scene of the crime wearing the exact same hoodie Joy had owned, and that coincidence was finally going to be examined today.

Delia eyeballs Joy over the rim of her glasses then looks to Jonathan Ryan and nods.

'Mr Ryan, can you call your next witness?'

'I can indeed, Your Honour. The prosecution calls Tobias Masterson to the stand.'

Masterson's suit looks at least two sizes too large for him as he sweeps his way down the aisle to a sea of synchronised swivelling heads on both sides of the gallery. He has a lacklustre presence, like that of a clichéd geek, what with his round John Lennon-style specs sitting loose on his pointed nose and his tie hanging below his nether regions – ironic given that he is the managing director of Pennsylvania's largest fashion distributor.

'Do you swear to tell the truth, the whole truth and nothing but the truth?' the court clerk asks as Masterson stands, awkwardly fidgeting, in the witness box.

'I do.'

'Mr Masterson, can you state your occupation for the court, please?' Ryan asks when the witness has sat.

'Sure. I run the company PeppaTrue – we are a stockists and distribution company based outta Pennsylvania.' Masterson spoke with a high-pitch nasal squeal, as if somebody was constantly pinching his nose.

'You stock fashionwear for some well-known high street stores, correct?'

'We stock up to eighteen different retail brands throughout the United States.'

'And you are managing director for the Pennsylvania branch of that company, yes?'

'I am.'

'And that company stock and supply Urban Outfitters with some of their fashion wear?'

'We do.'

'Did your company distribute the Pink Sasoon Ladies Hooded Top in the early spring of 2005 to Urban Outfitters?'

'We did.'

'Interesting. And just for the record...' Jonathan Ryan walks over to the television screen and presses at a button, 'this hooded top, seen here in this footage...' the screen blinks to the infamous three seconds of a figure walking into shot just outside a small residential garden, a mere one-thousand yards from where Oscar and Reese's bodies were found some two years later, 'is the Pink Sasoon Ladies Hooded Top, right?'

'We are without doubt certain it is. The Pink Sasoon Ladies Hooded Top has distinct trimmings. They are all red. A red zip as is visible in the footage at some points; the red band at the waistline and the red band on each cuff are also visible on the footage at some points. On certain freeze-frames the stitching on the side pockets and around the shoulders is also visible. It's the Pink Sasoon Ladies Hooded Top. One hundred per cent. The top is that distinctive. And even though this footage was shot in the early hours, we know the colours, we know the details.'

'Okay, thank you for your expertise in that regard, Mr Masterson. And for the record, Your Honour, that has never been disputed by anybody. All concerned are willing to accept that the hooded top in this footage is the distinct Pink Sasoon hooded top.' He narrows his lips, then turns to the witness again. 'Now, Mr Masterson, I want to move to another side of your expertise. I am right in saying that Urban Outfitters were the *only* store to stock the Pink Sasoon Ladies Hooded Top, yes?'

'Yes.'

'But more specifically, it was the Pennsylvania-based Urban Outfitter stores, only, right? This product didn't go nation-wide?'

'That is absolutely correct. It was a trial run of a fashion item by a local designer who Urban Outfitters' buyers are often willing to give a break to. That kinda thing happens often. Items come and go all the time.'

'Interesting. Thank you, Mr Masterson. And as managing director, you keep records of all stock coming to and from your warehouses, right?'

'Of course.'

'So, can you tell me and indeed the court how many Pink Sasoon Ladies Hooded Tops you supplied your Pennsylvania-based Urban Outfitter stores with?'

'Yes. They went on a trial run in three of their stores. And in total, we distributed ninety items.'

'Just ninety, for the whole State?'

'According to our records, each store received thirty Pink Hoodies; ten in size small, ten in size medium and ten in size large. It was a typical trial run.'

'And were any of the hoodies returned to your warehouses unsold?'

'Yes, almost half of them. Forty-three of the ninety.'

'Meaning only forty-seven were ever purchased from an Urban Outfitters?'

'Yes.'

Delia moves to pick up her pen, but she doesn't scribble any notes. Not yet, anyway. Because the witness hasn't revealed anything knew – nothing that hadn't been revealed in the original trial. But she knew something was coming...

'Now... a Mr Mathieu Dupont testified on that very stand two days ago, Mr Masterson, and was questioned about the figure in the CCTV footage being five foot, and three quarters of an inch, or five foot, two inches – but in regard to the hooded top itself, that wouldn't make a difference, right?'

'I, eh... I'm sorry. I don't know what you mean, Mr Ryan.'

'I mean, you don't make individual hooded tops for specific individual heights, right? There isn't one for somebody who is five foot, one and a different one for somebody who is five foot, two.'

Masterson puffs out a laugh.

'Of course not. These particular hooded tops only come in three sizes. Small. Medium. Large.'

'It's that straightforward?'

'That straightforward.'

'So, in that case, somebody whether five foot or five foot, two would be wearing a small hooded top, correct?'

'That is most likely, yes,' Masterson says, biting on his bottom lip and then looking to the judge as if fearful he had said anything out of turn. She glances at him, then looks towards Ryan, her eyes squinting. But she doesn't say anything.

'So, do you know how many Pink Sasoon Ladies Hooded Tops were distributed to Urban Outfitters in size small only?'

'Yes. As mentioned, each of the three Urban Outfitters received ten small hoodies, so that means thirty.'

'Thirty. Interesting. And how many out of that thirty were sent back to your warehouse unsold?'

'Fifteen. The hoodie wasn't a big hit.'

'So, if only thirty of these small pink hooded tops were ever distributed, and fifteen were sent back, that means this hoodie here in this footage,' Ryan points to the screen again, 'could only possibly be one in fifteen, too, right?'

'One in fifteen, correct. That is the famous fraction.'

'You see, Your Honour, our defendant here today was one of those one in fifteen. Because she purchased this small Pink Sasoon Ladies Hooded Top when visiting Pennsylvania with her husband, Shay Stapleton. He was away on a tour with the Dublin GAA squad when Joy flew out to meet him for the last five days of that tour in April 2005. She purchased this hoodie for seventy-nine dollars on April tenth, during that trip.'

Ryan walks to his desk, bends down and picks up the infamous hoodie, all wrapped in a clear plastic cover, as if it had just come back from the dry-cleaners and hadn't, in actual fact, been hanging in a dusty warehouse filled with shelves of trial evidence for the past eight years. The problem investigators had when it came to the hoodie was that it gave no indication of Joy's involvement in the death of her two young sons. The top wasn't of interest to investigators until the CCTV footage had been found some two years after the children had been reported missing. And in that time, the top had been worn and washed by the defendant an incalculable number of times. Meaning that, like the scene of the burial itself – given the two years it took to come across it – the hooded top had been rid of any possible DNA evidence dating back to the time of the crime.

'Also, for the record, Your Honour, in the original trial this was stated, but I would like to highlight again, investigators put a call out through national channels looking for anyone in Ireland who might have, coincidentally, like Mrs Stapleton, purchased one of these tops back in Pennsylvania in 2005. Nobody came forward. Not then. Not since. Which means, we firmly believe that Joy Stapleton was the *only* person in this entire country who owned a Pink Sasoon Ladies Hooded Top at the time Oscar and Reese Stapleton were murdered. However... since then, and for extra investigative measures for this retrial, we also put a call out to people in Pennsylvania to speak with women who may have owned the small version of this hooded top back when it was on sale in 2005...' Ryan walks towards the judge. 'Your Honour, I give you twelve statements from witnesses from Pennsylvania, all of whom say they did indeed buy that top back then, and, crucially, confirming they were not in Ireland during the period in which Oscar and Reese were murdered. We have narrowed the field even further. If it was hard to believe the coincidence excuse back when Mrs Stapleton first blurted it out, then it's almost impossible to believe it now.'

'Mr Ryan,' Delia calls out, hammering her gavel repeatedly. 'You will not assume the belief of this court. I am the judge here.'

She eyeballs him over her glasses. Though she knew what he had just delivered was pretty golden. He had literally chipped away at any notion of coincidence.

'Sorry, Your Honour, what I'm trying to say is... it was always argued by the defence that it was mere coincidence that a figure wearing that exact hooded top was seen so close to the scene of where Oscar and Reese were buried. And now we know it to be an even bigger coincidence than was claimed in the first place. In the original trial it was stated that it could only have been one of fifteen people in the entire world in that footage, well today we know that it could only have been one in three.' Ryan turns and faces the witness. 'Thank you, Mr Masterson. Your time is very much appreciated.'

Delia scribbles onto the paperwork in front of her as Jonathan Ryan takes a seat. Then she glances at Joy before raising an eyebrow at her defence lawyer.

'Mr Bracken, I assume you have questions for this witness...'

'I do indeed, Your Honour.'

Bracken gets to his feet, walks himself directly to the witness box and grips the edge of it, squinting up at Masterson.

'Mr Masterson,' he says, 'you are Pennsylvanian, are you not?'

Masterson's brow dips, causing his glasses to slip down his narrow nose.

'I am indeed, yes,' he says, pushing them back with a stab of his boney middle finger. 'I was raised in Roxborough, but have lived in Philadelphia practically my whole adult life. Since I was twenty-two in fact. So that's thirty-four years.'

'I'm an Irishman,' Bracken says. 'And like you, I have moved towns. I was born in Cork. I moved to London. Then to Dublin. So, what I'm getting at here is, we move around, don't we?'

'Move?'

'As in, we don't just stay in the same place, do we?'

'I, eh... guess not,' Masterson says, turning to the judge as if to ask if she is as flummoxed by Mr Bracken's questioning as he is.

'It's human nature to move around,' Bracken says, holding his hands out and shrugging his shoulders. 'It's not just Irish folk who move around, is it? American people move around too, don't they?'

'Yes.'

Masterson hunches his shoulders up and down, the wrinkles on his forehead now forming a deep V.

'In fact, Americans like to move around Ireland specifically... Let me tell you that in the year 2008, nine-hundred and eighty-seven thousand people travelled from America to Ireland. On November 2nd of 2008, when this footage was filmed,' Bracken says, pointing at the screen still on loop, 'and according to Fáilte Ireland statistics, eighty-eight thousand Americans were travelling in Ireland.' He inches closer to Masterson. 'I assume you haven't spoken to all of those eighty-eight thousand people, right?'

'Mr Bracken,' Delia calls out.

'Sorry, Your Honour. It's just that this witness seems willing to sit in this witness box during this very important trial to rule out the possibility of coincidence when indeed the coincidence cannot *totally* be ruled out. This witness hasn't spoken to everybody who owned a Pink Sasoon Ladies Hooded Top. We don't even know that the top in this footage is definitely a small, do we, Mr Masterson?'

Mr Masterson looks at the judge, as if she is going to protect him again. But she just looks over her glasses at him, awaiting his answer.

'It looks like a small,' he says.

'Sir, you do not know for certain whether that top is size small, do you?'

'No.'

'And, Sir, you do not know everybody who travelled from the States to Ireland in November, 2008, do you? So, therefore you cannot totally rule out the fact that one of those many travellers might, just might, have been from Pennsylvania and just might have been wearing one of those tops.'

'Well, as Mr Ryan has proven to the court with that new paper-work... he has ruled out many more people since the original trial. That dilutes the possibility of coincidence to one in three—'

'Mr Masterson,' Bracken shouts, his irritation stretched. 'Is it or isn't it a fact that you simply do not know for certain that somebody may have travelled from America to Ireland in November who owned one of those Pink Sasoon Ladies Hooded Tops?'

'Yeah... It's a fact.'

'You can't possibly know for certain, can you?'

'No.'

Masterson shakes his head and looks down at his own lap, as if he's just been scolded by his mother.

'Exactly,' Bracken says. 'You can't possibly know for certain. That's our questioning complete, Your Honour.'

1,120 days ago…

Joy's cell door swept open, but she didn't turn in her bed; assuming it was just one of the prisoners dropping by out of sheer boredom. But then she heard the squealing whistle of hard-soled shoes against her concrete floor, before a familiar, agitated sigh exhaled.

'What are you still doing lying in bed? It's gone half eleven.'

She held her eyes closed with annoyance before mustering up enough energy to turn over on her mattress.

'Chill out, Aidan. Ye sound like me da. Ye think you can order me about?'

Aidan swung his jaw from side-to-side.

'Well, actually, I *can* order you about. I am a *prison officer* in Mountjoy Prison, and you are a *prisoner* in Mountjoy Prison,' he hissed through his clenched jaw. 'Now listen up… you have a visitor. And you need to go see him now.'

'Is it my lawyer?' she asked, sitting upright and rubbing at both eyes. 'Is it?'

'I think it is, yeah,' Aidan said, sounding exhausted. He stepped outside and waited for her to throw on a sweat top and slip herself into her trainers before she joined him.

They didn't say another word to each other as he escorted her around the maze of landings and into the bowels of the prison, eventually leading her into an office she had never been in before. Aidan had grown frustrated with Joy's moping about and had long since started to treat her as just another prisoner. He had no idea she was constantly moping about because she was hungover from the effects of the meth she was smoking most nights.

'Howaya, Mr Bracken?' she said, entering the office with as much of a smile as she could muster.

Like all of the offices in Mountjoy Prison, this one was freezing cold. The walls were bare concrete, as was the floor, and a cramped, cheap wooden white desk took up pretty much the entirety of the floor space.

Bracken stretched a hand across the desk and gripped hers in it.

'I've got some great news for you,' he said.

It had been a year since Gerd Bracken had first surprised Joy out of nowhere. They had sat then, for that first meeting, just as they were now – across a cramped white desk in a freezing cold office – where he explained to her that Bunny the dog, who had been a key cog in her original trial, had been exposed as a fake. Bracken promised Joy there and then that he was going to do all he could to get her conviction quashed. And she became fully convinced he would get her out, because he proved to her that he had a history of overturning convictions. None of them were murder convictions, of course, and none held the magnitude her case did. But she couldn't help but get excited; especially as prison life had turned so unbearable for her – much, much worse than it had ever been. If it wasn't for the crack of light that Bracken brought to her, Joy was sure she'd be contemplating suicide by now.

'Remember I said to you that we'd need something more than the dog?' Bracken said as Joy stared across the desk, heavy-eyed.

'Yeah,' she replied.

'Well, what we've figured out is that we need to convince the judges in the Criminal Courts of Appeal that it's feasible that when you claimed that a woman captured in the CCTV footage with the same unique pink hoodie that you owned was merely a coincidence, that you may very well have been telling the truth. You know this, right? Either the woman in that pink top is you and you murdered Oscar and Reese, or the woman in that pink top isn't you, and the police have got this wrong from the start.'

'Yeah,' Joy said, nodding her head.

'Well, we found an expert – he's from France – who is willing to testify that the girl in the CCTV footage couldn't have been you.'

'Couldn't have been me...' Joy said, changing the direction of her head from nodding to shaking, 'how?'

'He invented some technology that can read a person's exact height from camera footage. And he is insistent that the girl in that footage is too small to be you.'

Joy's mouth popped open and she held two fists up and shook them, as if the football team she supported had just bulged the back of the opposition's net.

'And this will seriously be enough to get me outta here?'

'Well...' Bracken cocked his head to the side, 'I'm confident it's enough to win us a retrial... and if we get a retrial, we'd certainly have a good shot of getting you out of here.'

Joy leaned over the table and bear hugged Bracken's tanned face, smothering it into her boney chest.

'You look a little better,' he said when he was finally released from the hug and was flattening down his hair with his hand. 'Have you stopped using?'

Joy nodded her head, then swallowed the lie. She hadn't quite stayed off the meth as she'd promised Bracken she would, but she wasn't taking it on such a regular occurrence as she had been months prior. Though only because Nancy couldn't get the stuff into the prison as readily as she once could. The dodgy screw from Maple House who had been smuggling the meth in for her had left his post, and so they couldn't get as many crystals into the prison as Nancy would have liked.

Although Joy found it tough to wean herself off the drug, she also took solace in the silver lining not being able to get the meth inside afforded her. Not only did she no longer have to stress about prison officers finding the drugs sellotaped to the understem of her toilet bowl, but she had promised Bracken – the only person in the world who seemed as if he wanted to help her – that she would stay clean. Though it was still a prison she was residing in, of course, and so every now and then a prisoner would manage to smuggle some measurement of meth inside. And when that happened, Nancy would jump all over it. And Joy would be expected to join in.

On the rare occasions that Nancy would get her fix, she was fine with Joy – as if they were in a happy coupling who would laugh and joke and smoke and orgasm together. But during her come downs, Nancy could be a nasty bitch. She would physically attack Joy; not in any extreme way, but she would often take her frustrations out on her by shoving her or slapping her or kicking her.

Just two months prior, during a comedown and whilst she was judging Joy to be turning the pages of the newspaper too loudly, Nancy took two handfuls of Joy's curls and pinned her against the cell wall. Then she grabbed at Joy's throat and held a firm grip until Joy's face turned puce and she eventually collapsed. Nancy ran, leaving Joy to be later found by Aidan who, in a panicked state, had to scream for medical attention before Joy eventually came back around. She claimed she fainted from low blood pressure, but Aidan was far from convinced.

Although Joy was wary and constantly conscious of Nancy's bi-polar episodes, she never really felt in fear of her life. She knew she'd be subjected to the odd shove or slap, and that a small cut on her lip or a bruised hip from crashing off the concrete walls would often appear on her skin. But trying to stay on Nancy's good side was the best way for her to survive Elm House.

'Are you sure?' Bracken said. 'You don't seem very convinced, even if you do look a little more pink in the face.'

Joy held her eyes closed for a second, and within those seconds she decided she couldn't risk lying. Not to him.

'Well, once or twice somebody has snuck some meth in and I've had a drag off a joint, but that's it... it's seriously only been once or twice since I last met with you and made a promise that I wouldn't touch it again. Twice... maximum.'

Bracken leaned his forearms onto the desk and pouted a sorrowful glare at his client.

'You promised me you'd stay off the drugs if I was going to help you, Joy.'

'I will,' she said, grabbing his arm, 'I won't take another drag. I promise. I won't. I'll do whatever it is you need me to do in order to get me out of here.'

'Well,' Bracken said, leaning back in his chair, 'it may take a while, but I am certain we have enough new evidence to convince the Court of Criminal Appeals that you should be awarded a retrial.'

'How does that work?' Joy said, her eyes squinting, her curls shaking from side to side.

'Well, three judges sit on the Court of Criminal Appeal and, in basic terms, the only way to convince them to order a retrial is to bring new evidence to the table. They really need two pieces of new evidence – two things that would pour doubt over the original trial that convicted you.'

'And we have the fact that Bunny the dog is a fraud... and now this guy... the French guy... suggesting that whoever that was in the pink hoodie in that CCTV footage can't be me...'

'Exactly,' Bracken said, grinning his veneers, 'well, really what's new is the technology this guy has come up with. That's what the judges in the Court of Criminal Appeal will be swung by; something that's been invented in the intervening years since your original trial that can further pour doubt on the original case built against you.'

'I'm gonna get out!' she told Aidan as he escorted her back to her cell.

He stopped at the top of a set of stairs and turned to face her.

'I'm happy for you, Joy. I am.'

'Well... tell your face,' she said, grinning.

He fake-smiled, then dropped it abruptly as he turned to continue down the steps.

'Hey... what's up with you?' She grabbed his shoulder, 'Didn't you just hear me. I'm gonna get out. Why aren't you happy for me?'

'I am happy for you. I just wish... listen,' he said, looking at her square in the eye as she now matched him for height what with her standing one step taller than him, 'getting through the Courts of Criminal Appeal is as far from easy as you think it is. Very, *very* few get offered a retrial. And I mean *very* few. They don't like to order retrials because it really is the justice system admitting that the justice system might have got something wrong. Then if... even *if* you get a retrial, there are still no guarantees.'

'Jeez,' Joy said, blowing out her cheeks, 'way to piss on my Corn Flakes.'

'I'm not pissing on your Corn Flakes.' Aidan leaned into her to whisper, in fear of anyone overhearing them; his face inches from hers. 'I'm happy you are getting this opportunity to get your case heard again. I am. It's just... I know these things can go on for ages... years. And in the meantime, you're still in here, and you're still under her thumb. And you're still vulnerable.'

'Nancy?'

'Shhh,' Aidan said, before he turned around to continue descending the stairs. 'Joy, when you first came in here, I was worried for you, but you seemed to fit in well. You were much nicer than you... than you've been the past couple of years. When Christy left, you seemed to wither right into the arms of Nancy Trott. I've seen the cuts and the bruises, and I hear stories about how she treats you. I found you flat out in your cell a few weeks ago, don't forget.'

'Wow... are you, eh... are you in love with me or something?' Joy said, grinning again.

'Shhh,' Aidan hissed, then he paced down the landing as quickly as he could, her jogging behind to keep up, until they reached her cell without a further word said.

Though Joy didn't have to stay locked up in her cell for long. She, along with half of the prisoners from Elm House and half from Maple House, were due their hour in the yard.

The yard didn't offer much. It was a long rectangular tarred stretch, fenced off by sixteen-foot fences that were topped off with swirls of barbed wire. There were some cigarette packets and paper bags, likely filled with weed or other contraband, caught in the barbed wire that were too tricky for anybody, even the officers, to get to. There were also two basketball courts lined out on the ground, and two hoops at either end, minus the nets. Though nobody ever played basketball. In fact, Joy hadn't remembered ever seeing a basketball in the five years she'd been inside. The prisoners would just stand around the yard, shooting the breeze as if they hadn't spent much of the last few years doing exactly the same thing. Joy often found it odd that they could come up with new things to talk about. Though she rarely came up with anything, because she rarely talked anymore. She'd just stand around Nancy and her cohorts, nodding when she needed to nod, shaking her head when she needed to shake her head and laughing when she needed to laugh. But today she was bursting with an energy she hadn't felt in years... not since way before she was an inmate.

'I think I'm gonna get out!' Joy excitedly spat out, holding up her fists and shaking them. 'My lawyer says they have the cadaver dog and now another expert who is going to prove in court that it wasn't me in the CCTV footage with the pink hoodie.'

'Wow,' Nancy said, exhaling her cigarette, 'you've finally got somebody who's gonna say it was a coincidence after all, huh?'

'Huh-huh,' Joy said as those around her laughed.

'Yeah, right,' Nancy said.

'Whatcha mean 'yeah right'?'

'I mean, you seriously think anybody's gonna believe that's not you in that pink—'

'Holy shit!' Linda said, interrupting Nancy by tapping her on the shoulder. Then she stretched her arm over that shoulder and flexed her index finger into a point. 'Look who's coming this way.'

Joy turned, but as she did, Nancy leaned into her.

'Don't you fuckin' dare say anything to her, you hear me?' she whispered with a snarl. 'You're mine now. If she tries to get pally-pally with you again, I will make your life miserable. Just tell her to fuck off, okay?'

'Well, if it isn't Missus Joy Stapleton,' a voice called out.

And before Joy turned around, she knew that she was going to be greeted by beautiful brown skin, stained yellow teeth and heavy, red eyes.

'She has nothing to say to you, Christy,' Nancy said.

'Huh... Me and Joy are best friends, ain't we, Joy?' Joy stared wide-eyed at Christy, the life she once lived inside the confines of this prison flashing before her eyes. 'Joy?'

Joy said nothing.

'She ain't talking to you, you crazy ass junkie hoe.'

Christy tutted.

'Nancy Trott, I will fuck you up. I will tear you to shreds in this very yard, you hear me, girl?'

'We're not surprised to see you back in here, Christy, whatcha rob this time?'

'Bite me, Linda,' Christy said. Then she put her arm around Joy and pulled her closer. 'Was hoping we'd be on the same yard times... I'm in Maple House this time. Now let's catch up, sista, huh? How you been getting on without me?'

Joy's heart stopped momentarily, then she shrugged Christy's arm from her shoulder.

'You heard Nancy,' Joy said, her voice shaking 'I don't wanna have anything to do with you. So do one, Christy. Fuck off. And don't ever come near me again.'

1,119 days ago...

Joy's routine hadn't changed in the five years she'd been inside, because the prison system's routine hadn't changed in those five years either. Her door would click open, as would the majority of them on the wing, for breakfast at eight-thirty a.m., then she'd be locked back in her cell from nine-thirty for an hour before she'd have to go for her first shift at work in the laundry room. Lunch would then be between one and one-thirty, before another hour-long lockdown after which there'd be an hour's access to the games room or the TV room before another two-hour shift back at laundry. Dinner at her usual bench, and sat right next to Nancy, would follow for an hour before all of the prisoners were locked back up in their cells from seven p.m. until the doors clicked back open again the next morning, just for that whole routine to start up again.

For the hours that she was locked in her cell, Joy really only ever did one of two things; she either read a fiction book which she would swap with the librarian who called by, cell to cell, each and every Thursday afternoon, or, when she didn't feel like reading, she'd lie on her thin mattress in foetal position and stare at her photograph of Oscar and Reese. It was still hung in the exact same spot she had hung it on the very first evening she arrived here, after Aidan had gone to the trouble of finding her some sellotape.

She felt bad about telling Christy to fuck off the day before. But that guilt was battling against the waves of optimism that were also swaying in the pit of her stomach. Gerd Bracken seemed rather confident he was going to put an end to this nightmare for her. And when she got out, she wouldn't have to worry or stress about junkie criminals like Christy Jabefmei or Nancy Trott no more.

'Psst,' Nancy said, standing in the doorframe of Joy's cell as Joy was laying there, staring at the smiling faces of her two sons. 'C'mon, time for our shift... and time for us to celebrate.'

'Celebrate? Celebrate what?'

'To celebrate whatever it is your lawyer said to you yesterday. Look...' Nancy held a small plastic bag in the air and it twisted from her pinched fingers, making the crystals glisten. 'Cost me a few quid, but I wanted to celebrate... with you.'

Joy didn't say anything, not until they were both hid at the back of the laundry room where Nancy was licking two rizla papers together.

'I, eh... I'm not gonna have any,' Joy said. 'Not this time.' Nancy glared up at her as she lit the joint. 'It's just my lawyer made me promise I wouldn't do it anymore... I don't wanna ruin my chances of a retrial. You understand, don't you, Nance?'

Nancy took one step closer and lit the joint just inches from Joy's face.

'Don't be fuckin' ungrateful. Get some of this into ya. We're celebrating. We're celebrating you. I had to transfer a hundred

quid for this. And I did it to spend some time with you. C'mon...
it's been ages since we had a little fumble. Linda's keeping eyes out
for the prison officers for us... Let's enjoy ourselves.'

Nancy exhaled a large cloud into Joy's face.

Joy gulped, then waved away the smoke before stiffly shaking
her curls from side to side.

'No, I'm not taking it... I don't want any.'

'Get it fuckin' into you. I want a good high and a hell of a finger
fuck from you this evening. It's been way too long. C'mon, baby,'
Nancy said, softening her voice and rubbing a fingernail down
Joy's cheek, 'I miss you. I miss us doing this together.'

She pressed the joint to Joy's lips, but Joy shook her curls even
more fervently.

'No.'

The slap was loud, though not loud enough to be heard by the
prisoners who were down the other end of the laundry room, overseeing the unloading of bed sheets with washing machines
tumbling around them. Joy inhaled sharply through the gaps in her
teeth, trying to rid the stinging sensation, but then Nancy's fist
struck her nose. Hard. And when Joy fell to the ground the kicks
were plentiful. And painful. *Very* painful. Especially the kicks to
the ribs.

1,118 days ago...

'C'mon. I love you. You're my best friend. You're more than a
friend,' Nancy said.

She was sat, on the grated floor of the landing, her back against
Joy's cell door which Joy had requested be locked after her attack
the previous evening. The prison officers agreed to her request,
though Aidan was furious that she wouldn't go on record as admitting it was Nancy who had beaten her up. She was well aware by
now, used to prison life, that ratting would only cause her more
harm. She had learned that was why the nastiest prisoners, like

Nancy Trott, thrived inside; because snitching is seen as being a totally unforgiveable act in the eyes of every prisoner. It was the one trait that was frowned upon more than any other. Ratting was deemed worse than the most heinous of crimes; even murder – even the murder of your own sons.

Joy slowly sucked in a painful breath while moving over in her bed; her ribs burning. Her two eyes were bruised yellow; much like they had been for her first full month inside prison.

'I didn't mean to hit you. Or kick you. I just wanted to celebrate. And I took offence to you turning me down, that's all. Come on. You're my best friend. I love you.'

But for the entirety of the one-hour Nancy was sat on the landing with her back to Joy's cell door, only distracted by Mathilda strolling by on three separate occasions as she walked her rounds, Joy didn't answer her pleas for a truce. She kept quiet as a mouse.

When the call came up for all prisoners to return to their cells, Nancy slid a note under Joy's door and then slumped back to her own bed for lock up.

Joy turned on her mattress upon hearing the note being slid inside, sucking in further breaths through gritted teeth. Then she mustered up enough energy to bend forward, through the pain, and pick it up.

I love you. I can't go on without you. x

She squinted at it; feeling it odd that Nancy was going on and on about how much she loved her when she had never so much as uttered that word before. Perhaps Nancy's emotions were being smothered by guilt. Or perhaps she was just being the manipulative and conniving cunt Joy knew she could be.

'Fuck you, Nancy,' she whispered to herself.

Then she heard a key turning in her lock and, in a panic, she grabbed at her bible and slid the note inside the back cover, just before Aidan appeared.

'I heard she was sitting outside your door the whole of the past hour. You need to make a formal complaint about the beating. We can't do anything until you do. Come on, do this. We can get you off this wing, onto another one.'

'You've been saying that to me for years, Aidan,' Joy said, while grimacing in pain as she sat back down on her mattress.

'She's never gonna leave you alone, y'know?'

'I'm fine, Aidan. Anyway, I'll be getting out soon.'

Aidan pursed his lips, while staring at the bruises under Joy's eyes.

'Joy. There's still every chance you are going to spend the rest of your life in prison. Nancy's in here for a long time, too. You don't want this to be a regular occurrence.'

'I told you before, Aidan,' Joy said, grimacing again while pressing a hand to her ribs, 'you're not me da. You can't tell me what to do. So, with the utmost politeness and respect, can you please just fuck off and leave me alone?'

Aidan raised his eyebrows, then let them drop back down before he paced out of her cell, slamming the door shut behind him.

Joy slapped the pillow in frustration. Then she turned to face her two boys, as the tears began to stream down her face.

⁕

Delia licks the tip of her thumb, then flips over the top sheet of paper and continues to read.

She has been going through the testimonies of the twelve females from Pennsylvania who had provided witness statements and proof that they once purchased a Pink Sasoon Ladies Hooded Top, in size small, for the past half-hour. She's just beginning to read through the last of these statements when Aisling walks into her office; a bottle of water, a packaged sandwich and a fruit bar in her hands.

'Here you are, Delia,' she says. 'They didn't have the ham and cheese one, so I just got you plain ham again.'

'You're a darling, Aisling. Thank you.'

Aisling places the lunch on her boss's desk, beside the shards of glass that have fallen from the photo frame and then turns to leave.

'So, eh... what did you make of Tobias Masterson's testimony this morning, Aisling?' the judge asks, looking over the rim of her glasses at her assistant.

Aisling smiles to herself before spinning back to face Delia. She loves being asked about the trials; feels really valued when probed for her opinion.

'Well, if the chance is now just one in three of that being Joy Stapleton in the footage and not one in fifteen as we've always thought, then that sure is a big difference... Those statements you are reading, they sure do make a huge difference to this trial, right?'

'But what about Bracken's cross examination... suggesting that Masterson couldn't have known everything; that it may not even be a small-sized hooded top in that footage?'

'I mean, it was good cross... under the circumstances. You've taught me the difference between good and bad cross. And there aren't many better than Gerd Bracken at delivering one.' Delia smirks a proud grin. She loves how enthusiastic and studious Aisling is about her chosen career. She reminds her of herself. 'But is his cross that pertinent when you think of how coincidental it would all have to be to actually align? I mean, this footage was shot one-thousand yards from where Reese and Oscar were buried. On the night detectives are certain they were buried – the night before Joy rang in her missing person's report. It'd be some coincidence to think that isn't Joy in that footage, right?'

Delia winks at her assistant.

'Thank you, Aisling,' she says. 'I, eh... appreciate your input. Now, I got to get through this.' She nods down at the paperwork on her desk.

'Okay, well, I'll leave you to read while you are eating lunch. I'll knock on your door ahead of the resumption.'

Delia rips open the sandwich packaging as Aisling exits her office and takes a large bite before continuing to read. But she doesn't get very far before she is disturbed again. This time by her phone vibrating against her desk.

A text message.

From Eddie Taunton.

Convincing testimony today, huh?

'Conniving mother fuc—'

Delia only gets out half of her mumble, just about stopping herself from producing another swear word. She hadn't sworn since she was a teenager up until this week. Now she can barely stop herself; certainly not when Eddie Taunton pops into her mind.

She picks up her phone and finger taps a response.

Depends on your definition of the word 'convincing'.

Then she places her phone back down and continues reading. The witness statements have all been flawlessly prepared, clearly overseen by Jonathan Ryan for a final edit before they were signed by the witnesses and handed over to the judge. The statements don't throw up any surprises. Most detail how and when each witness purchased a Pink Sasoon Ladies Hooded Top from Urban Outfitters. Some even go so far as providing photographic evidence of them wearing the top. One statement even had the actual receipt from the hoodie's purchase, dated October 10th – the exact same day Joy had purchased hers.

Some investigative work had been done ahead of the original trial to track down Pennsylvanian owners of the hooded top, but the prosecution didn't deem it overly necessary. They were certain Joy was the only person in Ireland with one of those hooded tops, and they were convinced they would get a conviction from a jury based on that. Besides, it wasn't that easy in those days. But the evolution in social media in the years since Joy was first convicted has been so dramatic that it became much easier to track down folk anywhere in the world. And so, when Ryan put out social media posts to Pennsylvanian folk with an image of the pink hooded top, it was no surprise that a few women, who had purchased one back in the day, finally came across the posts. He knew if he got statements from as many of those women as possible, then that would be viewed as pretty convincing evidence to a judge. He outdid his expectation. He got twelve. Leaving the chance of the woman in the CCTV footage being Joy as only one in three in the whole world.

Delia flipped over the penultimate page of the written testimonies but got distracted by her phone vibrating again just as she was finishing up.

She's guilty. Can only be her in that footage.

Delia stares at the message, then puffs out a snort of laughter. Not because she finds the text particularly funny. But because she still can't get over the brazen manner in which Taunton is transparently blackmailing her. So, she thumbs at her phone again.

I will be the judge of that.

Then she places the phone back down on her desk and gets back to her reading.

'Judge McCormick,' her desk phone spits out Aisling's voice, causing Delia to tut, 'Mr Bracken and Mr Ryan are both here to see you.'

Delia holds her two hands over her face and silently grunts into them.

'Send them in, Aisling,' she says.

A light knock is heard at the door, before it swings open and Bracken appears, grinning his veneers into the dimly lit office. Jonathan Ryan, taller but much slimmer, is stood behind him, peering over his shoulder.

'Come in, gentlemen. I've only the one visitor's chair here, so rather than look favourably on one of you, how about you both just take one step inside, close that door behind you and stand where you are... what's the issue? Why are you here before I've even finished my lunch?'

'Ma'am,' Ryan says, 'I have reservations about the cross examination Mr Bracken has led me to believe he has planned for the next witness.'

Delia sighs loudly, before rifling through the larger document on her desk until she locates the sheet of paper she is looking for.

'Mr Bracken, is this true?'

'Your Honour, the next witness cannot be relied upon to offer honest testimony.'

'Excuse me, Mr Bracken. *I'll* be the judge of that. In fact, I already *have* been the judge of that. I've allowed the witness.

You've known this witness would be testifying for weeks and although you raised an argument against it before, you are already aware of my judgement on this. Testimony from this witness is valid. Very valid.'

Bracken sucks on his cheeks, then slides himself into the chair opposite the judge, crossing his legs as he sits.

'With all due respect, Your Honour. This witness has history of very heavy Class A drug use.'

'She's clean now!' Ryan spits.

Delia waves an open palm upwards.

'Mr Bracken... firstly, stand!' she says. He heaves himself to his feet and throws his hands into his trouser pockets. 'Secondly, you're bringing this argument to me at the eleventh hour. I'm not quite sure what your ploy is with regards delaying this trial. You seem to be throwing clinks into the mix constantly. We spent much of the first day of this trial arguing witnesses and written statements when you had been made privy to the witness structure three full weeks before the trial began. I thought you were a much better prepared defence lawyer than this, Mr Bracken.'

'Your Honour, with all due respect, I am one of the most prepared lawyers in this country. I am not delaying this trial at all... in fact, I am aiming to have a quick resolution to what has clearly been a grand miscarriage of justice. I am eager to get my client out of prison as soon as possible.'

'Well then what is your problem, Mr Bracken?'

'The fact that the next witness is a heavy drug user and cannot be relied upon to tell the truth.'

'You have known about her appearing as a witness for quite some time... this is what I mean by you coming to me with issues at the eleventh hour.'

'Your Honour, this witness—'

'No. No, Mr Bracken. We will not be having this discussion now. The time for that argument was weeks ago. You raised some concerns then, but I informed you of my decision. And my decision still stands.

'But, Ma'am.'

'Enough!' Delia shouts. She picks up her sandwich and takes another large bite from it, leaving Bracken and Ryan standing and staring at her as she chews.

A light knock is heard at the door, before Aisling enters.

'Delia, shall I delay the restart of the trial, seeing as you three are...'

'No need,' Delia says, swiping the sleeve of her robe across her lips and then snatching at her bottle of water, 'these two gentleman will return to the courtroom ahead of resumption. I shall be there in a couple of minutes.'

'But, Your Honour—'

'Off you go, you two,' Delia says, brushing her hand at them, unwilling to listen to any more of Bracken's groaning.

The two lawyers turn around like two sorrowful teenage boys to be greeted by the infamous hooded top, hanging from the back of Delia's door. Then they pull that door open and leave.

'I'm sorry,' Aisling says. 'I didn't want to disturb what was going on... but just felt I'd need to inform the court clerks if there was going to be a delay. Is everything okay?'

'No problem at all, Aisling,' Delia says as she twists the lid back on to her water bottle. 'Just Mr Bracken chancing his arm, trying to get the next witness null and voided.'

Aisling thins a smile as she picks up the empty sandwich packaging from Delia's desk.

'I've ordered a new frame for this photo,' she says. 'From Amazon. It should arrive by the end of the week.'

'You are a darling,' Delia says as she stands up, sweeping the crumbs down her robe with her fingers while taking in her husband's smile through the cracked frame. She misses him so much. No more so than when she has a major decision to make. Bouncing arguments off Callum is just not the same as bouncing them off Ben. Callum didn't quite inherit the genius level of constructive nous his father had, even if he is proving to be a fine trial lawyer himself.

'Right, I need to get back to the grind. This witness should be interesting.'

'She sure will,' Aisling says. 'If anybody knows the defendant's state of mind straight after she was found guilty, it's this witness, right?'

Delia arches one of her eyebrows and nods slowly at Aisling, then she makes her way back down the corridor, turning left to face the young woman dressed in black up ahead of her who carries out her usual routine of opening the side door and nodding into it to note the imminent arrival of the judge.

Delia glances across at Bracken as she climbs the three steps up to her chair, then she knocks at her desk once with her gavel, silencing the murmurs of chatter.

'Mr Ryan,' she says, 'can you please call your next witness?'

'I can indeed,' Ryan says getting to his feet. 'Your Honour, we call Miss Christine Jabefemi to the stand.'

CHRISTINE JABEFEMI

Ain't normal I see the inside of a courtroom. The four times I been sent down, I cut deals every time. I always admit I'm guilty if I get caught. That way I get less time. Don't think I'd ever have the patience to sit through a trial anyway… barely able to sit through this. But I promised Jonathan Ryan that I'd be here, dressed all nice and being all sober. So, here I am. Dressed all nice. And being all sober. Don't know how people manage to do this all day, e'ry day.

'Ms Jabefemi, thank you for taking the time to be with us today.'

'Call me Christy,' I say, 'Christ with an extra Y.'

He smiles. Like a little pretty boy. The exact same smile he offered me when I first asked him to call me Christy all those months ago now, after he dropped by to talk to me bout this retrial. He wanted to know all about my relationship with Joy after she had been first sent to Mountjoy.

'Christy it is then,' he says. 'So, Christy, can you tell the court about a prison sentence you served in 2012?'

I snort, then move the microphone closer to me.

'I was in for burglary and theft in 2012. For a seven-year stretch. Ended up doing almost three years. Should have been less. But the fuckin' parole board—'

'Excuse me, the witness cannot use such language in the courtroom,' the judge says, smackin' her hammer off her desk like a crazy

lady. If she thinks that scowl is supposed to frighten me she can think again. I ain't the bitch on trial here today.

'We apologise, Your Honour,' *Jonathan says as he walks towards me. He leans in, covering the microphone with his hand.*

'Christy... as I said, no foul language. Let's just get through the questions and answers like we said, okay?'

I wink at him. He's such a cute little man-boy; I likes me them cute little man-boys sometimes; especially if they have dimples like he does. He walks backwards a few steps, then looks up at me again.

'Christy, if you could just answer the question directly... You were sentenced for seven years in 2012 for burglary and theft, and served almost three years of that in prison?'

'Yeah.'

'Okay... and you happened to be sent to Mountjoy on September sixth of that year, yes?'

'Yeah,' *I say nodding my head. Though I only know that cos he told me. Otherwise I don't remember dates.*

'That happens to be the day Joy Stapleton was also sentenced. Is it true that you both travelled together to Mountjoy Prison in the back of a police van?'

'Yep.'

'Good. Now, you spoke on that journey and when you entered the prison, you were both sent to the same wing within the prison, yes?'

'Uh-huh. Elm House.'

'Did you strike up a friendship with Mrs Stapleton?'

'Yeah. We sure did. I guess. I mean we spent time with each other. I tried to protect her. I'd been in prison befo', so I just tried to help with the small details. Ye know it's the small details in prison. How to get your hands on a new toothbrush. What books you can take from the library... how to keep yoself warm at night... those kinda details.'

'You, in a sense, took her under your wing, correct?'

'Like a Mamma birdie,' *I say. And I laugh. But nobody else does. Cos this courtroom full of snooty-ass bitches.*

'And, as you said, you spent almost three years in prison then. Did you spend all of that time on the Elm House wing?'

'Yep.'

'And did Mrs Stapleton serve all those years with you on that wing, too?'

'Think she's spent all her time on that wing... I don't know. It's been a lot of years since I've been back inside.'

'But, you were in effect neighbours in Mountjoy for all the years you were there that time?

'Yep.'

'Friends?'

'Yep?'

'Close?'

'I took her under ma wing, as I told you. I was her mamma birdie. There are a whole lotta screwed up women in prison, and I guess she looked so small and lonely and frightened. Hell, she was shakin' in the van the first day I met her.'

'Thank you, Christy. So, you were close friends for almost three years. Then you were let out of prison, but arrived back there some two years later, correct?'

'Yep. But that was bullshit. I shouldn't—'

'Enough, Mrs Jabefemi,' the judge says, slamming her hammer again.

'Sorry,' I say.

'If the witness could refrain from profanities.'

'I will, Ma'am,' I say, noddin' ma head at her.

'It's insignificant whether you feel you were rightly or wrongly sent back into prison, Christy, in terms of this trial. What is significant is what Joy Stapleton said to you during the small stretch of time you spent in prison during that sentence, isn't it?'

'That it is. That's when she told me she did it. That she killed her two boys. She confessed. Came crying to me one day, saying things hadn't been the same in prison since I left, and everything came out. It all poured outta her.'

I look to Joy. Her lawyer has his hand lightly gripped around her wrist, just in case. But she doesn't react. She just stares straight ahead.

'She confessed to you that she killed Oscar and Reese?'

'Yep. And that she buried them in the woods in the mountains. And that it was definitely her in that CCTV thingy... everything. She poured her heart out to me.'

'Wow, Your Honour,' Jonathan says, turning to look up at Judge Delia. I don't know whether she believes me. I hope she does. But she looks like the snootiest bitch of all the bitches in this courtroom. So I dunno. 'Now carefully and to the best of your memory, can you detail what Joy said to you exactly?' Jonathan asks.

'It was a long time ago, but I remember. I remember like it was yesterday because it was, well... it was Joy Stapleton finally confessin'. She said, "I did it, Christy. I couldn't put up with them crying no longer. I strangled them and killed them. Then I went up the mountains and buried them." She told me it took her three hours to dig out a grave and then she dumped the bodies in there and then she went home and got drunk.'

'Quite a lot of detail...'

'Yep. She just opened her heart to me.'

I look at her again, through the curls covering her face so I can see her eyes. But she won't look at me. Little bitch.

'So, you are here to testify today, Christy, that Joy openly confessed to you inside the confines of Mountjoy Prison during your six-month sentence in 2017, yes?'

'Yep. Sure am. The Lord God sent me. He said, he said, "Christy, you need to make sure o' justice for those two little innocent boys." So here I am. Making sure justice is served. She can't get out of prison. She's a killer. Worse than a normal killer. She kills her own.'

I stare at her again. I really want her to look at me, to see me. Bitch embarrassed me. She made a show o' me, telling me to fuck off in the yard that time. She payin' for that now. You don't fuck with Christy, sista.

She just keeps looking down at the desk in front of her, her lawyer still holding a loose grip round her wrist. Then I see him let go, and he stands up and stares at me. I didn't even see Jonathan sit down. Now it's this guy's turn? Jonathan told me not to be intimidated; that this fella will bring up my past and won't paint a pretty picture. But all I have to do is sit here and take it and not overreact. Then I can walk out those double doors, back to my freedom, back to ma little bedsit. While Joy here will be going back to Mountjoy. Back to those shitty little cells the rest o' her life.

'May I call you Christy, too?' he says.

'You may indeed, Sir.'

'Christy, you just said Joy Stapleton confessed to you that she killed her two sons. Can you detail for the court where this conversation took place?'

'Eh...' I scratch at the side o' my hair. 'In her cell in Elm House.'

'Really?'

'Yep.'

'It's just that during this period, in 2017 when you were in for a six-month sentence for theft, you were not based in Elm House, were you?'

'Eh... nope.'

'So how could you possibly have been present there for a conversation with Joy Stapleton at this time.'

'I must have... must have been allowed in. Somehow. Sometimes we wander.'

'You must have been allowed in... to Elm House? But this simply doesn't happen, does it? Prisoners don't wander block to block in Mountjoy Prison, do they?'

'Well, eh... maybe it happened somewhere else and my memory is a little... I don't know... fuzzy?' I laugh. But none of the other snooty fuckers do. I know Jonathan certainly won't be laughing. He be screamin' inside. He told me this lawyer fella would ask all about where this conversation with Joy is supposed to have taken place. Because when I first told him, he recorded me and I said it had happened in Joy's cell in Elm House. So, he told me I should just stick to that, even if this lawyer fella kept suggesting it couldn't have happened there. But I didn't stick to it like he told me. It don't matter.

'So now your memory is a little fuzzy on where this actual

conversation took place? Is your mind fuzzy on the content of the conversation, too, perhaps?'

'Nope. She told me e'rything.'

'Really?'

'Yep.'

'She just spat it out one day to you... just like you testified here today?'

'Yep. She wanted to get it off her chest. She had been depressed since I left the prison and just wanted me back as a best friend, y'know, so she just told me e'rything.'

'Well, Mrs Stapleton says no such conversation came up during your six-month sentence in Mountjoy Prison in 2017. In fact, she says she had no conversation with you at all during this period. That she saw you one day in the break yard, but that she ignored you.'

'She lyin' cos we did talk.'

'Did you talk many times during that six-month stay?'

'Nope. That was it.'

'Hold on. You are telling me you only had that one conversation in 2017 and she openly admitted everything to you?'

'Yep.'

'Now I find that hard to believe. Especially as you've already admitted to your mind being fuzzy – which is the exact word you used.'

'Well you should believe it, cos it's true, Sir.'

'And you are to be trusted, Christy, yes?'

'I am a woman of God, Sir. I am honest and true.'

'You were fired from your job as warehouse worker in Cribbins Closets in 2019, Christy. Yes?'

'Yep.'

'For what reason?'

'Because they ass holes.'

'Mrs Jabefemi,' the judge calls out, slammin' that hammer again. It's a good job I don't have a hang-over... good job I kept clean these past three weeks.

'Sorry, Yo' Honour,' I say, 'won't happen again.'

'You may answer the question properly this time, Christy,'

Bracken says. 'You were sacked from Cribbins Closets for what reason?'

'Cos they say I stole from the till.'

'You stole from the till?'

'That's what they say. Sacked my sorry ass in front of all the folk working there.'

'So, you were sacked for stealing on the job?'

'I didn't steal nothin'.'

'But that is the reason they sacked you, yes?'

'I guess so.'

'And you were thrown out of a hostel called The Inn Take in early 2011. why was this?'

I breathe out loud. Right into the microphone.

'I stole somebody's watch.'

'You stole somebody's watch?'

'I didn't do it.'

'You just said you did.'

'Well, I just sayin' why I was thrown out, s'all. They threw me out cos they say I stole the watch. But I didn't steal jack sh—' I stop myself befo' the judge slams that hammer again.

'Okay, Christy. Now let me go back a bit. You were first sentenced to prison in 2008. Yes?'

'Think that was ma first time, yep.'

'For what?'

'Theft.'

'Theft. Correct. And you spent nine months inside. You then went back to prison in 2010 correct?'

'Yep.'

'For what reason?'

'Theft, I guess. And I got eight month that time.'

'Yep. That's correct. Then the third time you got caught, you were sentenced to seven years for theft with use of an illegal weapon in September of 2012. Which is when you spent almost three years on the same wing as the defendant. You got out in 2015. Then in late 2017 you were back in Mountjoy for six months for...'

'Theft.'

'Yep. Theft.'

'See where I'm going with this, Christy? You were sacked from the only job you've ever held, according to my records, for theft. You were thrown out of a hostel for theft. You have been arrested, charged and imprisoned on four different occasions for theft. And yet here you sit before us, asking us to trust you as you testify about a conversation that simply didn't happen because it couldn't have happened.'

'It did happen!' I say.

'You ever been reliant on illegal substances, Christy?' he says, taking a step closer to me. I was told this would come up.

'You know I have.'

'When did you start taking drugs?'

'When I left home, back in... I don't know... late nineties or whatever.'

'And when was the last time you took drugs, Christy?'

'A long time ago. I'm clean now. I don't do nothing like that no more. I am a woman of God, Sir.'

'Last time... roughly?'

'I don't know, Sir.'

'You don't know... has it been weeks? Months? Years?'

'Years.'

'Years? Well, now that can't be the case, can it, Christy? I mean, I have here...' he walks back to his desk and picks up a sheet of paper. 'Records of you being accepted onto the Desoxyn trials at the Lilac Clinic in Blackrock back in February of this year, for a course of Desoxyn. Desoxyn, for the record of the court, is a legal substitute for methamphetamine. Did you need a substitute for meth in February, Christy?'

'Well, maybe it hasn't been years. But I bin clean fo' months. Ever since I did that clinic trial at Blackrock,' I lie.

'Really? It says here that you left the trial after only four days?'

'Whatever.'

'Whatever? Christy. Your history suggests you are a woman who has relied on Class A drugs for the best part of twenty-five years. It *also suggests you are untrustworthy, given your records of consistent theft, isn't that correct?'*

I start swishin' ma hands around on ma knees. This ass hole really rilin' me up. Jonathan told me he would. But I thought I be strong enough to get through it. Any time I play with my hands like this, I know I need me some meth. It's been three weeks now since Jonathan put me up in a hotel and told me to sober maself up befo' I took the stand. But tonight... tonight when I get back home, I'm gonna get straight on the phone. I need ma fix. I gotta get me some shit, just to get over this shit.

'Yeah. I guess ma history does suggest I'm a drug taker and that I'm untrustworthy,' I say. Then I shrug one shoulder at him. 'But I tell ya somethin', mister lawyer man, I ain't lyin' bout this. She told me she done it. That gal confessed to me.'

Joy was practically skipping behind Mathilda, her arms swinging by her side, a smile stretching across her face.

'And he said – and these are his words because I chose there and then to remember them – "there's a great chance" – a *great* chance, Mathilda!'

'Cool,' Mathilda said as she waddled her way around the maze of landings to lead the excitable prisoner back to Elm House.

'Are you not happy for me?' Mathilda shrugged her shoulders, not even bothering to turn around. 'Where's Aidan? I need to tell Aidan. Why didn't he bring me to my meeting with Gerd Bracken, I know he's rostered to be working today?'

Mathilda cleared her throat.

'He eh... was called up for a meeting with the Governor.'

'Well, I guess I'll tell him when I see him.'

Joy continued to skip and grin while following Mathilda all the way back to Elm House. Bracken had just informed her that her retrial had been officially granted – all three judges in the Criminal Court of Appeal agreed that the fresh evidence brought to them was enough to warrant Joy another day in court. The consensus seemed to be, in the judges' summoning up, that while they felt Mathieu Dupont's technological breakthrough to be less than one-hundred percent scientific, the fact that Bunny the Dog had been found to be a fraud in a court of law overseas was ample reason to order the retrial. Which was odd, Bracken had told Joy when delivering the news, because he thought it'd be the other way around.

'So now we have to start planning for the retrial... what we need to concentrate on is convincing a jury or a judge or whatever road they go down with this that you are not the woman in that CCTV footage. If we can pour doubt on that, then I think we have a great chance of finally getting you out of here.'

'When will the retrial be d'you think?' Joy asked, her face beaming, 'think I'll get out before Christmas?'

Bracken puffed a laugh out of the side of his mouth, then he leaned forward.

'Joy... this will take some time. Again. It may even be up to another two years before we get back into a courtroom. We gotta join the queue... and I can't tell you how long that queue is. Besides, with your retrial, who knows what way the justice system will even try it. They might not see a jury as being suitable... I mean, who doesn't know about the Joy Stapleton case? So, this could rumble on and on...'

'Two more years?' she said, grimacing.

But it didn't dampen her spirits. She was high as a kite. Especially after Bracken said he had to leave her to it because he had scheduled a press conference and was about to let the whole nation know that Joy Stapleton had been ordered a retrial – and that Ireland's most infamous prisoner may have been innocent all along. The Joy is Innocent campaign will be abuzz. Half of the nation will say, 'I told you so.'

'Listen, listen,' Joy squealed, clenching up her fists and excitedly shaking them at her fellow inmates as soon as she arrived back in the TV room, 'I've got it! I've bloody got it! A retrial.'

'Well, holy shit,' Linda said, standing up and hugging a bouncing Joy.

Nancy remained seated on the worn sofa, her arms folded as she stared over Joy's shoulder at the TV.

'Right Said Fred.'

'Huh?' Joy said, her face scrunching up at Nancy.

'Right Said Fred. Which 80s pop band had a hit with a song titled *Don't Talk, Just Kiss*? Right Said Fred. It wasn't one of their big hits, but I was a fan back in the day....'

Joy looked over her shoulder at the repeat of *Tipping Point* playing on the screen.

'Didn't you hear what I just said, Nancy? They're giving me a retrial. They confirmed it at the Courts of Criminal Appeal this morning. My lawyers out there talking to the press right now as we speak. It's official.'

Nancy heaved herself up from the sofa, by griping a clawed hand to Linda's knee.

'I'm happy for ya. I am.'

She slapped Joy on the back, then refocused her stare to the TV screen.

Joy's relationship with Nancy had been awkward and undefinable ever since she beat her up almost a year ago. But Nancy kept claiming her undying love for Joy until Joy eventually gave in and forgave her, but only because it made her life easier to not be ignored by the entire wing, all of whom had begun to blank her because she wouldn't speak to Nancy. The two of them had been back talking for months now, but their relationship was undeniably strained. And awkward. They rarely spoke, not until Nancy felt horny and would sidle up to Joy and insist on being fingered. Joy wasn't receiving any fingers in return, not anymore. But that was fine by her. She'd just close her eyes, give Nancy all four fingers until she couldn't take them no more, then they'd both get back to folding bedsheets before being locked up for the night.

'Has anyone seen Aidan?' Joy asked, her fists still clenched with excitement.

The heads around her shook, then some of the inmates leaned into her for a celebratory embrace; though they seemed unsure. But only because while they knew they should be happy for Joy, Nancy had set an unenthusiastic tone to receiving Joy's news, and the ambience had fallen flat. Joy's fists released and the bubble of excitement began to dilute in her stomach.

But just as it did, in the midst of the awkward silence that followed a couple of the loose hugs she received from her so-called friends, she heard the voice she'd been waiting to hear. He was outside, asking if Joy was back from her meeting yet.

'Aidan, Aidan,' she shouted, running towards the door of the TV room, 'I got it! I got it! They're giving me a retrial.'

She stopped short of hugging him, only because she knew it to be frowned upon. But she so desperately wanted to. Instead, she stood in front of him, ringing her hands and smiling from ear to ear.

Aidan bit the bottom of his lip, then, in seeing Joy's excitement, beamed a grin at her, before reaching a hand to her shoulder.

'I'm so happy for you,' he said. Then the grin dropped from his face.

'What is it? What's wrong?' she asked, her smile dropping too.

'It's your father,' Aidan said, his fingers squeezing at her shoulder, 'I'm sorry, Joy, but he didn't wake up this morning.'

---

774 days ago...

She closed her eyes softly, allowing the gentle breeze to tickle her curls. Then she inhaled a fresh breath of air. It had been a year since she'd felt a breeze. The large sixteen-foot fences and walls around the prison made it nigh on impossible for winds to penetrate.

When she opened her eyes again, it was the green that stole her gaze; the grass, the stems of the flowers, the leaves of the trees that stood tall only fifty-feet away. She'd never found a tree more interesting to look at; had never even thought to stare at one for so long. But here she was, enraptured in its bulging trunk and the thick branches that bent and arched away from it. The leaves seemed luminous, and the flowers, in rows all around her, were so multi-coloured that it seemed as if the brightness of the outside world had been heightened since she'd last been out here.

Aidan stared at the profile of her face as she soaked in the tree, then he jangled the cuffs a little, and ever-so-slightly rubbed his knuckles against hers.

She blinked herself back to the present, glancing at Aidan quickly, before glaring down at the hole in front of them.

'We lay to rest Noel Benjamin Lansbury. Noel, may you rest in peace in the arms of our Lord.'

Six strange men, all dressed in black suits and shaking with cold, balanced the coffin on to two leather straps, before slowly lowering it to the bottom of the grave.

Joy looked around herself at the pitiful attendance. Two of her father's old workmates – one of whose name she had forgotten – and good old Pat Traynor; the one friendly neighbour everybody adored from the tiny cul-de-sac Joy had grown up in. There were a gaggle of women, none of whom Joy recognised, and two nurses from the home Noel had spent the past six years residing in; noticeable because they wore a ribbon around their necks that was emblazoned with the care home's logo – just to ensure their attendance was noted, Joy assumed. And then there was Ray De Brun. For some reason. The detective who spent all that time with her, telling her he was going to bring her boys back before he finally showed his true colours and arrested her for their murder. She knew he had spoken to her father multiple times during the investigation, and that he had once paid a visit to his care home to pass on his regards, but she was surprised he was here for the funeral. He had thinned his lips when he saw Joy enter the small church cuffed to Aidan. In fact, he made the same face everybody in attendance made at her when she met their stare. They all seemed to lose their lips and offer a very subtle nodding of their heads.

She got distracted by the breeze picking up, rustling through her tight curls, so she closed her eyes again as the priest mumbled a prayer, and inhaled fresh air through her nostrils. Then she noticed everybody blessing themselves and before she caught up with the act, not easy when you're handcuffed, most of the crowd had begun to disperse.

'You, eh... you wanna go, or hang on a bit?' Aidan said.

Joy looked back over her shoulder, towards the marked police car in the car park that had two police officers inside, waiting to escort her back to Mountjoy.

'How long will they give me?'

Aidan shrugged a shoulder.

'Let's stay until they call you, huh?'

She smiled at him, then subtly allowed her knuckles to brush off his again. He looked so handsome in his long navy double-breasted overcoat.

'Wanna join me on my hunkers?' Joy said, raising her cuffed arm. And then Aidan slowly lowered to his hunkers, before Joy joined him, staring down on to the top of the coffin.

'That was weird seeing all those old faces,' Joy said.

'Nobody really said anything to you, did they?' Aidan replied, squinting through the breeze towards the gate at the far end of the cemetery where the small gathering were filing through the over-sized gates.

'Nope,' Joy said, 'But I know what they all would have said to try to console me: that he died in his sleep, so he went out in a good way. But he didn't. Did he? You actually couldn't go out any worse than my dad did. First, he lost his wife just half-way through her life, then his two grandkids go missing. Then his daughter is all caught up in the storm and wrongfully sent down for two life sentences. I mean... no wonder he was in a mental home by the time he was in his mid-fifties...' She sobbed a little, but then steadied herself. Her dad was only sixty-one when he passed; he got a decade more than her mother. But those ten years were as miserable as life can possibly get. The Lansbury's were once one of those enviable families – always by each other's side. Noel and Monica had been a proper partnership. Never shaken. They had tried for almost seven years after getting married in 1979 to have children, but it turned into a struggle. It wasn't until they had been for multiple tests that doctors got to the bottom of the problem. It was Monica; her eggs were limited. *Very* limited. She had one chance at IVF, and even at that there were no guarantees. But it worked out. Nine months later Joy arrived, kicking and screaming. The trio were inseparable until Joy was swept off her feet by a Dublin hero when she was just eighteen. And then, sometime not long after that, their whole lives turned into a nightmare from the first day Monica was diagnosed with breast cancer. She passed away not knowing Joy was pregnant with a grandson she would have just doted on. Joy didn't know she was pregnant either. Not

226

until the following week, when she was still in the throes of her grief.

'It's such a shame you never got to tell him you had been offered a retrial.'

'Pffft... that's typical me though, isn't it? I had literally come looking to tell you in the prison, then I wanted to go call him to let him know. He would've been so happy for me.'

Aidan glanced at Joy's profile.

'At least you've got all that to look forward to though, huh?'

'What have I to look forward to, though? Even if I do get out... where would I go? Who am I getting out to? I've nobody. Not a husband no more. Not a son no more. Not a parent... Not even a friend.'

She sniffed up her nose, determined not to cry, then she gently took another of those fresh inhales through her nostrils, just to steady herself.

'Listen,' Aidan said, pinching Joy's fingers between two of his. 'I just want to say, cos I didn't really get a chance to yesterday, but... I'm super happy for you. Thrilled. You gotta keep this to yourself because us officers, we're not supposed to say anything like this, but...' he looked back over his shoulder, towards the car park, 'I've always thought you to be innocent. Always. From before I even met you.'

Joy stared into Aidan's blue eyes.

'I know you did.'

'I was glued to the coverage of your trial just as I was finishing my training as a prisoner officer. It's funny. I often wondered that if you were convicted whether or not I'd ever get to meet you in Mountjoy. And there you were on my very first day, the very first prisoner I ever got to escort to a cell. Funny how life works out sometimes, innit? But I was hoping I'd never meet you, because I never believed you should have been sent to prison. I thought your trial was bullshit. I knew the dog was bullshit, knew the CCTV couldn't be proven. I truly hope they over-turn your conviction at this retrial. I mean, I'll miss ya 'n' all... but...'

He shrugged a shoulder at her and smiled.

'Why d'ya have to be fuckin gay?' she asked, beaming a smile back at him.

'Why? Do you still fancy me?' He laughed out loud. 'Don't think I've ever forgotten you tried to kiss me.'

Joy held her free hand to her face, to smother her embarrassment with it.

'Has anyone else been trying to kiss you lately?'

'Ahh, that'd be telling, wouldn't it?'

'Go on... tell me.'

'No. It's nothing. Nothing. It's the gay scene, isn't it? Loadsa chances of one-night stands, very little chance of actually finding somebody you want to see again after those one-night stands... typical.'

'Ye filthy sodomists,' she said, giggling. And then Aidan shouldered her. He didn't mean to push her that hard, but she stumbled and fell, and then he fell on top of her as the cuffs dragged him down. He immediately got up. Offered his free hand to help Joy to her feet, before he brushed down his knees in a fit of giggles.

Then he stared over at the two officers sat in the front of the police car and was relieved to see them sat still, unmoving.

'I'm serious, Joy,' Aidan said, gripping her hand again. 'I looked into your case as much as I could. And I know you. I've gotten to know you well over the past six years, despite our ups and downs. You're no murderer, Joy Stapleton. I know you're not.'

Delia's stare hasn't left Christy in quite some time – not even to glance at Jonathan Ryan as he is posing his questions. She has been fascinated by this witness, intrigued by the testimony she has just provided. Though the witness certainly has come across as troubled, what with her swearing on the stand and Bracken delving deep into her long history of theft. Yet Delia has been left feeling there was a sense of sincerity in how the witness spoke about Joy. Delia was wondering, as she studied Christy's heavy, bloodshot eyes, whether the witness possibly believed wholeheartedly that Joy confessed to her, even though Joy never did. Perhaps the drugs had played their part in convincing Christy she heard what she wanted to hear. The alternative theories were probably just as likely. Maybe Christy is aware she is lying, and at some stage decided to just turn on Joy. Or maybe, just maybe, Christy was actually telling the truth. Maybe Joy did confess to her.

Delia scribbled a question mark in her notes, then turned to Jonathan Ryan as he approached the witness box again.

'You have been clean of drugs for some considerable time, Christy. And you have begun to turn your life around... correct? I mean you haven't been in prison since 2017. And here is Mr Bracken trying to tear down all of your progress by bringing up your past. Christy, if I can ask you to say again what it is you came here to say... is it true that inside Mountjoy Prison in 2017, Joy Stapleton confessed to you that she had murdered her two sons?'

'Yep, it sure is. She confessed to me. She did.'

'Thank you, Christy Jabefemi, for your time. You are now free to leave.'

Delia stares over the rim of her glasses at the witness as she climbs down from the box before hobbling her way down the aisle. Then the judge pulls back the sleeves of her robe to check her watch just as Christy is pulling back the double doors, and notes that it's just gone two p.m. So, she sucks through her teeth, and stares down at Jonathan Ryan.

'Are we calling it a day, Your Honour, or would you like me to introduce my next witness?' he asks.

'Let's, eh...' Delia hesitates, 'let's take a quick recess. Fifteen minutes. Court will resume at two twenty precisely.'

She bangs down her gavel once, then gets to her feet and rushes out the side door. She offers a thin smile to the young woman dressed in black and – all of a sudden – she just collapses, her back sliding down the wall until her ass reaches the cold tiles.

'I just need to sit... sit anywhere but in there,' she says to the woman dressed in black, before producing a long sigh. 'You couldn't just give me ten minutes, could you? I, eh... I know my office is only twenty paces away, but I just feel as if I need to breathe before I walk again.'

'Sure thing, Judge McCormick,' the woman dressed in black says. Then she turns on her heels, leaving Delia to sit alone in the overly-lit hallway, her head in her hands.

She tries to steady her breathing as she soaks Christy Jabefemi's testimony into her mind; trying to gauge it within the context of everything else she has heard over the course of this retrial. She couldn't make it all the way to her office because she was jaded; and she is jaded because her filtering system has been working overtime – her mind splintering in so many different directions.

Then the side door sweeps open beside her, and her son appears.

'Oh hey,' he says, blinking at the sight of his mum's legs stretched across the tiles. 'Was just coming to see you.'

'Course you were,' she says, puffing a laugh into her hands.

'That was some testimony, huh? This is over – she's guilty. This retrial paints her even more guilty than the original.'

Delia removes her hands from her face.

'Really?'

'Mum... don't tell me you don't agree? I mean, you're not still thinking about that bloody cadaver dog, or Mathieu Dupont's testimony, are you? Mum...' Callum takes a step closer and stands over his mother. 'This is open and shut. Just deliver the guilty verdict and get me out of this mess.'

'Making it all about yourself again.'

'Mum, this will destroy me.'

'Calm down, Callum,' she says, whispering and then pointing at the courtroom door he had just exited. 'You think that witness was reliable... really? Ponder this for a second, yes? Joy Stapleton murders her two children, then keeps it secret from the entire world for the past twelve years. She doesn't tell a soul. Not one of her loved ones, not her best friend, not her husband. Not a police officer. Nor a doctor. Nor a psychiatrist. Yet despite keeping it a secret for so many years from so many loved ones and so many professionals, she just happened to let it slip to a prison junkie? Of all people. Really? You think that's plausible?'

Callum circles his foot on the checkered tiles.

'You allowed the witness.'

'I allowed her because I thought it'd be beneficial to hear the testimony of the person Joy spent most of her time with just after she was incarcerated. I was intrigued to understand how different Christine Jabefemi's opinion of Joy Stapleton would be compared to anybody else. Even as much as Shay Stapleton's. Or Lavinia Kirwan's. I wanted an insight into the convicted Joy. The Joy who was behind bars... to see if she was any different post-conviction to how she was pre-conviction.'

'Exactly,' Callum says, 'and that's what you got. Joy admitted to a prisoner that she did it. You got what you wanted...'

'Just because I allowed the witness, doesn't mean I have to buy everything she testified. Christine Jabefemi is hardly a model witness.'

'She is a witness who knew the defendant—'

'Shhhh,' Delia whispers. 'Keep your voice low. Besides... I'm the bloody judge here, okay? Only I know why I allowed Christine Jabefemi to testify. Only I can glean from her testimony whether or not she is being sincere.'

'Mum, I don't give a shit,' Callum says, keeping his voice low, but his tone curt, 'about Christine bloody Jabefemi's sincerity. I just want to know you are going to do the right thing; that you are going to get me out of this mess.'

'I thought you were getting yourself out of the mess,' Delia says, folding her arms.

'The private eye hasn't got back to me. I've left about half a dozen missed calls on his phone between last night and this morning. He said he was looking into things... But I'm not sure he's going to be quick enough. He might not get much information for me before this trial ends. You've only one bloody witness left now anyway, haven't you? Final arguments will be tomorrow. You might even have a verdict back by tomorrow afternoon.'

Delia rolls her eyes to stare up at her son, and then snorts out a laugh.

'That won't be happening. I'll be taking my time. Let's see what Detective Ray De Brun has to say anyway.'

'Well, hopefully De Brun will be able to convince you of Joy's guilt again. Because I think you have somehow been slanted on this... you seem like you're determined to acquit her...'

'Slanted? Me?' Delia holds a hand to her chest. 'Determined to acquit? Where did you get that from?'

'Well you keep constantly arguing with me about it. I keep telling you she's guilty, you keep pushing back.'

'I'm not pushing back on guilty. I'm just not jumping the gun like you are. Besides, I've taken all of my emotion out of this. You clearly haven't. I haven't told you I am leaning either way yet. Because I'm not leaning either way. It's too early for a judge to pass judgement. And you need to learn that, son. You should have learned that already. I'm assessing every witness testimony and every slice of evidence being offered up just as I'm supposed to. So, stop assuming you can read my mind. If you could, you'd be able to tell that I haven't made my mind up at all, yet. Far from it, in fact.'

They both pivot their heads and stare up the hallway as a sweeping of feet brushes its way towards them.

'Sorry, Judge McCormick,' the young woman dressed in black says as she walks into view. 'I was asked to get back to my post because it's 2:18. Court is set to resume in two minutes.'

'Oh crikey, that fifteen minutes flew,' Delia says, readjusting so she's on all fours before she steadies herself to her feet. She then puffs out her cheeks and slaps her son between his shoulder blades. 'Time to get back to it, Callum,' she says. 'Take your seat. I'll be in in one minute.'

Callum pulls at the side door and disappears, but not without huffing and puffing.

'You can let them know I'm coming,' Delia whispers to the young woman dressed in black, then she, too, pulls open the side door Callum has just disappeared through, and nods inside.

'All rise!'

Delia winks at the woman as she passes her, then she climbs her way to her highchair.

There is a lot of chatter in the courtroom, but that's only because most of the gallery didn't bother leaving their pews for the short fifteen-minute break, preferring instead to debate Christine Jabefemi's testimony with the folk sat next to them.

'Mr Ryan,' Delia shouts, arching her eyebrows over her glasses and putting an end to the chatter.

Ryan stands and straightens his tie.

'Your Honour, I call Ray De Brun to the stand.'

A rotund, bald man with an overgrown grey moustache, rises from the middle of the gallery, apologising with whispers as he brushes past attendees in his row, before pounding his heavy frame down the aisle and up into the witness box.

Instead of paying attention to the witness being sworn in, Delia reshuffles the paperwork in front of her, then gives up looking for the sheet she needed when Ryan takes to the middle of the courtroom floor.

'Thank you for your time, Detective De Brun.'

'Ex detective.'

'Yes; ex detective. You retired in...'

'2016.'

'After how many years on the force?'

'Forty, exactly.'

'Impressive. And how many years as a detective?'

'Thirty-two.'

'You were one of longest serving detectives in the history of the state when you retired, correct?'

'So they tell me.'

'Well, thank you for your service, Detective De Brun. Let me ask you this... in those thirty-two years you led the investigation on some of Ireland's most notorious cases... But, of course, the reason you are here today is because you were lead detective on the Stapleton case, correct?'

'Yes. I certainly was.'

'From day one, right? When Reese and Oscar Stapleton were reported missing, who was the first detective assigned to the case?'

'I was.'

He fingers the blunt-edges of his moustache, then scratches at the aging freckles that are forming a map on his scalp.

'You worked on the case for over two years; two as a missing person's case and then a further two months after that when it turned officially into a murder investigation, right?'

'Yes. And I stayed with this case all the way through to conviction.'

'So, it would be fair to suggest you know this case better than anybody?'

'I've certainly poured more hours into it than anybody. And I can also say that I've poured more hours into the Stapleton case than I did any other case in my entire career.'

'Impressive. And you say you saw the case all the way through to conviction. It was you who literally arrested Joy Stapleton for the murder of her two sons in January of 2011, correct?'

'Yes, I did.'

'And can you tell us why you arrested her?'

'Why I arrested her?'

'Yes, Sir.'

'Well... because she murdered her two sons.'

RAY DE BRUN

'So, it would be fair to suggest you know this case better than anybody?'

'I've certainly poured more hours into it than anybody,' I say. 'And I can also say that I've poured more hours into the Stapleton case than I did any other case in my entire career.'

It's true. This case was a nightmare for me right from day one. And it's a nightmare that never seems to want to end. Not with half the country believing she's innocent – judging the entire case on tabloid headlines. They don't know the case like I do. Nobody does.

'Impressive. And you say you saw the case all the way through to conviction. It was you who literally arrested Joy Stapleton for the murder of her two sons in January of 2011, correct?'

'Yes, I did.'

'And can you tell us why you arrested her?'

'Why I arrested her?'

'Yes, Sir.'

'Well... because she murdered her two sons.'

Ryan pauses for a gasp from the gallery after I say that. And it arrives right on cue. Only because he set it up. He told me, when we rehearsed what I was gonna say up here, that there'd be a gasp when I bluntly delivered the line "She murdered her two sons." I think it's a guy who works in his law firm who produced it. But it seems to work. The courtroom has fallen silent, and the judge is scribbling away on her notes.

'So, you investigated this case from day one, Detective De Brun, and worked on it for over two years – put more work into this than any other case, you say?'

'It was more than two years. It was two years between the case opening as a missing person's case and the eventual arrest for double homicide. But I worked on it a lot more after that. The original trial took almost a further two years to come around... and I worked hard on the case all the way up to that. Heck, I'm still working on it today.... sitting here.'

'Yes... much more than two years, that is correct. And the state thanks you for your dedication to true justice. But just to go back a bit... past the second year you worked on this case, you arrested Joy Stapleton because, as you have just said, she murdered her two sons. Why were you and the police force so convinced of Joy Stapleton's guilt?'

I blow through the bristles of my 'tache.

'In missing children's cases, in particular, it is always key to look closest to home. In eighty-four percent of child abduction cases the culprit is found to be a family member or somebody closely associated with a family member.' Jonathan Ryan told me the statistic last week, told me it would fit in nicely with my testimony; certainly after Sandra Gleeson tried to throw me under the bus when she was sitting up here last week. 'I know an ex-colleague of mine testified here to say that we were focused on Joy Stapleton from the get-go, and that's because the statistics inform us that is the right approach to take. We rule out who we can with a matter of urgency. And we managed to rule everybody associated with Oscar and Reese out – all except for Joy. In fact, we only got more and more suspicious of her involvement as time went on.'

That's all totally true. We ruled out Shay straight away because he had been in Roscommon, lounging about in the Grand Hotel on a work trip. Shay's parents had alibis, as did Joy's father. Their closest friends and associates all accounted for. Lavinia Kirwan was on a date; Shay's best mate Steve Wood was at home with his then-girlfriend. One by one we found we could strike all family and friends from the list. Yet Joy's name remained there. In capital letters. Highlighted.

'Can you tell me when you, personally, first became suspicious of Joy Stapleton?'

'Personally? At the end of day one of the investigation... when I heard the phone call for the first time.'

'You mean the phone call Mrs Stapleton made to 999, to report that her boys had been abducted?'

'Yes. I listened to it at about eight p.m. on the first evening, and I was shaking my head listening to it. Especially as I'd just spent much of the day with Joy, consoling her.'

'Well, I think now is a good time, Your Honour, for the court to listen to the tape.'

The judge nods her head and then Jonathan Ryan holds a finger to the ceiling as if he's the conductor of some invisible orchestra up there. There's a small clicking sound, then a pause, before a crackling ringing blasts through the speakers.

'Hello'
'Somebody took my boys. They are gone. They are gone.'
'Your children are missing, ma'am, is that what you said?'
'Yes. They were on the green in front of my house. And somebody took them. My boys have been taken. They're gone.'
'Give me your address, ma'am.'
'Yes... yes... It's ninety-three St Mary's Avenue, Rathfarnham... please get here as quick as you can. My boys! My boys!'

Seventeen seconds long that call is, before Joy hangs up. It must be the thousandth time I've heard those seventeen seconds. And I am under no doubt that I have heard a guilty mother every single time.

'Can you tell us why you felt suspicious of Mrs Stapleton as soon as you heard that call, Detective De Brun?'

'The whole country has heard that call by now... it was all over the news for many a year. There's still people arguing about it online today. And I see people arguing that Joy sounded too over the top when she was screaming down the line; that she was being too dramatic an actress... but her screaming is not what was suspicious about the call for me.'

'Well, what was suspicious?'

'Her words, "Somebody took my boys".'

'And that was suspicious because?'

'It sounded to me as if she had already decided what her narrative was going to be – that her sons were abducted. She said it right from the off. She didn't say they were missing. She said they were taken. That somebody took them.'

'Interesting. But that only raised your initial suspicion, correct? It wasn't a smoking gun for you. You couldn't have been certain she was guilty because of the phone call alone?'

I shake my head and mouth a 'nope' – popping the 'p' sound into the microphone.

My thoughts on the phone call were, in truth, just instinctual suspicion, but detectives live and die by the art of using their instinct, and it always pisses me right off that so many people are keen to play that skill down. My instinct... my gut... it never let me down in forty years on the force. Certainly didn't in this case. I believed Joy Stapleton murdered her two boys from day one of this investigation. And I was dead right. We didn't take our eyes off her during the process of the missing person's case, but we had nothing to go on for such a long time. The dog evidence was never a clincher for us. In fact, there was no clincher for two years – not until the bodies were found. Then we turned the heat up on her. Nobody else seemed to suspect a thing. I remember Shay, God love him, storming up his garden path one day when he saw me coming to his house and asking me out straight if I was genuinely considering Joy as a suspect. He had tears running down his face. I'm not sure Shay has ever been fully convinced of Joy's guilt, and he certainly let that be known at his testimony yesterday – but his mind has been clouded by too much emotional attachment. It's been really sad watching him go downhill over the years. The poor man is living in a warped universe. I'm surprised he hasn't gone mad. Though I did notice when I saw him at the courts yesterday *that he has aged terribly. Such a shame. He didn't deserve this life.*

'Even though you brought in the cadaver dog who indicated a body or bodies may have decomposed in the Stapleton household, you still didn't arrest Joy Stapleton, did you?'

'We had so little to go on. No bodies, no evidence whatsoever. It seemed to the naked eye as if the boys had just vanished into thin air. Only we had spoken to Joy's best friend Lavinia Kirwan who I know also testified at this trial and she had told us Joy had been acting strange for a couple of months leading to the boys' disappearance. We also observed changes in Joy as the case was on-going ourselves. The psychologists who spoke to her during the course of the investigation very often reported that Joy would speak like a fantasist; saying she always felt Oscar and Reese would grow up to be superstars or superheroes or something like that. And she was also observed as having a natural ability to emotionally manipulate... we saw her manipulate those out searching for Oscar and Reese, she tried to manipulate some of our police officers, too. She even manipulated her own husband, Shay. It was just a subtle personality trait she had. But we zoned in on it. She was a strong voyeur, too. She would stand back and watch everybody; watch the investigation unfold... She knew everybody's business. She also had a history of abuse, albeit small. Her father used to smack her when she was younger. And I have to tell you, Mr Ryan, that all these traits I have just mentioned; a fantasist, emotionally manipulative, a voyeur, a history of abuse... they are all the traits associate with killers. It's just that Joy Stapleton doesn't look like your everyday killer. Even though she is one of the most cold and calculated killers I have ever come across.'

Everything I'm saying is true, apart from the history of abuse thing. That was minimal. One time at the start of the investigation, during what he thought was routine questioning, her father, Noel, admitted he used to smack her as a toddler – only if she was naughty, mind. It was no big deal. But it helped with our argument of listing traits Joy has in common with other murderers. The other traits I've listed – a fantasist, emotionally manipulative, a voyeur –

they are all traits Joy genuinely possesses. In abundance. She killed those boys and tried to hide it from us as we investigated. But she wasn't doing quite as good a job of it as she thought she was. We were on to her all the time. We just couldn't find the bloody evidence to nick her. Which is a great shame. I'm aware more than anyone that the evidence is light-weight in this case. But I always felt when we got that CCTV footage of the pink hoodie, even though her face wasn't shown in it, that we had enough to put her away – certainly enough for a jury made up of everyday people to put her away. But a judge, somebody who knows law inside out, well... now that is a different type of persuasion. And I'm worried... I'm worried Joy might get out. She doesn't deserve her freedom. That's why I'm testifying again here today. And why I rehearsed with Jonathan Ryan what I needed to say. We have to get this right. We need to convince the judge she has to uphold the original verdict.

'And then two years later, a member of the public happened upon the bodies and the investigation dramatically changed from there, isn't that correct?'

'Yes. A dog walker.'

'But the scene or the bodies didn't give you as much evidence to go on as you would have liked...'

'Nope,' I say, shaking my head. 'All that was left of Oscar and Reese was bone. And the scene itself had long since weathered away any indication that might have led us to a suspect. I mean studies on the bones suggest there was no sign of a struggle and therefore it is likely Oscar and Reese knew and trusted their killer, but there was no direct forensic evidence at the scene by the time we got to it, no.'

'But then, a few days later you came across the CCTV footage.'

'Then we found the CCTV footage, yes. And everything changed.'

'Everything changed?'

'We knew we had her. That is Joy in that CCTV footage, just yards from where the bodies were found. She is walking back down the mountain on the night we believe her sons were murdered and dumped in that wasteland. It was the night before she reported them missing with the phone call you just played to the court.'

'You have no doubt she is responsible for killing her two sons, do you, Detective De Brun?'

'None whatsoever,' I say, leaning closer to the microphone. 'Listen, Joy Stapleton had no alibi for the night we believe the boys were killed. She says she was at home alone with them, but she has no witness to back that up. There are also no witnesses whatsoever to the crime Joy claimed; that they were snatched from the green area in front of their garden. Then she makes a mistake by telling 999 when she made the emergency call exactly what she wanted her narrative to be. Then she acted with all these strange behaviours over the course of our investigation, right in front of us. And then, low and behold, she was spotted on CCTV footage not far from where the bodies were buried. She is as guilty as they come. It just took us a couple of years to be able to provide proof of her guilt. Which we did, of course. This case went to court, let's not forget that. And that court found her guilty. And the court found her guilty because she is guilty.'

'Detective Ray De Brun, thank you for your time.'

I release a sigh of relief as Jonathan sits back down beside his legal team, but I know I'm only half-way through this – with the worst half yet to come. I can't stand Gerd Bracken. I mean, his cause should be so worthy – trying to get innocent folk out of prison. But this guy isn't interested in the justice of it at all. He's only interested in making a name for himself. He's a narcissist – there's no doubt about that. As soon as that cadaver dog, Bunny, was outed as having made a mistake in a case in England a few years ago, he jumped all over Joy Stapleton because he thought if he could over-turn the most infamous case in Ireland's judicial history then he'd make an even bigger name for himself. He's a disgrace. There's no way even he can believe Joy Stapleton is innocent. The smarmy prick literally lies to himself for a living.

'Ex Detective,' he says appearing in front of me, his legs standing slightly wide apart, his hands clasped against his stomach, 'correct me if I'm wrong, but you have just testified here today that you felt Joy was guilty for two whole years but you couldn't arrest her because you couldn't prove it in a court of law, correct?'

'Correct.'

'Correct? So, the cadaver dog. The voyeurism you accuse my client of having, the personality traits you have testified here today suggesting she proved to you, without providing us any proof whatsoever, the phone call that in your opinion she is acting in... all these pieces of evidence you were building up against my client... they weren't enough for an arrest?'

'No. They weren't.'

'Good,' he says, 'then I can throw most of my questions away. Because, ex Detective, I was going to ask you about all these nuances and redundant pieces of evidences, or opinions as I would label most of them. But you have just admitted to us all under oath that these are pretty much redundant because they weren't enough to warrant arrest.'

'They weren't enough to warrant arrest, but I wouldn't call them redund—'

'Now, ex Detective,' he says, talking over me and looking all smug, 'that only leads us to the CCTV footage then, doesn't it? The only reason you arrested Joy Stapleton is down to that CCTV footage, correct?'

'It's not only down to the CCTV. We built a case around her....'

'Yes, but a case that wouldn't, in your words, have led to a conviction without the CCTV, right?'

I cough and fidget in the chair.

'I guess so.'

'Well, not "I guess so". I know so. Sure, you just said that yourself on the stand.'

'Okay. Then, yes. We would not have got a conviction without the CCTV.'

'And yet we've all seen the CCTV footage. And nobody can see a face in that CCTV footage. All we see is a figure walking past a garden wall in a pink hooded top, isn't that correct?'

'We know it's Joy.'

'You don't know it's Joy. You can't possibly know it was Joy. Besides, there was never any footage found of this figure going up the mountain. Only down. How do you explain that?'

This argument irks me. Has always irked me.

'She likely walked up on the other side of this street where the CCTV didn't reach. Or maybe she even went up the mountain via a different way. Truth is, we've never quite known exactly how she got up there. How she got the boys up there. But we know she did it. Because we found film of her coming back down that mountain. On top of that, Mr Bracken, this argument was addressed in the original trial. We only found footage of Joy walking back down the mountain. But it is Joy. We know it's Joy.'

Bracken puffs out a small laugh.

'You keep saying that, ex-Detective. But you can't possibly know for sure that is Joy in that footage, can you? You can't see more than the rest of us can see with all due respect. You're not a superhero. You don't have x-ray vision, do you, ex-Detective?'

'Mr Bracken,' I say, leaning towards the microphone, 'don't let the conspiracy theories fool you. A woman walking away from the scene of the crime wearing the only hooded top in the whole country which we know Joy owned, a woman of Joy's height and description, on the exact night the crime took place... Let me tell you, Sir. There is no conspiracy to be had here. There is no coincidence. There has never been any such thing as a coincidence in this entire case.'

349 days ago…

'We don't even have to prove it was a coincidence,' Bracken says. 'We just have to pour doubt on the case the state proved against you in the original trial. When Ray De Brun testified in that original trial, his expertise was given too much credence. The jury bowed down to him. They took him at his every word. But I'm gonna tell him out straight when we get him on the stand in the retrial that he's not superhuman, that he doesn't have x-ray vision and he can't possibly know that was you in that CCTV footage more than anybody else on this planet can. I'll prick his ego a little bit.'

Joy smiled, while both of her knees bounced up and down under the desk. She had been animated anyway; because the opportunity of freedom was now very much in sight. But after Bracken just informed her she could be set for millions in compensation if she got out, her elation has immeasurably elevated.

She was still grinning, still bouncing her knees when Aidan knocked lightly on the door before pushing it open.

'Time,' he said.

He winked at Joy when she joined him on the landing, and after she had said her goodbyes to Bracken, and she and Aidan were alone, she gripped onto his arm.

'I've got a date. Eighth of December.'

'Really? Less than a year away. You could be out for Christmas, huh?'

She gripped his arm even firmer, but then he had to shrug her off when they heard the footsteps of another prison officer coming up the stairs behind them. So, they walked, as they were supposed to, the inmate in front of the prison officer and in total silence, until they arrived back at Elm House.

She updated the prisoners she normally sits next to for meals, and while some were already excited by her court date, interest really began to inflame when she mentioned compensation.

'He said it could be millions. I mean... if I get out in December that'll mean I'll have spent eight years in prison. Wrongfully. Think they'd give me a million for each year? I'd be super rich!'

'You'd take that eight million over having your two sons, would ya?' Nancy said, cutting right through the excitement that had just fizzled across both sides of the bench.

Joy chose to ignore Nancy's negativity, and turned away to stare down the line of women on her side of the bench.

'He said the reason it took so long for them to agree to a court date was because they couldn't figure out how to run a retrial for me. Some members of the judicial board wanted a jury, but they were overruled by the Chief Justice, because they don't think they'd be able to find an unbiased jury. Too many people know about me, apparently. The Joy is Innocent campaign has lovers and haters in equal measure, my lawyer said.'

'Well, if I was a juror on your retrial, I'd let you out,' Linda said, pouting her lips and blowing a kiss across the bench. 'So... what way are they gonna do it?'

'One judge, and that's it.'

'So, all your lawyers have to do is convince one person, huh?'

'That's all,' Joy said, 'and my lawyer said I have a much better chance with somebody who knows law inside out rather than a jury of nobodies. He's really confident I will be let out. *Really* confident.' She made a screeching sound that cackled from the back of her throat and those sat around her, gripped by her excitement, squealed too. Nancy Trott didn't, though. She just stood up, snatched at her tray, whispered something into Linda's ear and then left them all to it to giddily celebrate Joy's court date. Joy had noticed everybody around her was smiling just as wide as she was. Except for Linda. Linda's smile had well and truly been wiped off her face by whatever it was Nancy had just leaned in to whisper to her.

'Oh, hey,' Joy said, pushing the door to her cell wide open.

'Hey,' Linda said.

'Whatcha doin' in my cell?'

'Just lookin' for you.'

'Sure, you know I'd be in the laundry room now – it's my shift time.'

'Oh yeah,' Linda said, her brow frowning. 'So whatcha doing back so early then?'

'I, eh... have a headache. Think it's all the excitement of yesterday. Mathilda said I could come back to my cell and have a lie down.'

'Oh...' Linda said. 'Well, eh.... Hope you feel better soon.'

Then Linda pulled open Joy's cell door and walked out.

'Eh... well what did you want me for?' Joy shouted after her.

'Oh, don't worry about it. I'll come back to you when you're feeling better.'

Joy scrunched up her face in confusion, then picked up the book she had loaned from the call-by librarian the previous Thursday and sat up on her mattress, her back resting against the cold concrete wall beside Reese and Oscar's photograph.

She was only three chapters in when she had another visitor. It was the fat red-headed prison officer who she remembered from her very first day who escorted her and Christy to the prison in the back of the van. She was never given his name, and had only ever seen him in passing when she was brought through Maple House on her way to her own private visitations.

'Joy Stapleton, stand up!' he ordered.

She looked confused, but slammed her book closed before slowly getting to her feet.

He pulled back the sheets on her bed before pivoting his head from side to side, his hands on his hips, whistling. Then he strolled towards the toilet seat in the back corner of her cell and immediately reached downwards.

Her mouth popped open when he stood back upright and held out his hand, from which was hanging a rather large bag filled with glistening crystals.

---

347 days ago...

Joy was worried; stressed. But her overall feeling was one of sheer anger. She knew she'd been set up; knew who had set her up. So, as she sat on one of the uncomfortable office chairs – which reminded her of the chairs she used to sit on at school – in another cold office, she dug her fingernails into her palms to try to dilute the frustration erupting from within her.

'If you don't mind, Gov, I'd like to sit in on this meeting. I, eh... I was asked by the prisoner to be here, and with your agreement, I'd eh...'

'Stop stuttering, Aidan,' the Governor snapped. 'Why on earth would a prison officer ask to sit in on a disciplinary hearing at the behest of a prisoner? I've been working here thirty-two years and I've never heard of such a thing.'

'It's just, eh...' Aidan looked at Joy and swallowed, before turning back to the Governor. 'Literally my first job as an officer here was to escort Joy to her cell. We've been in this prison the exact amount of time, only difference being that I get to go home every so often, though not that often, right?' he said, puffing out a laugh. He paused to allow the Governor to catch up with the joke, but too much time passed and the Governor's face remained stern and unflinching. He just glared at Aidan, waiting on him to explain himself. 'And, eh... I guess what I'm saying is that I know the prisoner well. I have worked in Elm House since my first day, and I see first-hand what goes on down there. It's not the worst House in this prison by any stretch, but I know who's in control and who's up to what. I firmly believe Joy was set up, Gov.'

'No!' the Governor said, and Aidan's face dropped. 'You can't sit in on this hearing. Get your ass out of here and you,' the

Governor said pointing at Joy, 'better explain yourself! Over three hundred euros worth of methamphetamine... what in the world are you playing at?'

Joy dug her nails deeper into her palms as Aidan squirmed his way out of the office. She had never been intimidated by the man sitting in front of her. In fact, she always thought him to be fair and reasonable – as the majority of the prison staff had been. But this was different. The Governor wasn't being his usual jovial self with her. He was pissed. Really pissed.

'Please, please don't tell my lawyer. Please don't let this story get out to the newspapers. Please. I beg you. I'm only eleven months away from my retrial, Sir, and I... I promise.' She held her hands up. 'I was set up. Linda Wood and Nancy Trott set me up. I know they did. I saw Nancy whisper something into Linda's ear yesterday. Then I found Linda lurking in my cell for no reason. Next thing I know that red-headed officer was calling by and searching my entire cell.'

The Governor leaned back in his chair, removed his glasses and washed a hand across his jowls.

'Oh, Joy, you haven't given me an ounce of trouble in all the time you've been here...'

'I know, Sir. Because I'm not one for trouble. I shouldn't even be here in the first place. I've never done anything wrong in my life. Stole a pencil off a friend of mine in primary school once... s'about all I can ever remember doing wrong. I didn't kill my boys. I didn't. And my lawyer will prove it in my retri—'

'Enough!' the Governor said, raising his voice and holding up his hand to signal that Joy should put a stop to her rambling defence.

He sat more upright, hooked his glasses back over his ears and sighed.

'I will keep this internal. Nobody else will know. I will ensure this story doesn't leak. But I'm gonna remove you from Elm House and place you in isolation for two reasons: one, as punishment for holding contraband in your cell, and two, for your own protection.'

251

'Eh... thank you,' Joy said, unsure of herself. 'How eh... how long will I need to spend in isolation, Sir?'

'Eleven months.'

'Eleven months! But, Sir, that'll bring me up to my retrial.'

'Exactly!' he said.

❖

Delia felt refreshed; as refreshed as a Criminal Court Judge could possibly feel at the tail end of a major trial. The uptake in her mood was somewhat influenced by the fact that the trial was coming to an end. But she was mostly feeling upbeat because she turned off her phone last night, poured herself a full bubble bath – as well as a full glass of Massolino Parussi Barola – and ordered Callum out of the house. She wanted, no, *needed*, an evening without distraction; does her best thinking when bubbles are hugging the cheeks of her face, and a glass of red is swirling in her one dry hand. The bubbles and the wine have proven, over time, to be the best lubricant to start the cogs of her mind-filtering process.

She lay there last night filtering out the fascinating new evidence brought by Mathieu Dupont, suggesting it simply can't be Joy Stapleton in that infamous CCTV footage; filter-processing what was and what wasn't significant about the fact that the cadaver dog, Bunny, from the original trial had since been exposed as a fraud; filter-processing the emotional pull of Shay Stapleton's testimony – and that, in stark contrast, to Lavinia Kirwan's; filter-processing the alleged confession made to former inmate Christy Jabefemi, and then filter-processing the rather convincing and direct testimony of lauded ex-Detective Ray De Brun.

She circled through the entire trial and then back through it all again while she soaked. She even had to refill the bath with hot water when the temperature dipped too cool an hour and a half in. Yet she was still far from making up her mind. Which was fine. Because she wasn't supposed to make up her mind. Not yet anyway. Not until final arguments were heard.

There were times, during her filtering process, when images of her son's erect penis would flash before her. Then arched bushy eyebrows would stain her thoughts further. But the warming serenity of the bath and wine saw to it that those flashes were kept to a minimum. She knew Eddie Taunton would have tried to reach her multiple times last night – which is the main reason she'd turned her phone off. So, it was no surprise when she arrived at her office just gone eight a.m. to find he'd left four voicemails on her desk phone. She didn't listen to any of them though; didn't need, nor want to. Whatever Eddie had to say for himself, Delia was going to judge this trial independent of his meddling. She'd get to his blackmailing in time.

'Morning,' Aisling calls out as she opens the door to Delia's office, she too looking more relaxed than she has over the course of the retrial – most likely because she has a tendency to mirror her boss's moods. Though Aisling was also aware that her workload and stress levels were about to dramatically reduce after today. And she needed a break... even more so than Delia did. She had two children at home; both under six years of age.

'Final arguments, then we're done, huh?'

'Yes. Sorry about all the late hours you've been doing over the course of this trial. You can get back to seeing your children soon.'

Aisling giggles.

'Seeing them for bath time and putting them to bed is enough,' she says.

Then Aisling's desk phone begins to ring outside and her assistant turns to rush towards it.

'No need... I can pick it up here,' her boss says.

Delia stabs at a button, answering the call and placing it on speaker.

'Hello.'

'Oh, Judge McCormick herself,' the familiar voice of Gerd Bracken says. 'I, eh... we need to talk, Your Honour. As a matter of urgency.'

'Well, we are talking, Mr Bracken. Used to be the only useful thing you could do on a phone in my day.'

A silence breezes through the speaker, and in the time that it does, Delia creases her brow at her assistant, aware something intriguing was about to be said.

'My client has had a rethink. She eh... she wants to go on the stand.'

'What!?' Delia replies, her voice high.

'Joy Stapleton wants to testify, Your Honour.'

'Is this your idea of a game, Mr Bracken?'

'No... no, Your Honour. We're being totally honest. Joy has shown more eagerness to put her own version of events across as this retrial has gone on, and especially so since Lavinia Kirwan's testimony earlier this week.'

Delia stretches both arms across her desk, spreading her fingers wide.

'I wouldn't put it past you to have planned this out, Mr Bracken. The defence have had their time... Mrs Stapleton opted not to take the stand before her retrial.'

'Your Honour, with all due respect... Joy Stapleton on the stand suits both the prosecution and the defence. I'm sure Jonathan Ryan has many a question he would like to ask her. And, personally, I'm glad I will have the opportunity to get her innocence across when she's up there. Either way, two trials have now taken place over whether or not Joy killed her two sons back in November, 2008 and not once have we ever heard from the defendant herself. She was advised not to testify in her original trial by her defence team and – to be totally transparent with you, Your Honour – we also advised her not to testify during this retrial. But now she is insistent... she wants to go on record. Under oath. She told me last night that she feels she has to do this... that she has to stand up for herself. She can't go back to prison, Your Honour. She wants to fight for the freedom and justice she is owed. She is entitled to fight for herself...'

Delia stares up at her assistant to see Aisling squelching her lips before quietly leaving the office, pulling the door quietly behind herself.

'Your Honour...'

'I'm still thinking,' Delia hisses. Then she swipes up the hand receiver of her phone and exhales heavily into it.

'Okay,' she says. 'I'll allow the witness.'

25 days ago…

Isolation had been long. And boring. *Really* boring. It was as if the days had lasted weeks and the weeks had lasted months.

Joy had to keep reminding herself that the Governor had done her a good turn by not allowing the story to leak outside of the prison walls. But while her excitement for her retrial was growing, she still felt largely frustrated by the fact that she was punished so harshly when it was so clear and obvious that she had been set up.

Initially she didn't mind being sent to isolation, but that's because she was comparing it to her time spent there in the early days of her incarceration. Back then, she was sent to isolation under caution, because her life was under threat. So, she was given all the luxuries and protection prisoners get, such as multiple hours of yard time, and a TV in her cell. But this time, because she was there under the grounds of punishment, there was no TV – and she could only visit the yard once, on her own, for one hour a day. The first time she had been in isolation was also bearable because she often had Aidan for company. But this time it was Mathilda and a new female prison officer called Anya – who was tall, thin and beautiful, like an Eastern European model – who took shifts looking after her. And neither fancied much conversation with Joy, except to order her around.

Joy had hoped Mathilda at least, who she had known for eight years now, would have melted her hard exterior somewhat, seeing as Joy's retrial had been granted and many of the national newspapers were now beginning to lead with stories suggesting her innocence. But Mathilda still treated Joy the same way she treated every other prisoner inside Mountjoy – with an evident air of superiority that she almost thought it beneath her to converse with her.

Joy's spirits had been further dampened when Aidan paid her the only visit she had had from him in all the months she was in isolation. He had been allowed to come see her, to let her know face-to-face that he was leaving the prison. The catering business he had started with his brother had finally taken off – enough for both of them to move into it full-time anyway. Besides, his relationship with Joy had been, for years, too much of a concern among the staff of the prison, and his insistence on backing her after drugs had been found in her cell was the final straw for the Governor. Although he informed Joy that he was standing down to concentrate on his catering business, she knew it was more likely a mutual agreement with the prison's board. While she painted on an excitable face for Aidan as he revealed his new business plans to her, her stomach was tossing and churning like a washing machine. She knew in that moment, more than any other over the years, that she *had* to win this retrial. There was no going back to Elm House for the rest of her life. Not without Aidan there.

Though it was Elm House she had been led back to last night. But for the first time since she'd arrived in Mountjoy she wasn't holed up in E-114, but E-108 – the cell right next to Nancy. She taped the photograph of her two boys to the wall, hoping that she'd be taking it down in a few weeks' time once her retrial had granted her her freedom, then she left her cell to go to the dining-room, flanked by Mathilda.

The atmosphere fell silent as she walked to the counter and took a plateful of lasagne from the prisoner serving it. Then she turned around and looked about herself, wondering where she should sit, feeling like the new girl all over again. Those eleven months had seemed a hell of a lot longer than eleven months, even though nothing on the wing seemed to have changed.

'Over here,' Nancy shouted from the middle of the largest pack of prisoners. Then she stood up, showing her shock of red hair, before waving her hand, beckoning Joy towards her.

Joy wandered over, slowly and uncertain, as Nancy ushered some prisoners to move along the bench so that there was room for Joy next to her.

'Great to see you,' Nancy said, wrapping both of her arms around Joy while trying to avoid the plate of lasagne she was gripping with both hands. 'Sit down. Sit down.' Nancy patted the bench next to herself. Then she immediately began asking Joy about isolation until they were finally conversing as if no time had passed at all. As Nancy repeated how much she missed Joy, all Joy could think was, *'You set me up, you devious cunt'*. But she didn't tell her face what she was thinking. Because her face smiled and frowned along with whatever it was Nancy was saying.

Although Joy's pleas to the Governor, that her drugs bust wouldn't leak outside the prison walls, were adhered to, she couldn't keep the punishment from her lawyer. Gerd Bracken was initially fuming, but Joy was keen to put his mind at rest.

'I swear I was set up. I was set up. Believe me. Please.'

Bracken made her undergo a urine test, just to prove that she hadn't been using, which did return, thankfully to him, a negative result. He needed those results in case the story ever leaked out and was brought up in the retrial. That way he'd have some proof of her innocence with regards use, at least. Though he doubted it would be brought up in the retrial. He only knew the Governor of Mountjoy to be a man of his word.

She took a seat opposite Bracken and let him know that her reintroduction to Elm House the night previous had gone as smoothly as she could have imagined.

'It's as if I hadn't been away at all,' she said, shrugging her shoulder.

And then they got down to the business Bracken had called in to the prison to discuss.

'Okay, it's less than a month until the retrial starts,' he said, 'and my assistant and I have finalised the layout of the case we're bringing to the court.'

Joy's knees began to bounce under the table.

'We're going to start with the cadaver dog, bring its owner to the stand and have him admit to the judge that the dog never had the pedigree to determine the presence of decomposing bodies. But even if he's arrogant enough to not openly admit that on the stand, we'll easily be able to get him to say that the dog had been found as a fraud in another case – and that will make an instant impact on Judge Delia. She's a stern judge, but one of the finest in the country. So, what we've been working on for the past months is a strategy of trying to convince her that a lot of doubt exists in this case, which is totally different than trying to convince a jury of twelve.'

Joy nodded her head, then muttered, 'go on.'

'Then we'll bring Mathieu Dupont to the stand. I've mentioned the name to you before... he's the French guy whose technology may or may not have a huge impact on the judge. We're taking a small risk in that we'll be comparing the height he deems the woman in the CCTV footage to be against the height you are on all of your prison records... which is out of sync when we look at them. But I'm confident his testimony will go over well. If it does, you'll be a free woman in a matter of weeks. If it doesn't, the whole retrial could go either way.'

'Well, just make it go well,' Joy said, her two knees bouncing now.

'We're going the best way we can, Joy,' Bracken said. 'And then... and then... listen, because this might make you happy, or upset in some way or... I don't know what...'

Joy's knees stopped bouncing and her nose stiffened.

'What?' she said.

'It's great news, I want you to know it's great news.'

'What is it?'

'Shay is going to testify. For you. He's going to say on the stand that he doesn't believe you murdered his boys... *your* boys.'

'Really?' Joy said, her eyes widening.

'We think it'll win the judge over. This could be the game-changer, Joy. Depends on how well Shay does up there.'

'Oh my God,' Joy said. And then she puffed out a laugh that produced both snot and tears. Bracken had to rise from his to lean over and rub her back in consolation.

'I should also say, in opposition, that the prosecutors have a big bullet in their gun, too,' he said, sitting back down. 'Lavinia Kirwan. She's still convinced you did this, Joy. And she's been added to the witness list for the prosecution. We just need to hope Shay's testimony outweighs hers in the eyes of the judge.'

Joy wiped the tears away from her cheeks, using the sleeves of her sweat top, then shook her curls at Bracken.

'It's crazy... my life in the hands of all these people... husbands, friends... detectives... bloody dog handlers. I mean... ahhh, I actually don't know what I mean.'

'I understand what you're trying to say,' Bracken said, placing his hand on top of hers. 'It can't be easy.'

'I mean why can't I get up there? Why don't I get to defend myself? If Lavinia is gonna get up there and call me a child killer, then surely I have a right to let the court know that she's just a jealous bitch who has always envied me.'

'No, no, no,' Bracken said, shaking his head and taking his hand off Joy's.

'Why? Why can't I defend myself?'

'I've told you, Joy. It just gives the prosecution too many opportunities to trip you up. Even though you're innocent, their job will still be to get you to act on impulse. And if they wind you up on the stand, it could go horribly wrong for you. It's never a good idea for the accused in any murder trial to take the stand... trust me.'

'It's just so unfair. The whole nation has had a say on whether they think I'm guilty or innocent. I seem to be the only one who never gets a say. That's just... it's just...'

'Listen.' Bracken placed his hand on top of hers again. 'We would consider putting you on the stand at the very end of the trial,' he said, 'but if we do, it's only because we'll be feeling things haven't gone as well as we would have liked. If you do end up on the stand, Joy, it would literally be a last roll of the dice kinda thing.'

JOY STAPLETON

I comb my fingers through my hair, then retighten the scrunchie around my heavy pony-tail. Gerd Bracken said it'd be a good idea if I removed all the hair from my face, so that it doesn't look as if I am trying to hide.

Playing with my hair seems to have stopped my hands from shaking. And my heart doesn't seem to be thumping as much as I thought it would as soon as I sat up here. Maybe I can do this. Maybe I just might be able to turn this whole trial around.

'Mrs Stapleton,' Bracken says.

'Call me Joy, Mr Bracken, please,' I say, snapping the scrunchie tight and then bringing my hands to rest on my knees.

'Of course... Joy.' He smiles his big teeth at me. 'Your world turned upside down on November 3ʳᵈ, 2008, correct?'

'It did, Mr Bracken. That's the day my boys were taken.'

'Can you tell the court when you first realised they were taken?'

'Where I live – lived – there's a green patch of grass straight across from the house. I often brought the boys over there. Reese would kick a football around and Oscar would bundle about after him. It's all very safe. It has a rail around the edges of it. Well, most mid-mornings the three of us would potter over and have a bit of play time there. It's literally thirty yards straight across from the house... Well, on this particular day, we were there playing and then

I realised I hadn't put the dinner on. I was going to do a chicken, and wanted to oven-roast it for a couple of hours. So, I went back to the house... which is the biggest regret I'll ever have in my life... to baste the chicken and throw it in the oven. I was four or five minutes. Four minutes. That was all. And I left the hall door open.'

'And when you came back outside?'

'They were just gone. They weren't there no more. I knew instantly somebody had taken them.'

'And what happened next?'

'I called out their names. But there was nobody around. Nothing. I knocked into my neighbour – it's the only other house that overlooks the green – but he wasn't in. Then I panicked and...' I sob. My first sob on the stand. Only one minute in. Shit. I need to get my act together. 'And then I rang the police.'

'That's correct, Joy. Almost immediately upon noticing your children were gone, you made this phone call.'

Bracken points his finger to the ceiling and there's a click sound, before the ring tone starts.

'Hello'

'Somebody took my boys. They are gone. They are gone.'

'Your children are missing, ma'am, is that what you said?'

'Yes. They were on the green in front of my house. And somebody took them. My boys have been taken. They're gone.'

'Give me your address, ma'am.'

'Yes... yes... It's ninety-three St Mary's Avenue, Rathfarnham... please get here as quick as you can. My boys! My boys!'

Every time I hear that recording even I find myself listening out for my acting skills. As if I can't even convince myself that I didn't kill them.

'Joy, it is the prosecution's claim that you are acting during that phone call. Given that I've now heard that recording about two hundred times, I'm a little baffled that they would suggest you were acting, because it sounds so legitimate to me. So raw. So emotional. For the record of the court, you weren't acting, were you?'

'Of course not.'

'You've never studied acting, never did an acting course?'

I sniffle up my nose, then remove a tissue from the pack Bracken had promised he'd place in the witness box for me.

'No.'

'No amateur dramatics... nothing like that? You weren't part of the local theatre group?'

'No.'

'The prosecution have argued, during this retrial and indeed at your original trial, that you were too keen to suggest your boys had been taken, but that's easily explainable, right?'

'Well, I was right. Wasn't I? They were taken. Two years later their bodies turn up, so I was right all along. They were taken. Somebody took them. It's not as if a four-year-old and an eighteen-month-old went on walkabouts and ended up in a shallow grave, is it? I never quite understood why they fixate on me saying they were taken. It's obvious they were taken. It was obvious at the time. There was nowhere else for them to go.'

'Thank you,' Bracken says, pursing his lips at me. He told me he'd do that every time he felt I needed to take a sip of water. So, I do. He's planned this all out. Well, apart from the fact that I'm up here in the first place. He said to me two days ago that he needed me to take the stand, that he felt the judge would really benefit from hearing from me. I'm not sure I believe him, though. Because he told me only a few weeks ago that I shouldn't testify; that if I had to it'd only be because the trial wasn't going so well. But I'm gonna turn this around today. I have to turn it around. I have to convince Judge McCormick that I didn't do this; that the only reason I'm in this mess in the first place comes down to a stupid fucking coincidence.

'Almost two years passed before you realised you were a person of interest for investigators. Can you tell me when you first realised you were being investigated yourself for the disappearance of your sons?'

'At first, I knew I was a suspect, so was Shay, so was my father, our best friends. We weren't stupid. We knew they always look closest to home in investigations like this. I just wanted them to question me, then get out there to go find out who had actually taken Oscar and Reese. So, I thought they had moved on, after ruling all of our nearest and dearest out. I thought they were looking for their kidnapper. Then they started playing silly games by bringing the dog into our home and pretending he could sniff evidence of dead bodies... I mean...' I shake my curls and then gulp.

'Yes. And as a reminder for the court, that dog has since been found to be a fraud when it comes to investigations like this.'

'I knew he was a fraud at the time,' I say. 'Well, either that or somebody who used to live in our house before us maybe died in that bedroom or something. I really didn't know. I still don't know. All's I know is that I had nothing to do with this. But they fixated on me because everybody else had alibis... whereas I was just home with the boys until...' I sob. 'Until they were taken.'

I snatch at another tissue and press it into my eyes.

'A lot of time passed without any progress in the investigation, then a dog walker came across the bodies in a remote part of the Dublin mountains... what happened then?'

'After their bodies were found, they started bringing me into the police station again, asking if I knew anything about the place where Reese and Oscar had been buried.'

'And did you?'

'Of course not,' I say. 'I knew nothing. I still know nothing. I still don't know who buried my boys in that shallow grave. And neither do the police, because they haven't looked past me.'

'And soon after the bodies were found, you were arrested, correct?'

'Yeah – five weeks later. But only because of a coincidence. I swear, Your Honour,' I say, turning to the judge while balling up the tissue in my hands, 'it's just a coincidence. That's not me in that footage. That is not me. That is not my hoodie. I swear.'

Her face softens a bit, probably to match mine. But I genuinely have no idea what she thinks of me.

'So, you have been through the unimaginable, Joy,' Bracken says. 'Your boys are snatched from just outside the house and after two years have passed a detective comes to you to say a dog-walker has *found their bodies. Then within a few weeks of their bodies being found, you are arrested for their murder?'*

I nod.

'If you can answer audibly,' the judge says.

'Yeah... yeah. I mean, it's such a big tragedy in so many ways. How can they do this to me? How can the justice system get this so wrong?'

Bracken purses his lips at me again and I reach for the glass of water, noticing that my hand is now quivering.

'It's terrible... terrible.... terrible,' Bracken says holding his chin and shaking his head. I know that he is biding time for me to compose myself. *'This is the biggest injustice this country has seen, in my opinion. And it all came down to three seconds of CCTV footage that shows a video of what looks like a woman walking past a house wearing the same hooded top as one you happened to own, yes?'*

I place my glass of water, using both hands to hold it steady, back down onto the shelf.

'When they showed me that footage, I knew it couldn't have been me. But then when they started to suggest it couldn't be anyone else, I just told them that it was a coincidence that somebody was wearing the same hoodie as me. One of the police started laughing at me when I kept saying that word. Then it was all over the newspapers, that I was defending myself by claiming a coincidence... but it's true. It is a coincidence. I don't know what else to call it. That is not me in that footage.'

'I know it's not, Joy. I do,' Bracken says. He told me he was going to say that. "An extra blanket of security while I was on the stand" he called it.

I take another swig of water, and in the time I do, I notice he has moved closer, glaring up at the witness box from just below.

'Joy, you didn't suffer with post-partem depression after the boys were born, did you?'

'No,' I say. And I say it as clearly and frankly as I possibly can. *'We were happy. I was happy. We were one big happy family. I don't know what else to say about being accused of having post-*

partem depression, because it's just not true. I know Lavinia Kirwan sat up here earlier in the week and said that I was suffering with depression before my boys went missing, but that is a very obvious lie. Shay admits he didn't think I was depressed around that time. My dad admits he didn't think I was depressed. Because I wasn't depressed. I wasn't suffering with depression at all. I was happy. We were happy. Then it all.... Then it all....' A loud sob leaps itself up from the back of my throat. And suddenly the tears pour from eyes. And my nose. I pinch at the tissues and cover my face with them, my shoulders shaking. That fuckin' bitch Lavinia. She's such a jealous fucker. Always has been. She hated that I was prettier than her. Hated that I snagged myself a Dublin footballer while she was left on the shelf.

After steadying my breathing behind the mask of tissues, I remove them from my face, then mouth a sobbing 'sorry' at Bracken.

'You have nothing to apologise for, Joy,' he says. 'It's the entire state who owe you an apology. Now,' he says, moving even closer, so close his fingers are clinging on to the edge of the witness box, 'do you know how many days you have spent in prison for this crime that you did not commit?'

I spray from my mouth as I let out a puff.

'Days... no?'

'Two thousand, nine hundred and ninety-nine,' he says. I make on 'O' shape with my mouth. 'That's right. Tomorrow will be your three-thousandth day inside Mountjoy Prison. Three thousand days, Your Honour. Three thousand days for a crime she did not commit. Three thousand days incarcerated for a crime that unearthed zero eye-witnesses. Three thousand days incarcerated for a case that offers up zero forensic evidence. Your Honour, this is the biggest miscarriage of justice in the history of our nation, and you are the only one who can put it right. I am done with my questioning, Your Honour.'

He reaches out his hand to me and squeezes my fingers, and as he does, I wipe another tissue across my face with my other hand. Then Jonathan appears, standing in front of me – all set and ready to convince this judge that I am a fucking child killer. I hate him. I hate Jonathan Ryan. He's an arrogant cunt.

'You are the only person in the country who owns one of those hoodies, Joy – right? You know it is not a coincidence that that hoodie was filmed a thousand yards away from where your boys' bodies were found on the night we believed they were first buried there.'

Wow. Straight into the coincidence. Fucker wants to squash my argument from the get-go. But I'm not for moving.

'It wasn't me. So, it has to be a coincidence.'

'I find that hard to believe, Joy.'

'What I find hard to believe, Mr Ryan, is that my boys are gone. Forever. And I've been holed up in Mountjoy Prison ever since, accused of murdering them. That's what I find hard to believe.'

He hangs his bottom lip out, then inches closer to me. And in the time he does so, I look over at Bracken, to see if he was impressed with how I answered that question. But his face is void of expression.

'Joy, your mother passed away... when?'

'Second of February, 2003.'

'2003... so just before you gave birth to Reese, right? Your first son came along eight months later?'

'Yes.'

'And then Oscar was some two and half years after Reese?'

'Yes.'

'Okay... I just wanted to get my timeframes right. So, your mother passed just before you became a mother yourself?'

I sigh out loud.

'Yes.'

'Get to your point, Mr Ryan,' the judge calls out. And I stare at her, surprised she's sticking up for me. Maybe I'm not as far behind in this race as I thought I was. Maybe the judge likes me. Maybe she believes me.

'Sorry, Your Honour,' Ryan says. 'Joy, you have testified on the stand here today that you did not suffer with any depression when your boys were born, but in truth you must have been feeling grief stricken, right?'

'I grieved the death of my mam, yes. But I'm not one to... to...'

'Not one to, what?'

'To mope. Life is what it is. I was sad my mother only got half a life. But I was also looking forward. I knew I had lives yet to live. One was literally inside me when I was at my mother's funeral.'

'So, you did grieve your mother's passing, or you didn't?'

'No, I did. Of course I did.'

'Of course you did,' he says, unbuttoning his blazer and looking smug. Then he strolls back to his desk and picks up a sheet of paper. I've no idea what he has in store for me.

'Do you know what the second most prominent trigger for post-partem depression is, Joy?'

I sigh out of my nostrils, then shake my head.

'Out loud, Joy, please,' the judge orders.

I lean closer to the microphone and whisper, 'no'.

'Grief.' He stares at me, while scratching under his chin. I don't know whether he's expecting me to answer that. But he didn't ask a question. So, I just eyeball him back while pinching at the balled tissue in my hands.

'You gave birth to two sons within the immediate years following the tragic loss of your mother and you don't feel you suffered from any post-partem depression?'

'I didn't. I loved being a mum.'

'You were spotted one thousand yards from where you buried your sons after killing them, Joy.'

'I did not!' I stand and scream. But my screaming is drowned out by Judge Delia hammering onto her desk.

'Mr Ryan, you know well it is your job to ask questions and not make judgements in my court room.'

He stands there still trying to look smug, but she just made him look like her bitch.

I toss the hard ball of tissue onto the shelf, then sit more upright and try to steady my breathing. Bracken told me that Ryan would do this, that he would constantly try to wind me up. I swore I wouldn't react. But I couldn't help it that time. Besides, the judge seems more pissed off with Ryan than me.

'Let me rephrase that, then,' Ryan says, 'I put it to you, Joy, that in a bout of depression, after you lost your mother and then gave birth to two boys, you lost control of yourself, killed your sons and buried them in the Dublin mountains.'

I grind my teeth. And as I do the judge looks at me, as if it's my turn to talk, even though he didn't ask any question... did he?

'Mrs Stapleton, the lawyer has put a claim to you... how do you respond?' the judge says.

I unclench my teeth.

'You can put that claim to me all you want, Mr Ryan. I didn't kill my boys.'

'So, after all these years you are still saying it is a coincidence that your unique pink hooded top – the only one in the country – was filmed near the scene of the crime?'

'It is a coincidence.'

'Well, it's a coincidence that didn't convince your best friend, isn't it? A coincidence that didn't convince the detectives in charge of your boys' murder investigation. And a coincidence that didn't convince this very court of law over eight years ago.' My teeth immediately snap tight again. I'm literally keeping my mouth shut until he asks a question. Bracken made me swear I wouldn't offer up any information that Ryan doesn't specifically ask for. 'Mrs Stapleton, isn't it quite apparent to you that this defence you have – of coincidence – is difficult to be believed by anyone... not even your best friend?'

'Former best friend. I haven't spoken to her in a decade.'

'Yes. Because she believes you killed both of your boys in cold blood.'

The whole room goes silent... waiting on my response. But I just sit there, staring back at him, not saying a word, my teeth snapped shut.

'Now, Joy,' he says, taking a stroll back to his desk to pick up a sheet of paper. What the fuck has he got for me now? 'I'm going to read out a text exchange between you and your husband Shay from

February 14ᵗʰ, 2008. This is just over half a year before you reported Oscar and Reese as missing persons.

What. The. Actual. Fuck?

'"Hey," it starts, "you didn't think to check your schedule?" And then Shay replies, "Jesus it's only one night a year, we can rearrange." And then you reply, "I'm thinking of rearranging my whole life, never mind one fucking dinner." Rearrange your whole life... what does that mean, Joy?'

'Oh, please,' I say, gripping on to the shelf. 'We were having an argument about Valentine's night. I thought Shay was going to arrange something romantic for us. But I had just found out, because he had rung me just before I sent that text message, that he wouldn't be home that night; that he was in some other county... staying at some hotel.'

'You were having an argument?'

I sigh, and then throw both of my hands in the air before they slap down on to my lap.

'Seriously, Your Honour,' I say, looking to the judge. 'Is he seriously trying to convince you I murdered my two boys because I was expecting dinner with my husband on Valentine's night?'

The judge doesn't answer, she just turns back to Ryan.

'Well, that's not all, Joy,' Ryan says, 'I have another text message here dated earlier than that, December, third, 2006. This is Shay texting you, "Where are you?" You took almost three hours to reply to him. And when you did, you wrote, "I am taking a little time for myself. Jesus." He replied straight away saying, "Well, of course that's no problem. But perhaps we can talk about it rather than you just racing off without telling me. The boys were just left here. I don't know what to even make them for lunch." Joy, you never replied to that text.'

'So,' I say, shrugging my shoulders.

'Well, it just makes me wonder... fond of abandoning your sons, were you, Joy?'

'You little,' I grip the shelf, digging my nails into it, the blood shooting up my neck and into my face, 'you little—'

'Calm down, Joy,' Bracken shouts towards me.

I try to steady my breathing, then I turn to the glass of water Bracken said I should turn to every time Ryan tries to rile me.

'Your Honour, if she could answer the question.'

I look to the judge. She just nods at me and I audibly sigh. What am I playing at? I need to calm the fuck down.

'I went into town to treat myself for the day,' I say as calmly as I possibly can. 'It was one day out of I don't know how many that I had to myself. What do you want me to say? You found, out of hundreds of text messages, two that might suggest me and Shay were arguing. Well whoop-de-doo, Mr Ryan – ain't you a genius. Yes, on one or two occasions me and Shay had an argument. Do you know a married couple who don't argue?'

'Joy, I asked you a simple question, and the court would appreciate an answer to it. Were you fond of abandoning your sons?'

'Of course I wasn't,' I shout. At the top of my voice. Then in the silence that follows, I manage to become conscious of reducing my tone. 'As I said, that was one time I went and had an afternoon to myself. I never abandoned Oscar and Reese. Ever.'

'Well, that's not true, is it, Joy. It says right here in this text from Shay that you left the boys without any lunch.'

'They were with their father, for crying out loud. I left them at home with their father! Do you have children, Mr Ryan?'

He glances at the judge briefly, then nods back at me.

'I have a son, yes.'

'Your wife ever leave your son with you?'

'With all due respect, Joy, I am not the one on trial here today for killing his son, now am I?' I grip the shelf again to try to contain my shaking hands. The arrogant smug bastard. 'So, let me move on, Joy. Tell me this, why did you confess to the killings of Oscar and Reese to Christine Jabefemi.'

'I did no such thing.'

'Well, now, Christine, despite her personal struggles, is a woman of strong faith. She stands to gain nothing from this trial. So, why would she admit that you confessed to her?'

'Because she's crazy. That woman does more meth than I knew

273

even existed in Ireland. She is a thief. She steals and robs and lies her way into getting her fix.'

'But you did confess to the murders to her, right?'

'No, I did not!'

'Joy, I have met with Christine Jabefemi multiple times over the past months. We have tested her for drug use. She has not used in all the time I've known her. In fact, I've just known her to be a fighter who is determined to stay clean. She has proven to be a courageous and honest and hardworking woman to me. Now, you on the other hand claim you had a happy marriage, and now here we have proof that things were not so rosy in the Stapleton household at all, sure they weren't?'

'You're a liar,' I snap, 'you are lying right now saying that Christy is hardworking and honest. She's a thief, for crying out loud. She's been a thief her whole life.'

'Calm down, calm down,' the judge says, hammering again. 'The court will ask this witness to refrain from raising her voice and reacting in the manner she just has.'

'But... but,' I stutter to the judge, 'but he's... he's...'

'Just answer the questions put to you, Mrs Stapleton. This is the reason you have been allowed on the stand... so you can answer the questions put to you.'

I swallow, then find that I'm rubbing circular patterns into my thighs with my hands. As if that's the only way I can remain composed.

'Our life together was happy. Just like Shay said when he was sitting up here earlier in the week. There were two of us in that marriage, and both of us are saying we are happy. Yet you somehow think you know better, Mr Ryan, do you? You know more about my marriage than me or my husband do?'

'Well, I wasn't asking about your marriage,' he says, offering me a smug grin, 'I was asking about your family. And while it was good to hear from your husband during this trial, and whilst it's good to hear from you, we can't hear from Oscar or Reese, can we? Because they're dead. And they're dead because you killed them.'

'I... I.... Your Honour, Your Honour,' I say, spreading my arms out with panic etched all over my face.

'Mr Ryan,' the judge says, 'please ask a question, or be done with your witness.'

Please be done with me. Please be done with me!

'I have a few more questions, Your Honour,' he says.

Shit.

He walks back to his desk, picks up a small remote control and then pinches his fingers at it. And when he does, an image flashes up on the screen in the middle of the courtroom. A picture of my boys. The same picture I have sellotaped to the wall of my cell.

'They were very handsome boys, very handsome boys, don't you think?' he asks me.

I just hold my eyes shut, then I rework the scrunchie in my hair, because my palms are actually beginning to burn with how hard I'm rubbing them against my thighs.

'Yes. Very handsome. They looked like their daddy.'

'What would you imagine they'd be doing today, if they were still alive?'

'Huh?' I say, before eyeballing the judge. But when she doesn't look at me, I glance across to Bracken. He just nods his head. So, I lean closer to the microphone.

'Well,' I sob, 'Reese would be sixteen now. And Oscar would be almost twelve. They'd be... I don't know... typical boys.'

'Think they'd have been training to get into the Dublin football team like their daddy?'

I take another tissue, then fold it over in anticipation of another loud sob.

'Probably. I mean... Yes. Who knows?'

'They would have been happy children though, right? With the world at their feet. A whole life ahead of them?'

A sob does come. But it's a quiet one. And I just find myself ripping at the tissue while nodding my head.

'Yes.'

'Well then why did you take their lives away, Joy?'

The smarmy cunt.

I'm on my feet. My arm fully outstretched, my finger pointing. The tissue raining to the ground in pieces.

'How fuckin' dare you!' I snarl through gritted teeth.

And then Bracken is suddenly on his feet too, rushing towards me while the judge is hammering down a racket.

And the flashes I get when my head is spinning start illuminating in front of me. Those fucking flashes. They haunt me; have haunted me all these years. But it's not the flash of their lifeless bodies that haunts me. And it's not the flashes of holding a chloroform-filled rag over their mouths to shut them the fuck up that haunts me either. Nor is it the flashes of dragging their bodies into a shallow grave. It's the flash of a camera that truly haunts me. A stupid fucking camera. I still see the flash of it every time I close my eyes.

❖

When the gallery finally settles, Delia consciously begins to inhale and exhale deeper... just to dampen her own emotions.

She stares at a Joy, whose sobbing shoulders are being dragged into a one-armed squeeze by Bracken, before announcing that the court will take a recess for ten minutes, ahead of each side's closing arguments.

Her heart feels heavy as she solemnly takes the three steps down from her highchair and pulls at the knob of the side door.

'Oh my,' she says, bending over to rest her hands on her knees as soon as the door has closed tight behind her.

'You okay, Your Honour?' the young woman dressed in all black asks.

Delia pants for breath, then shakes her head, still folded over.

'Tough going,' she says. 'I, eh... I'm just gonna sit here for a few minutes. Can you please make sure nobody disturbs me; that nobody comes out that door?'

'Sure thing,' the young woman says. Then she moves to stand in front of the door like a guard and clasps her fingers together.

Delia sits on the floor, her back upright against the wall, her legs stretched across the chequered tiles. She squints her eyes, the cogs of her filtering process beginning to churn. That may well be the heaviest testimony she has ever heard in all the years she's sat atop one of those highchairs. She looked so pained, did Joy, while she was up there. But why wouldn't she? Whether she's guilty or not, she's still bound to be pained. Of course she'd be hugely emotional. Of course she'd be prone to outbursts.

'Ryan certainly was trying to wind her up,' Delia mutters.

'Sorry, Your Honour?' the young woman asks.

'Don't mind me,' Delia says without looking up, her eyes still squinting down the length of her legs. 'Just thinking aloud.'

There's a scuffle at the door, as somebody from inside tries to open it while the young woman spins to grip at the knob with both hands, dragging it back shut.

'Excuse me!' Callum's voice sounds agitated, curt, rude.

'Judge McCormick has asked me to keep this door closed during recess,' the young woman says.

'It's her son. Callum. Let me out.' He yanks the door so forcefully that he almost sucks the young woman into the courtroom, then he paces outside without an apology where he almost trips over his mother's outstretched legs.

'Get back in that courtroom,' Delia snaps.

'Mum, you need to—'

'You heard me. Get back in that courtroom, Callum. The court official here has just told you *nobody* can come outside that door. You are now in breach of the court. Do I need to call security?'

'Mum, listen. The Private Eye—'

'Callum!' she screams, forming both of her fists into balls atop her lap. 'I need these minutes to consider everything I've just heard.'

'Course you do, but—'

'Callum!' she screams again.

He holds both of his hands aloft, then looks back over his shoulder at the young woman dressed in black.

'Okay... okay, Jeez,' he says, swivelling, then strolling back into the courtroom in a sulk.

When the young woman dressed in black pulls the door back shut, Delia offers her a smile.

'What's your name, sweetheart?' she asks.

'Ivy. Ivy Malone.'

'Well, thank you for your continued service of the courts, Miss Ivy Malone,' Delia says. Then she drops the smile from her face, re-squints her eyes and stares back along her outstretched legs.

She doesn't know where to begin dissecting Joy's testimony from. She is aware the media will make it all about Joy's outbursts. But Delia knows she doesn't have to complicate her filtering process by concentrating on the two occasions Joy stood in the witness to shout back at Jonathan Ryan. Delia needs to dig deeper than that. She needs to reach the fine lines in between the lines, and then begin the process of filtering them into the appropriate pockets inside her mind.

'Your Honour, that's the ten minutes you called for,' Ivy says, startling the judge. It didn't seem as if she had been squinting that long. The judge tuts, then scrambles herself to her feet, squeezes the shoulder of Ivy's black blazer and pulls the door open herself.

'All rise.'

The shout goes up late from the clerk as Delia settles herself back into the highchair, gripping her gavel tight.

She sighs heavily, then knocks lightly once.

'We have heard from the last of the witnesses in this retrial. It is now time for both the defence and the prosecution to deliver their final arguments. Mr Bracken...'

Bracken scoots back his chair to get to his feet, then strolls purposely to the centre of the courtroom floor, leaving behind his client whose face is still swollen from all of her crying.

'Your Honour,' he says, adopting his familiar stance of forming a steeple with his fingers. 'If there is doubt, then you must let her out. And there is plenty of doubt in this case. In 2010, my client was arrested and eventually sentenced to two life sentences for a crime she simply did not commit. Nobody has ever been able to say with any degree of certainty that she is guilty of the horrendous and heinous crimes she is accused of. Two life sentences for a crime one police officer working on the case testified in front of you to say was a deeply... flawed... investigation. Let me remind you what Sandra Gleeson said when she was on that stand, Your

Honour. She testified that investigators, "were only focused on one suspect from the outset." She said that only three seconds of CCTV footage out of five thousand hours that were viewed were ever deemed necessary to the investigation. Three seconds out of five thousand hours. That is a decimal of a percentage that begins with three zeros, Your Honour.' Delia scribbles notes on the paper in front of her as she maintains eye contact with Bracken. 'If investigators were only looking for Joy Stapleton in all of the footage they viewed, Your Honour, then what did they miss? Sandra Gleeson was an assistant detective on this case, and she believes the investigation was lacking from the outset... and flawed from the outset. That, in itself, Your Honour, is enough to excuse Joy Stapleton with an apology for her wrongful conviction. Sandra Gleeson's testimony pours all sorts of doubt onto the original verdict. And if there's doubt, Your Honour, you must let her out.' Bracken readjusts his standing position, shifting his weight from one foot to the other. 'But that is not the only doubt that has been poured onto the original verdict over the course of this retrial. Bunny the dog, Your Honour, who had been instrumental in Joy's original trial has, since that trial, been confirmed as a fraud. The dog did not have the skillsets required to even attempt to confirm the presence of decomposing bodies in the Stapleton home in early 2009. Bunny's handler, Mr Grimshaw – who sat in that witness chair last week – also lacks the skillsets and indeed qualifications for such a claim. Again, Your Honour, we managed to pour more doubt onto the original verdict in this case. And if there's doubt... you must let her out. Then we brought, to this court, brand new technology which was able to pour more doubt over the woman in the infamous CCTV footage... letting us know that this couldn't be Joy Stapleton. Because the height of the woman in that footage simply doesn't measure up to Joy. Y'see that's a metaphor for this whole case, Your Honour. Nothing measures up. Nothing measures up at all... Judge McCormick,' he says, taking two steps closer to the judge and staring up at her with his heaviest puppy-dog eyes, 'when there is doubt poured onto a case brought by the state – any case at all – it is proper legal procedure to dismiss the charges. After all, a case must be proven beyond *all* reasonable doubt. We, here, haven't just poured doubt on to this case, Your Honour, we have flooded doubt onto this case. My client has spent eight years, two months, two weeks and two days inside Mountjoy Prison for a crime she did not, and could not, have committed. If you are to release her tomorrow, which we strongly believe you should do given the amount of doubt flooded onto this case, my client – Mrs Joy Stapleton – will have spent three thousand days exactly behind bars. Three. Thousand. Days. For a crime she simply did not commit.' Bracken softens his face and releases his fingers from their steeple. 'I and my client thank you for your time, your diligence and your expertise, Judge McCormick, and believe that you will faithfully do what is right by these courts. That is our final statement – thank you, Your Honour.'

He produces his tilted head bow again, then paces back to his desk, and as he does Delia pulls back the sleeve on her left wrist before tilting it to her face.

'Mr Ryan, it is lunch time. But I'll leave it up to you. Would you like to deliver your final argument now, or...'

'Let's take the recess, Your Honour,' Ryan says.

'That okay with you, Mr Bracken?' Delia asks, flicking her eyes to the opposite bench.

Bracken curls up his mouth, shrugs his shoulders and nods his head. Then Delia bangs down her gavel once again.

'Okay, let's take half an hour. Court will resume at 1:40 p.m. precisely.'

Delia sucks on her cheeks as she heads out the side door, nodding to Ivy as she passes her.

But she's barely turned the corner of the first corridor by the time she hears a familiar calling – a calling she's heard almost every day of the past thirty-five years.

'Mum.'

She stops, and sighs as she spins.

'What is it, Callum?'

'I've got something to show you, though it'll make you wanna vomit.'

'Vomit?' she says, placing her hands on her hips, then squinting at the wry smile flickering on the corner of her son's mouth as he approaches her, his phone cupped inside his hand.

He swivels when he reaches his mother, to show her the screen, then he presses at the play button. As soon as he does, a scratching sound hisses from the speakers, before Delia baulks her face away.

'What the hell is that?'

'Keep watching, Mum.'

'Callum,' she says holding a hand to her face. 'Have I not seen enough penis for one woman this week?'

'Keep watching.'

The camera was between his legs, his balls hairy and tight at the bottom of the screen, his hands tight around his tubby mush-roomed-shape shaft. Over his fistful of penis lay a hanging belly, all hairy and matted with sweat. She couldn't see a face. Not until a neat side-parting of grey hair made itself visible. Followed by those unmistakable bushy V-shaped eyebrows. It looked as if Eddie was staring up over his belly at whatever footage he was masturbating to, totally unaware his laptop was filming him.

'Men. You really are all stupid, huh?' Delia says. Then she glances up at her son, producing a wry smile to mirror his.

'Where is he?'

'Canteen, I bet,' Delia says.

She pats her son on the back and then they both pace back up the corridor they had just walked down, before entering through the side door of the courtroom so that they can take the short cut to the canteen. But they don't need to travel so far. Because heading towards them are the same bushy V-shaped eyebrows that had just appeared in the video.

'Eddie...' Callum calls out, his voice echoing around the empty courtroom. 'You might wanna take a look at this.'

1 day ago…

Joy sighed with every exhale of breath she took as she slodged behind Anya.

The cringing hadn't diluted. Nor the anger. She was furious with herself… so much so she formed both fists into balls and let them hang heavy by her side as she was being led back to her cell. That was her one chance – the only chance she'd ever have – of defending herself. And she fuckin' blew it. Or at least she felt she had.

In between bouts of heavy sighing, she held her eyes closed and replayed all the times she had stumbled or stuttered on the stand. Then she'd cringe when she'd picture herself standing and shouting back at Jonathan Ryan.

'I'm a fuckin' idiot. I should've listened to my lawyer. I shouldn't have gone up there. I think I might've fucked it all up for myself,' she said to Anya, who looked even more like a model today because she had her hair all tussled into a loose bun and was dressed in a designer fitted suit to accompany Joy to and from the courts. But, as always, Anya didn't return conversation to the prisoner. She just kept her sculptured face stern until they reached cell E-108, before she pushed open the cell door, pointed Joy inside and then slammed it shut – even though Joy would have been allowed to roam around, given that cells were open and most of the other prisoners were in the TV room gossiping – about her, no doubt. Though Nancy wasn't. Joy had peered through the crack of her cell door when walking past just moments ago, noticing she was having her usual post-dinner nap.

But Joy chose to do just as she had done every evening of the past two weeks when she returned from court – she lay on her mattress in foetal position, and stared at the smiling faces of her two boys.

She didn't feel up to mixing with any of the inmates since she'd returned from isolation – and knew the only likely place she'd find peace and quiet during her retrial was on top of the plastic, blue mattress of her own cell, with the door shut tight. She had heard the prisoners were getting updates on her retrial through the RTÉ evening news, which, she realized as she lay staring at her boys' smiles, is what most of them were likely doing right now.

She thought about crawling out of her bed and heading down to the TV room just to listen to what the RTÉ reporter had to say about her time on the stand. But she couldn't summon the energy. Nor the courage. She felt that if she heard him report that she had made a fool of herself up there today then she might as well head back to her cell and end it all.

So, instead, she rested her ear onto her thin pillow and attempted to relive her testimony. She cringed when she replayed the first time she'd stood up to shout at Jonathan Ryan. "How fuckin' dare you!" she'd snapped. And then she filled with rage when she heard him accuse her, straight to her face, of murdering her sons. Especially as he was so close to her, almost all up in her face, just below the witness box.

'Uuuugh,' she squirmed, tossing and turning on her mattress. 'I'm gonna be here the rest of my fuckin' life.' She stared at the photograph of the boys, then turned over on her pillow, away from their faces and began to sob, her shoulders shaking, her throat gurgling. She was so overwhelmed. So exhausted. So devastated.

'Fuck. Fuck. Fuck,' she said, slapping her palm to the pillow right next to her face. She had done the exact same thing during her first night inside. Eight years, two months and two nights ago now. Three thousand days tomorrow. Sometimes those three thousand days feel like a lifetime ago to Joy... and yet on other occasions, her first night inside a cell seems as if it were only last night.

She managed to stop sobbing, then mustered enough energy to sit up; her teeth grinding, her jaw swinging. She knew the rest of the prisoners would be heading back to their cells for lock up soon. So, she stood up, yanked the sheet from the four corners of her bed and then pinched one end of it between her chin and chest so she could fold it neatly in half. Then she knelt down and began to roll the sheet up so tight that it turned into a long scarf. Seconds later, she was looping the scarf around one end, before gripping and yanking the noose as tight as she could get it.

'Fuck this shit,' she whispered to herself.

Then she reached for her bible.

⁘

'Get your filthy hand off me,' Delia says, shrugging her shoulder until Eddie's arm drops. 'I know what you do with that hand.'

His eyes widen, his neck roaring red under the collar of his creased shirt.

'Delia, you can't... you can't...'

Delia pushes a laugh through her nostrils, then tucks her chin into her neck so that she can look up at her boss over the rim of her retro-styled glasses.

'I mean, how stupid can you be, Eddie, huh? You know... *you know* people hack into laptop cameras... Sure you did it to him.' She flicks her head back towards her son who is beaming with smugness over her shoulder. 'You got beat playing your own game. But nothing seems to get in between a boy and his tiny best friend, does it?' She puffs out another laugh, then spins on her heels, storming back out through the side door of the courtroom, ignoring Eddie's calls.

'You gotta protect the verdict regardless, Delia,' he whisper-shouts after her. Callum has to hold a hand to Eddie's chest, to stop him from following the judge as she paces her way back down the corridors, where she eventually kicks her way into her office and plonks herself into the leather chair at her big oak desk.

She nibbles at half of the sandwich Aisling had left for her as she attempts to soak in the absurdity of it all. Then she holds her eyes closed to clear her mind of Eddie's hairy ball sack, so she can turn her focus back to the trial. Though her thoughts are delving much, much deeper than just the trial itself. Well beyond this one court case. She finds herself questioning everything she has ever believed in; the system in which her family had given over almost the entirety of their adult lives. Then, in the midst of her inner deliberation, Aisling's voice cackles through the speaker of Delia's phone, stunning the judge back to the present, informing her that she's due back in court again. Time is flashing by for her. It seems as if every time Delia begins to squint her eyes in deep thought, she is instantly snapped back out of it.

When she is sat back into her highchair in the courtroom, she eyeballs Eddie in the back pew, watching as he fidgets, firstly by folding his arms, then dropping them down by his side before he begins to comb his fingers repeatedly through his hair with both hands. He doesn't know what to be doing with himself. His face is now hot pink, his neck flaming red.

'Your Honour,' Jonathan Ryan says, approaching Delia's high-chair. 'Mr Bracken's final argument kept trying to suggest that there was no evidence in this case.'

Ryan holds aloft a tiny remote control, then pinches his finger at a button that blinks the large screen at the side of the courtroom floor back to life. An intriguing opening to his final argument.

'There's your evidence,' he says, pointing at the footage playing on loop of a figure in a pink hood walking by a garden wall. 'I'm not sure evidence gets more red-handed than that. This is Joy Stapleton walking away from where her boys were buried, about one-thousand metres from where her boys were buried, on the night we believe they were buried. The defendant was practically caught red-handed.'

He pauses, with his finger still pointing at the screen, allowing the footage to play on loop three more times.

'Talk about evidence,' he says, shaking his head. 'That is literally evidence in front of our own eyes. Mr Bracken says there is no evidence. Well, he should know that most murder cases don't get the luxury of evidence as hot as this. In most murder trials we don't get to see footage of the defendant walking away from the scene of the crime. The defence's argument, that this is mere coincidence, is frankly laughable, Your Honour. We know that Mrs Stapleton was the only person in Ireland to own this particular pink hooded top even before this retrial. But during this retrial, we had Mr Tobias Masterson testify on the stand to reaffirm that, and we also produced written statements from other purchasers of this pink hooded top from Pennsylvania which only further rules out the plausibility of coincidence. If a coincidence was difficult to believe for the original jury in this case eight years ago, Your Honour, then a coincidence must be impossible to believe now. This,' he says, pointing his finger at the screen again, 'can *only* be Joy Stapleton. This is the evidence that proves she murdered her two boys. Don't let it be said we don't have evidence. We have evidence.'

He strolls back to his desk, picks up his glass of water and takes a short, sharp sip from it.

'Your Honour, the accused's best friend since Primary School testified on the stand that Mrs Stapleton was suffering with some form of undiagnosed depression around the time Oscar and Reese Stapleton were murdered. After her mother had died, and with very little support from her overworked husband, Joy Stapleton slipped into an undiagnosed depression that drove her to do the unthinkable. The testimony from Lavinia Kirwan proves motive, Your Honour. Which means that, to this court, during this retrial, we have proven motive. And we have proven evidence.'

He points his hand at the screen again where the footage is still playing on loop.

'We also had distinguished Detective Ray De Brun testify during this retrial. Ray De Brun has been the lead detective on many of Dublin's most infamous cases. He testified here, in this courtroom, this week, that he is under no doubt whatsoever that Joy Stapleton murdered her two boys. He was asked quite bluntly if he had any doubt that Mrs Stapleton is guilty of this crime. And his exact response under oath was, "none what-so-ever." This is one of Ireland's most decorated investigators in the entire history of our state, Your Honour. So, now we have expertise. We have motive. We have evidence.'

He doesn't point his finger at the screen this time, but he does notice that Judge Delia glances to the footage as he melodically repeats his tag-line.

'Your Honour, the detectives in this case got it right by arresting Joy Stapleton. The jury in the original trial got it right by finding her guilty. And the judge in the original trial – Albert Riordan – got this case right by handing down a double life sentence. That double life sentence needs to be protected. It needs to be upheld. It has been made plain and clear during this retrial that the defendant is prone to outbursts. She made numerous outbursts directed at me today whilst on that stand; outbursts certainly not befitting a woman of innocence, outbursts that can only reaffirm to us that she ended the lives of her two young sons in the most inhumane act this country has ever—'

'You lying mother—'

Joy is dragged back down to her seat by Bracken, who has to add weight to both of her shoulders to steady her.

'See, Your Honour,' Ryan says. 'A hot temper. Another outburst. And that is numerous times today. It is far from inconceivable that on November 2nd, 2008, Mrs Stapleton had the mother of all outbursts. And that outburst led to her murdering her two boys, before burying them in shallow graves in the wasteland of the Dublin mountains. And we know she did this because we have expertise. We have motive. And we have evidence,' he says, pointing at the screen, this time with both hands. 'Your Honour, the prosecution rests its case.'

There's a humming of chatter in the gallery as Delia steps down and exits the courtroom.

Aisling chooses to stay quiet as the judge brushes past to enter her office; conscious the judge will be deep in thought.

Delia huffs as she sits into her chair, before wiggling at her mouse again. And as her screen takes its time to blink back to life, she stares at the sharp shadows the cupfuls of pens and the cracked photo frame of her family are casting due to the dim orange light above her head. She is thinking about the taglines used in both closing arguments, feeling both to be rather outdated. Though she does realise Ryan and Bracken were playing to the media as much as they were playing to her. They knew the newspapers would lap up the taglines for lazy headlines tomorrow, though she isn't quite sure whether 'If there's any doubt, you must let her out,' would be preferred by editors over, 'We have motive. We have expertise. We have evidence.' All she knows right this second is that she, personally, wasn't won over by either of the closing arguments. Though she won't be making any decision right now. That'll happen later. When she's sunken into a hot bath, with bubbles hugging her face and a glass of wine swirling in her hand.

A familiar knock rattles, causing her to tut.

'Come in, Callum.'

He shows his grinning face, then shuts the door quietly behind him.

'Did you see how puce he was sitting in the back of the courtroom? He's in some shock. He kept stuttering to me after you stormed off. The fat gobshite. I mean, I'll never get the image of his hairy balls out of my mind, but... drama finally over.' He sits into the chair opposite his mother and holds up both hands. 'You can, eh.... do as you were always hoping to do; see this retrial through a fresh set of eyes.' Delia thins her lips while continuing to squint at her screen, saying nothing. 'Mum... Mum. Whatcha thinking about?'

'Things.'

'What things? The closing arguments? I thought, personally, Bracken's was stronger, but Ryan's was more specific. I mean—'

'No, Callum. I'm not thinking about the closing arguments. I'm not even thinking about the trial. I'm thinking well beyond the trial. I'm trying to figure out a bigger picture.'

'A bigger picture? A bigger picture of what?'

'Things.'

'Things?' Callum sits upright. 'Mum... what the hell are you talking about? Things?'

'Just a bigger picture is all... anyway, my head's been stuck in this trial for way too long... I'm going to wait till I run a hot bath tonight, then I'm going to get my head into it. Tell me something. Anything to distract me. How's that fella you dated last weekend? You guys arrange a second date?'

Callum sniggers, then snatches at a pen from the cupful on his mother's desk and repeatedly clicks at the top of it.

'I'm actually seeing him tonight.'

'And have you told me what this guy does for a living, yet?'

'He's a cook of some sort. Runs a catering business with his brother.'

'Ah, nice. Someone who can cook, huh? So, he's gonna be the one then, is he?'

Callum sniggers again, then tosses the pen onto the desk.

'Why you wanna talk about me? I wanna know what you mean by 'bigger picture', you're not thinking of doing anything stupid, are you, Mum? What does *bigger picture* even mean?'

Delia swipes the glasses from her nose and rests them down beside her mouse before leaning back and twisting the butt of both palms into her eyes.

'Don't know...' she says, through a stifled yawn. 'I'm thinking beyond this trial – way beyond it. About the justice system as a whole.'

Callum creases his brow.

'So, you *are* thinking of doing something stupid. Are you gonna let her out, just to let the system come crashing down? You're not... you're not thinking of letting her out... are you? Mum, she's guilty. C'mon... you know that.'

'Well firstly, I don't know that, do I? Nobody does. Ryan says he proved red-handed evidence. He didn't. It's a figure in a pink hoodie. We see no face. So, we don't know for certain. Nobody does. But... secondly, does it even matter if we did know for certain?'

'Huh?' Callum says, sitting more upright.

'Eddie Taunton... I mean the absolute cheek of that man.'

'You're not... Mum... are you fucking serious?' He mouths the word 'fucking', the sound of the 'f' flicking off his bottom lip.

'You're gonna acquit Joy Stapleton just to throw a grenade on the system?'

'I don't know. I told you, I need a warm bath. I'll do my filtering process in there tonight and I'll... I'll—'

'Mum. Tell me you're not being serious?'

'I told you. I'm gonna think it all through tonight.'

'Mum, she murdered her two young sons. They were babies. She was videoed walking away from the scene for crying out loud.'

'We don't know for—'

'It's not a bloody coincidence, Mum. There is no coincidence in this case. You said that yourself. You said it years ago in your interview with Eddie Taunton. There is no coincidence in this case whatsoever. Never has been. This has been known as 'The Coincidence Case' for over ten years now, ever since Joy was first arrested. Coincidence this, coincidence that. As Jonathan Ryan said in his opening argument, there's no such thing as coincidences, not really. Hell...' Callum puffs out a snort, 'the only time I heard any coincidence in this entire trial was when they mentioned the date of the murders. Second of November, 2008. Same date as my graduation, wasn't it? Same night this was taken.'

He picks up the cracked photo frame from beside his mother's monitor and turns it to himself. He's still grinning back at his father when it releases from his grip, his thumb slicing on a shard, the frame swirling in slow motion until it crashes to the floor. Again.

'What the fuck?' he says, standing up and holding a hand to his chest. He bows forward to stare down at the photo; but not to see his father's proud face, nor his, nor his mother's. But to squint at the tiny figure in the background. A figure that had never caught his eye before. Joy Stapleton. Just over his father's shoulder. Her curls packed tightly into a pink hood.

Delia's brow is heavily creased as she chicanes herself around her desk. She stares up at Callum's paling face... then down at the photo. She lowers to her hunkers and inches her nose closer. It takes a long moment for her to finally see it; to notice the tiny figure in the background – a figure she hadn't noticed, not once, in any one of the ten thousand times she had glanced at this photograph over the years.

'What the fuck?' she says, opting for the exact same words her son had chosen.

Delia lifts her knitted jumper from the waist, taking her undervest with it and struggling, once again, to lift them over her head because she'd forgotten she had combed her glasses back into her hair. But she manages to untangle herself before tossing the garments to her bed. Then she unclasps her bra and pulls down her trousers – taking her cotton bloomers with them – before kicking her way to her birthday suit.

She normally basks in the quiet of the house; loves it when Callum goes out for the evening. But this quiet sounds too quiet. Eerily quiet. It's not calming her spinning head at all.

Callum didn't want to go out on his date and had actually texted him to call it off. But Delia forced him into a U-turn, demanding that she had the house to herself this evening; that she wasn't to be disturbed.

They had both sat for an hour in her office just staring at the photo, their jaws ajar, their eyes wide. Then, when Delia snapped out of her shock by shaking her head, she snatched at the photo frame and shoved it into her briefcase, loose glass and all.

'Mum... what you doing?'

'I'm going home to have a bath.'

'But... Mum... Mum,' Callum roared as she was pacing out of her office.

'Enjoy your date, Callum,' she shouted without looking back.

She stares at her body in the mirror, shrugging a shoulder at herself before tip-toeing the length of the carpeted landing that leads her straight into the bathroom. She dips her toe into the bath before sucking in through the gaps in her teeth. Too hot. So she runs the cold tap and begins to swirl her hand through the foaming water. The bathroom is consumed by steam, the glass of Massolino Parussi Barola standing tall on the edge of the bath fogged and dripping with condensation. She turns off the tap, then dips her toe in again for another temperature check. Perfect. She'd been looking forward to this all day. Even before she was stunned into the surrealist of silences by the most extraordinary of coincidences.

As soon as she rests her head on the back rim of the bath she squints through the swirling steam at the cracked photograph. She had sat it upright on the edge of her chest of drawers facing the bath so that she could soak it all in while the cogs of her mind-filtering process churned. She still can't believe it. Undoubted proof that Joy was walking back down the Dublin mountains on the night she dumped her son's bodies up there; caught in the background of a family portrait of the McCormicks as they stood, proudly, outside the Windmill pub celebrating Callum's graduation. One quick flash of a camera. And there it was. Proof; a single split moment caught in time forever.

'Justice?' Delia whispers to herself as she sinks further under the water. 'Or the justice system?' She picks up her tall glass of wine and swirls it before taking a tiny sip and resting it back down. 'Which is more important?'

She takes a deep inhale of breath before pushing her bum further forward, allowing her shoulders, then her neck, and finally her face to sink under the water. She opens her eyes when she's fully immersed and stares up through a gap in the bubbles at the steam as it swirls in a haze towards the high ceiling. Then one bubble releases from her mouth and buoys for a long moment on the surface... before it eventually pops.

0 days ago...

Joy glanced over at Mathilda and Anya who were both standing against the side wall of the courtroom all courteous and disciplined with their hands clasped behind their backs, their shoulders high and their chests puffed out. And as she stared at them, she was certain that Mathilda was smiling at her – her lips twitching, the sides of her eyes ever so slightly creasing. Joy squinted back for a moment, then lightly shook her curls from side-to-side, assuming she was just imagining things.

She pivoted on her chair to face forward when Judge Delia lightly coughed into the microphone, signalling she was about to begin. And as Joy sat more upright in her chair, Gerd Bracken reached a hand across to pinch two of her fingers between his.

'I have concluded my judgement of this retrial,' Delia said, leaning her forearms on to the desk in front of her. 'In all my years I have never so strenuously had to consider so many matters in one court case. Not only is this a retrial that meant I also had to consider testimonies from the original murder trial, but this is a unique murder retrial in that it is without a jury.' She lightly cleared her throat again and then swallowed, looking sincerely sorrowful. 'I meticulously examined all evidence and witness testimony brought to this court. And after considered due process, structured within the legal parameters in which I am honoured and proud to work in, time has now come for me to ask the defendant to please rise.'

Bracken squeezed Joy's hand. Then the entire defence team got to their feet in unison.

'Mrs Joy Stapleton,' the judge said, 'this court finds you not guilty of the crimes of which you have been charged and subsequently incarcerated for.'

There are audible gasps in the gallery. Joy releases from Bracken's grip so she can throw both of her arms around his neck, then she leans in and kisses him just beneath the ear. 'You are a free woman. You are free to leave this court a free woman. On behalf of the Justice System,' Delia continued, even though it was evident Joy was no longer listening to her – lost in a haze of elation, 'I would like to extend the first apology for your wrongful conviction.' She slams down her gavel. 'Court dismissed.'

A booming chorus of chaos sounded out as the judge stepped down from her highchair. Joy was sandwiched in a double hug; Gerd Bracken on one side of her, his assistant Imogen on the other. Then, over Imogen's shoulder, Joy noticed Anya and Mathilda making their way towards her, Mathilda definitely smiling now, Anya's stunning face still sombre and pouted.

'Joy, we need to conduct due process before we free you, as per the court's orders,' Mathilda said, holding her fingers to Joy's elbow. 'If you could step into the hallway with us.'

Joy nodded her curls while beaming a huge smile through her tears and then, flanked by Bracken, she followed Anya and Mathilda through a side door that led to a monochrome tiled corridor.

As soon as the heavy door was closed behind them, the chaotic mumbling of debate and discussion humming from within the courtroom instantly drowned to a near silence.

'I told ya all them years I was innocent, Mathilda,' Joy said, bouncing up and down on the spot, much like she used to when she'd get high on meth.

Mathilda nodded and pursed a thin smile at her.

'Listen,' she said, leaning in to Joy, 'I know you have just had the best news ever, but eh... we just got word after we arrived here this morning, and I'm sorry to have to tell you this... but it's, eh... it's Nancy.'

Joy stopped bouncing.

'Nancy?'

'She, eh... she took her own life last night.'

'What?'

Anya nodded once, like a robot.

'I know you've got a lot going on, but I know you guys were close and I thought I should tell you,' Mathilda said. 'Because well... she did it because of you, y'see?'

'Because of me?'

'She left a note. A suicide note. It said, "I love you. I can't go on without you." She didn't want to do her time inside with you not being there, Joy. She musta feared you were gonna be acquitted today.'

Joy pouted her lips and shrugged one shoulder.

'That's sad,' she said, before she began bouncing on the spot again. 'Now, what's this due process we need to go through, cos I just wanna get the hell outta here?'

Mathilda stared up at Anya, but Anya, as usual, produced nothing – not even the flicker an eyelash.

'There is no procedure,' Mathilda said, turning back to Joy. 'I just wanted to let you know about Nancy... that's all.' Then she pointed her whole hand to the back end of the corridor. 'Let your lawyers take you out that entrance down there... there'll be less media that way.'

Joy spent her first hour of freedom bouncing her knees up and down under a desk inside Bracken's office, celebrating with men and woman dressed in suits – most of whom she'd never even met before. She was buoyed, but already bored by her new-found freedom. Only because she felt she had to keep a fake smile plastered wide across her face for the sake of those in suits she knew she had to consider her heroes.

'I, eh... gotta go, I gotta go do... *something*,' she finally said. Bracken was reluctant to allow her to leave. He knew all too well that she had nobody on the outside world she could consider a friend. And when he informed her he had already booked a hotel room, she resisted – insisting she couldn't spend another moment of her life being holed up.

'I just wanna walk. I wanna feel... *free*,' she told him. Then she held him close, whispered a 'Thank you' into his ear, and left his office to wander the streets of Dublin city with the four fifty-euro notes Bracken had insisted she take from him stuffed into her back trousers pocket.

She strolled up and down the boardwalk of Bachelor's Walk, sniffing in the scent of the River Liffey as if, despite its stench, its air was as fresh as any air she had ever inhaled. She turned heads as she walked. There was no mistaking Joy Stapleton. But nobody approached her, except to shout an odd, 'I always believed you, Joy' or a 'Oh, look, it's yer wan' in her direction. Though most of the folk she passed were too silenced by their own shock to say anything. They just stood there, open mouthed with shopping bags hanging heavy from both hands.

It was only when she sat in the back of a taxi that she felt her thighs and calves begin to burn from the mileage she had covered. She only realised when she stared at the clock on the taxi's dashboard that she had been walking non-stop for over three hours.

Her thighs and calves still feel stiff now as she holds a finger to the doorbell while inching her ear to the glassed porch door so she can hear it chime through the house. Then she stands back and stares up and down the street, nibbling on her bottom lip. It doesn't look as if eight years have passed. Aside from the car in the drive next door being larger and wider than it used to be, she genuinely can't notice anything else that's changed around here.

He appears, standing in the frame of the front door glaring out at her from behind the glassed porch. His face is still as grey as his hair; his eyes a diluted blue.

She thought about what she would say to him repeatedly as she wandered the city centre streets, but as he is sliding the porch door across, she begins to lose all sense of herself and has to grip the wall that separates their garden from their neighbours with her fingers – just for some semblance of support. In case Shay is unreceptive. In case he steps out and snaps 'What the fuck are you doing here?'

'Joy,' he says. As soon as he steps into the garden path he glances up and down the street, much like she had done seconds ago. 'Come in. Come in.'

She stares straight into the living room as soon as she steps back inside the squared hallway. Shay hasn't changed much, aside from the overly-wide flat screen TV hanging over the fireplace. Her own face stares back at her; the mug shot of when she was first arrested. Then the screen blinks to a reporter standing outside the entrance to the courts, speaking into an overly large squared microphone.

'*Judge Delia McCormick delivered her verdict at 10:40 this morning; shocking some members of the gallery—*'

Shay stabs his finger at the remote control making the screen blink to black. Then he walks across his wife, taking her in as she glances around the room.

'I, eh... I don't know... eh... don't know what to, eh...' He scratches at the back of his neck.

'You don't have to say anything,' Joy whispers. 'You said it all on the stand, Shay. I'm just here to say... to say thank you.'

'I'm so sorry for all you've been through. I can't even begin to... I mean, my mind has just been jumping from one theory to another to another to another over the years and I...'

Joy steps closer to him and holds a hand against his elbow.

'You don't have to be sorry for anything.'

'I left you alone. With the kids. I mean... what was I thinking? All's I ever thought I wanted to be was a father. And when I became one, I bloody left you all to it... didn't I? I just went to do nothing in hotels. For no reason whatsoever.'

'Not for no reason,' Joy says, gripping his elbow tighter. 'You were earning crust for your family. You don't have to be sorry for anything, Shay. You've never needed to mutter the words 'I'm sorry'. I'm the one who left them on that green over there. I'm the one who's had to deal with that—'

'Joy,' Shay says, looking down at his wife, his eyes filling with tears, 'you need to stop blaming yourself. The entire state has blamed you for eight years and today that entire state has stopped blaming you. So, you need to stop blaming yourself.'

She takes one step closer and holds both her hands to his hips.

'I'll stop blaming myself, if you stop blaming yourself,' she says.

Shay stiffens his nose in an attempt to stop the tears from falling, then he leans down and kisses the top of his wife's curls. But as he does, his dam breaks, and he sobs snot and tears into her hair; his shoulders shivering. Joy reaches both hands up his back, and drags him as tight as she can to her, resting an ear against his chest.

'It's okay, Shay,' she whispers. 'I'm home now.'

SEE THE PHOTOGRAPH!

And see the real photograph from the true coincidence that inspired this novel.

Both photographs are shown at the start of this short video interview with author David B. Lyons in which he discusses all of the clues that lead up to the twist ending; clues you may have missed.

Click the below link to access the video right now.

www.subscribepage.com/coincidence

The End.

ALL OF DAVID B. LYONS'S NOVELS

The Tick-Tock Trilogy

Midday

Whatever Happened to Betsy Blake?

The Suicide Pact

The Trial Trilogy

She Said, Three Said

The Curious Case of Faith & Grace

The Coincidence

ACKNOWLEDGMENTS

Lin, thank you so much for being such a hero to myself, Kerry and Lola during the crazy year that was 2020.

Quite literally, without you being the best grandmother ('nanny') a grandmother could ever possibly be, *The Coincidence* would not have been written this year.

We thank you. We love you. We are indebted to you. Forever.

This book is for you.

I should also thank my own mother, seeing as I am thanking my mother-in-law. I'm so sorry I haven't seen you since February, Ma. Can't wait to catch up in person soon. I've missed ya lots.

To Kerry and Lola – thank you for always believing in me and thank you for being the best company anyone could wish to be locked down with.

Hannah, Margaret and Barry – your feedback, as always, is so greatly appreciated. I owe debts of gratitude to the wonderful Deborah Hart, too. As well as Rubina Gomes, Livia Sbarbaro, Kathy Grams, Sarah Hilton Rachel Wills and Eileen Cline. Your input, ladies, really helped shape this novel. And to my consultant for this novel, Andrew Harkness, whose experience and insight was invaluable to the construction of the plot. You're a gem, my friend.

To Julia and all of the team at MiblArt – thank you once again for designing such wonderful work for me. And to my editors: Maureen Vincent-Northam and Brigit Taylor – you two always make me look better.

Made in the USA
Monee, IL
02 January 2022

87694720R00184